Bona Fide Beauty
Bona Fide Book One

LANDRA GRAF

This is a work of fiction. Names, characters, places, and incidents are products of the author's imagination or are used fictitiously and are not to be construed as real. Any resemblance to actual events, locales, organizations, or persons, living or dead, is entirely coincidental.

Bona Fide Beauty

Bona Fide Book One

Copyright © 2018 Landra Graf

ISBN: 0-9909280-4-7

ISBN-13: 978-0990928041

DEDICATION

To my dear friend, Lori. This book wouldn't be here without you.

ACKNOWLEDGMENTS

I want to acknowledge all the wonderful people who've helped this book become a reality. From betas: Lora, Lori, Amanda, Cate, Kat, Sorcha, and many others who gave input from beginning to end. To my editors, Cara and Jax, you made Dev and Kat truly shine. To the lovely friends who've said a kind word of encouragement over the years and always inquired as to when this story would make its way to the shelf: Tonya, Christy, Becky — much love.

Finally, to my family who's constantly supporting me through hugs, kisses, and reminding me it's okay to step away from the computer a bit to enjoy the heavenly beauty around me.

CHAPTER ONE

When the doorbell rang, Kathleen Baum thought of her grandma's wise words. *Only religious cults or bad news rang a bell before nine in the morning.* It was a little past eight, and Kat had her purse in hand ready to leave for work. She opened the door and regretted the choice instantly.

"Good morning, Miss Baum," said the unwanted intruder, Pru Stone. The woman had been nothing but a menace over the last four months, and like grubs in a yard, just when Kat thought she was gone, she'd reappear.

"I'm in a hurry, late to work. Afraid I can't talk about the Bentonville Beautification Project, but just to reiterate, I'm not selling."

Pru tsked, swiping a tuft of blond hair over her shoulder while shuffling on her feet, the bright purple pumps she wore clacking against the stone walkway. "That's not why I stopped by this morning. You see, my friend Tom here"—she pointed to the blue-suit-jacketed gentleman behind her, the one analyzing the side wall of Kat's grandmother's house—"he's with the city code enforcement department. Some of the board members are concerned your house isn't to code, and well, the project is bringing more scrutiny to the houses around downtown."

"Are you fucking kidding me?"

"Miss Baum." Blue-jacket Tom came forward and extended a hand. A hand she refused to shake. He held her gaze for a prolonged minute and then gave up. "The inspection will take no more than twenty minutes. I can walk through quickly."

"Do you have a warrant?"

Tom scoffed, and that's when she noticed his shirt buttons were unevenly buttoned, causing an overlap of material at the bottom of his untucked shirt. "This isn't a television show, and I am here on the authority of the mayor."

"Prove it. For all I know, you're planting drugs for that evil bitch."

1

"Such language isn't becoming of a lady." Pru brought one of her manicured hands to her mouth as if to express outrage. Nails the same color as her heels, the woman was a genuine purple people eater.

"I never said I was one." Kat held her own manicure-less hand up, mocking the hoity-toity salute, and then swiped her ponytail back behind her shoulder.

Tom whipped out his credentials and an inspection form, signed by the mayor, giving him authority to request entry to her home. She had to be gracious, even if he held a gun to her head in the form of a signed piece of paper; Southern hospitality bullshit rules and such.

"Twenty minutes is all I have." Kat stepped to the left to let Tom into her house.

"I may need more time."

Damn it all to hell. "Do what you have to."

Pru stepped in behind him, but Kat shoved a booted foot and slack-encased leg in her way. "I don't think so, *lady*. He can go in, but you have to stay outside."

"Dogs in heat are friendlier than you." The thorn in Kat's side took two steps backward off her porch and onto the paved walk. "I gave you a chance to make a lot of money and put yourself in a good position to own a nice house locally, with plenty of time to move and get situated."

Kat's patience had left the moment Pru had shown up. Being held up from going to work was now the second layer of her shit cake, followed by inspector icing, and rude-ass comment sprinkles. "You mean selling my family's history for money? History is priceless; money can't buy that. This is my last tie to my grandmother, who, God rest her soul, gave me this house with the express interest of keeping it in the family. No silly project is going to make me give it up."

"Well, you may not have a choice." Her foreboding words coupled with a sickeningly sweet grin, almost worthy of a Cheshire cat, made Kat's stomach turn.

The woman had put on a good act, one with all the right words, the friendly phrases, and an excellent sales pitch— until she'd wanted Kat's house. There were things a person could accept and things they could not, and selling a family heirloom wasn't on the acceptable list. Not since her gran had made her promise to raise a family in the house and to ensure the home stayed standing for many more years to come. Three generations had been raised here. Kat would rather be hog-tied naked in the front yard than betray a promise to the woman who'd given her so much.

Shutting the front door in Pru's face, Kat trailed off to locate her unwanted house guest. She caught up with Tom in her bedroom investigating an exposed wall plug that needed a new cover.

"Pretty old place you have here. Bought it cheap, I take it?" Tom scribbled notes on his clipboard before scratching the side of his temple with the tip of his pen.

"No, it's been passed down through the family. My great-grandfather built it in the 1890s. My gran was born here. My mother was born here, too."

A surprised "hmm" was the only response her history lesson received as the inspector moved into the laundry room, then the kitchen. He didn't pay attention to the tile backsplash behind the sink or the rooster motif she'd helped her gran with to rid the future generations of the nasty daisy and patterned-orange wallpaper.

"We remodeled the kitchen nearly eight years ago. You should have seen it then."

"So you put in insulation?"

"Excuse me?"

"The walls," Tom replied, tapping on the wall above the stove, "they were insulated during the remodel?"

"You mean that pink foam stuff? We never cracked open the walls." Now she regretted speaking, especially when her response equated to more scribbles of pen on paper. She stayed silent the remainder of the short trek until they got outside. Tom wandered to look at the sides of the house.

Pru stood on the sidewalk, her thumbs wreaking havoc on her phone. "Whenever you're ready to put an end to this nonsense and sign the paperwork, let me know."

"The word 'no' isn't something you're familiar with I take it?" She inwardly winced.

Pru's eyes narrowed on her, assessing and giving Kat a once-over that made her skin tingle like she'd been found unworthy. Sure, Kat's no-nonsense slacks and blouse were standard and the color gray not exactly her best look, but her wardrobe, purchased economically from the nearest Goodwill, served her well.

"'No' *is* a phrase I'm used to hearing, but if there's one thing I've learned, it's that every 'no' is really just a 'not right now.' I have an important call to make. I'd appreciate it if you could occupy yourself with something other than verbal barbs for a few minutes."

Oh, the choice words rattling in Kat's head were about to fly, but Pru turned away, clacking back down the walkway to stand next to her black BMW. The woman's fingers keyed away once more, probably calling another hapless person whose home she wanted to steal. A beauty version of Miss Gulch, except Kat wasn't in Kansas anymore, not since she'd moved to Arkansas in her elementary school years.

Pru put the phone to her ear and smiled big with a loud and happy, "Hello."

Tom cleared his throat beside her. "Miss Baum, when is the last time an electrician has been out to the house?"

"I haven't needed one in the last four years since I've been the owner."

"How about a plumber?"

She shrugged. "I had one out to work on one of the toilets last winter, but otherwise nothing."

"The roof, water heater, furnace, or air conditioner been replaced anytime in the last ten years?"

"Not that I know of, but everything is working wonderfully."

"Glad to hear of your good fortune, but all of those items need to be updated according to Arkansas code, along with electrical wiring and foundation repair. You've got cracks all along the outside." He said all this while marking boxes and writing notes on his evil clipboard of death. "I'm also concerned you may have termites."

She shook her head. "Not possible. This bad boy is sprayed every six months. If there's one thing I won't abide, it's bugs."

"Regardless." The loud rip from Tom tearing the top sheet of paper from his board gave Kat an uneasy stomach knot. "You have four months to get it up to code."

"Four months?"

"Adequate time to get everything up to code, and my office can supply you with a list of contractors and businesses familiar with our county and city regulations if needed."

She took the paper and barely glanced at it. "If things aren't to code in four months?"

"The city will take the next steps in the process."

"What about the value of the home? My rights as an owner?"

"If the property is unfit to live in, your rights are forfeit and any expense to the city will be applied."

Another glance at the paper showed there were at least half a dozen red check marks, signs of things in need of repairs, or worse, replacement.

"Are you all finished?" Pru's voice intruded once more. Kat's eyes blurred for a moment, the tears threatening to burst forth. She'd keep controlled, or so help her...

"Yes, Mrs. Stone. All done, and Miss Baum has been provided her copy. I'll work with my secretary to set a date for the next inspection." Kat raised her head to meet Tom's serious expression. "Expect a letter from my office with the contractor information."

Pru didn't spare her another glance, just roped an arm through the housing inspector's and gave a smile. "You've been so helpful today. Can I offer you a quick breakfast down at Mesa Blue? They serve an excellent brunch."

Kat didn't hear Tom's reply. No, she swiveled away and marched back inside straight for her purse and keys. She needed to get to work, needed time to think, time to plan, because her bank account wouldn't solve this problem and no conventional method would either.

***

Devid Esposito had two problems: a clear work calendar and a severe lack of business dinners. For a business owner, those two things signaled a tempest of trouble on the horizon. All he needed was one happy client. One success story would keep Bona Fide Personal Image drowning in referrals for six months if the client had a lot of friends.

Too bad for Dev he'd yet to find the success story, the magic client. The extent of his schedule equated to a couple of private company professional image parties and one ex-college professor seeking a modern image. His buddy and Bona Fide co-founder, Mark, would tell him those numbers didn't bring in the cheddar. Yet Dev refused to help the type of clients who guaranteed the books would be in the black.

"Here's the completed questionnaire from Marshall Ashby," Victoria, their secretary and front desk receptionist, said. Her smooth voice brought him out of his musings. She placed a folder on his desk, and he took a moment to review her outfit. Black knee-length skirt, pleated belt, red blouse, white and black heels—one of his first female clients and she had accessed talents she'd always possessed with a little encouragement. If only they'd all turned out the same way.

"Thanks."

"Sure thing, but it'd be nice if I actually had some work to do." Her eyebrows lifted, dark brown eyes, similar to his, glowered at him.

Dev wanted to laugh at the serious look on her pale face. "For a woman who hates confrontation, you sure don't shy away from it with me."

She smiled wide. "Yes, just because I hate it doesn't mean I hide my unhappiness from people."

"Thank you for your continued vocal objections. You're welcome to report the issue to HR."

"You keep refusing female clients, and you won't need to worry about having an HR."

"Hearing rumors? Is Sheila or one of the others voicing concerns?" He wanted to tell her to mind her own business, worry about her own personal problems. Yet he'd learned long ago to bite his tongue and hold in the horrible things he thought. Those kinds of comments were intended to bully and intimidate, which broke spirits and self-esteem. He wouldn't be the type of person who cut others down when faced with his own deficiencies. Deflect rather than regret.

"We've all seen the latest financials, Dev. The ten people we have working for us saw them. Have you?"

He'd seen them. The company was struggling. In fact, without a significant enrollment push, they'd have to possibly lay off a few consultants. "Yes, but can we save the depressing talk for this week's investor meeting?"

"Whatever floats your boat, *boss*." Victoria put a little extra sarcasm in the word and headed for the door as his office phone began to ring. The number listed made his gut clench. Answering it meant opening the door to a conversation and potentially a confrontation he didn't want to have.

Victoria turned and frowned. "Don't keep the clients waiting. Isn't that what you always say?"

"It's not a client." Three more rings, and it'd go to voice mail.

"Who then? *Her.*" In the past four years, there'd only been one woman with the ability to invoke such a guttural tone from his secretary, reminding him of what the greeter to hell might sound like.

He let it go to voicemail, and then his phone beeped with a message.

"You know she'll call back right away like she always does. It's not like you're super busy."

"Didn't you have something to file before leaving?"

"Who's the one afraid of confrontation?"

He didn't like confrontation, especially with the caller, and like clockwork, the mere thought sent his desk phone jingling again.

"Answer it or I will," Victoria's tone was a far cry from her naturally sarcastic nature.

"Fine." He picked up the handset, and the plastic scratched against his facial hair. "Hello, Pru."

"Hello." Where once her voice had brightened his day whenever they talked, now she sounded fake to his ears.

Victoria posed in the doorway, lips pursed, stance locked, eyes glowering. He waved her away, but she ignored him. Typical.

"To what do I owe the pleasure of this call?" He tried to accent his voice to be as friendly as possible to one of Bona Fide's investors.

"I wanted to let you know your biggest success is two inches away from securing the last house for my Bentonville Beautification Project. With a few pieces of paperwork and some small formalities, it will be conquered in no time. So I thought we could go out for a celebration dinner and discuss the upcoming investor's meeting. Tonight or tomorrow, whichever works."

This week she'd secured a house for her project, last week the renovations on her house had been completed, and the week prior she'd secured the president's chair of her neighborhood's homeowners association. Every new accomplishment became another excuse to call him and invite him to dinner or for drinks. He had to play nice—she held a sizeable interest in his company, ex-girlfriend or no. Maybe it was time to get a little tougher, though. His more-than-friendly requests to keep things professional and declines to her invites had gone unheeded time and again.

"I'm happy for you and the latest accomplishment. Another notch on the belt is exciting, but I don't think we qualify for celebration dinners anymore."

He couldn't go backward, and Pru sat firmly in the "backward" column. He'd mixed business with pleasure one time and regretted it every day.

"True, but you were the one who wanted space and needed to label everything, which is common for men who are afraid to commit. I also know I come on a little strong sometimes, but that's nerves. We should at least talk about the investors' meeting."

The fact that she still held delusional ideas about them never ceased to amaze him, but to pin their relationship failures completely on his side of the fence was laughable. He'd been in love, deeply, until she'd shown him a few sides of herself he'd never seen before.

"We're not together for reasons I refuse to re-hash. As for talking, we can do that at the meeting." A headache was already brewing.

She sighed. "Dev, it doesn't have to be like this. Let me back in. I can help."

"Your help always comes at a price. One I'm not willing to pay." He hung up the phone before she could get another word out. Then he leveled his gaze on Victoria, who stood patiently waiting. "I refused another dinner, if that's what you're wondering. As for her advice, I don't want to hear it."

"If she's saying the same thing I am, maybe it's time to listen."

Dev shook his head at the idea. "Nope and nope. Now, get out of here. If we're so short on money, we can't afford to pay you overtime."

She gave him a stink eye and left without another word. Funny how she had been the one begging him to end things with Pru, pointing out how she'd step in to offer her own advice after clients left their consultants' care.

His own creation, a Frankenstein in the lobby of his company, thanks to his determination to help her. She always meant well, but her intimidating, take-no-bullshit attitude undermined his approach every time.

Minutes later he'd packed up his laptop and walked out his office door. Most of the lights in the other consultants' offices were dark as well as he headed down the main hall. Rounding the corner, he passed Victoria's desk. She was already gone, desktop computer in sleep mode, her favorite red jacket no longer hanging from the coat rack. *If I don't do something, there won't be a need for a coat rack or her desk.*

Turning his full focus on the glass-paned doors, he wasn't prepared for the head-down, focused-on-her-phone brunette who walked right into him. He put his hands up to keep her from causing a full on collision. His gentlemanly efforts earned him a rebuff.

"Watch where you're going, Metro Man."

"Excuse me?"

A pair of furious blue eyes lighted on him, and he finally got the entire story. Here stood a walking disaster with a divine figure, hideous, too-bulky clothing, and boots suited for the battlefield, not an office. *A project sure to be a success.* If he offered his services to women still.

"You almost plowed into me, and you've got that GQ look going for you, but I guess anybody who works here is expected to look a certain way."

Her mouth moved, and verbal vomit came forth. She would be perfect, except he couldn't go there… even if every instinct in his body told him to go for it.

"I think you walked into me, head glued to your phone. Do you work for the janitorial staff with the building owner?"

"I—what?" Her eyebrows hunched, and she growled. "Yep, just go ahead and assume what I do for a living. Have a nice night, asshole."

Dev massaged his temples as he watched the angry, short woman with the brunette ponytail and combat boots stomp off to god knew where. He'd send Victoria a text when he got to the car. The woman was a menace. *And I didn't even catch her name.*

CHAPTER TWO

Kat had officially hit rock bottom, standing in her cousin's office at Bona Fide Image Consulting after a day of no-luck dead ends. With her less-than-reputable credit, no bank would help her, and it'd take more than a personal loan of twelve hundred, the paltry amount offered by a local loan company, to complete the work. "Did you get my message?"

"I'm here, aren't I?" Her cousin Mark stood from behind his desk and motioned at her to shut the door. "Pretty ballsy move if you ask me. Why are you so desperate to save that old pile?"

She moved further into the room as he went to a cherrywood side cabinet. The office was done up in similar coloring and opulent to a ridiculous degree, similar to the bag o'douche she nearly ran into in the hallway. The autographed celebrity photos and college diplomas plastered on the wall, along with the multiple business recognition awards, and any unsuspecting person would think her cousin ran a financial firm. Instead he had partnered with his best friend and become chief financial officer for the personal branding and image consulting company they'd created. Yet he had the means to help.

"The old pile was our grandmother's home, your dad's home. It's the last family heirloom, and I promised her I'd keep it in the family." She'd died over four years prior, and Kat knew Mark and his family had stayed apart from Gran after his dad went to jail—at least until her funeral. Kat had been invited to her aunt's family dinners ever since.

"Family heirloom not worth much." He poured a glass of brown liquor. "Whiskey?"

"Sure." She wouldn't turn down a stiff drink, not when she needed to find common ground and get a little courage to restate her request. Letting her purse first slide off her shoulder into one of his dark cherry-colored

9

seats, she claimed her glass.

"Make sure to sip on it. It's not the swilling Jack Daniel's crap you're used to."

"I'll be sure not to swaller the whole fucking glass." *Damn.* She couldn't stop her smart ass even if she wanted to, but he needed to stop treating her, and anyone else for that matter, like they were all backwoods hillbillies. She took a sip, and sure as shooting, the whiskey slid down smooth, leaving a small trail of fire. Letting out her breath on an exhale, like her daddy'd taught her, she enjoyed the smoky taste left behind.

"Now, let me be sure I got this right. You want me to give you a thirty thousand dollar loan and work this out into car-payment-size payments?" He took another swallow of the caramel-colored liquid and then strode back to his seat behind the desk. The suit, the short haircut of his reddish-blonde hair, and the lack of facial hair gave him a professional, reputable look, but she drifted to the idea of mob boss as he steepled his fingers underneath his chin, the whiskey sloshing in its glass on the desk in front of him.

"Correct. Money for hefty size payments every month, and I'm even willing to accept some negotiated interest."

"Interesting offer. Let me counter. Agree to a personal image makeover with my company, and I'll give you the money."

"Thanks, but no thanks. I need money, not a new look." She'd be damned if she played dress-up Barbie for one of his consultants. Singing karaoke from a bar table sounded more exciting. "I'm looking for money without strings."

"Don't think of it as a string, think of it as an addendum to a contract. You're asking me for a favor, and I need one from you."

"Your consultants, based on dinner conversations, rack up some hefty bills for their clients—new clothes, salons, and all sorts of things." Mark had even mentioned how they provided consultations to a plastic surgeon in Little Rock. No knife trips for her and no needles either. She wanted to remain somewhat sane.

"I'll cover whatever money you'll need for the wardrobe renovation process, including shoes, hair, makeup, and any food expenses you may have from the scheduled meetings. You can bill it all back to me."

She swirled her own glass, watching the whiskey slide back toward the bottom before she swallowed the rest of it. A tingling in her feet set up residence. The feeling made her want to be brave, daring. Plus, there was no one else. If she didn't agree to Mark's solution, it would be time to admit defeat and start packing her bags. An image of Pru standing on her front step with a smug smile made her angry, fucking frustrated. No way would she accept defeat, not when she possessed a chance to stomp the bitch's face in the dirt.

"You have a deal." She stood, reached over the desk, and stuck out her hand.

Gran had always said the family would be there to help, especially when someone was stuck in a pile of shit up to the neck.

Mark's grip was firm and tight. "No backing out on me. I'll help, but I don't like liars or cheats." A sermon she'd heard from him more than once, all due to the sins of her uncle and some such jazz. She'd never met Mark's dad, but from how screwed up he'd become, the guy must have been a major asshole.

She grimaced and pulled her hand free. "I'm not a fan of asking for help. If there were any other road, I'd have taken it."

"If you stick to the deal, this will work out for both of us. Now, you'll need to be here tomorrow for your first appointment with your consultant. Second, it's your job to convince Dev to help you."

Kat stepped back. "What the fu—"

"You can't talk like that either."

"What a bunch of bullshit and you know it. How the hell am I supposed to convince your business partner to help me?"

Mark smirked. "Hopefully your clothes, language, and colorful personality will appeal to his tender sensibilities. And I'm not giving you any money or finalizing any contract until you've convinced him to help you."

She'd been told her blunt talk could be too rough for the white-collar world, her dress style not exactly what some would call "business professional," and her lack of fancy footwear intimidated co-workers. Yet her boss loved her presentations and attention to detail. Her yearly reviews were flowing with praise, and her personal relationships would be perfect if she'd start picking the right guys. For someone who didn't fit the mold, she'd proved pretty useful. If anyone could help, it would be this company, even if she didn't need help. But, "Having to convince my consultant to accept me as a client wasn't part of the deal."

"Another addendum."

"If you weren't my cousin, I'd kick you in the nuts. Wouldn't your mother be ashamed to find out you're conning me?"

"I learned from the best. The only difference is, I operate my cons legally, which allows me to call them business deals. And, threats on my nuts are nothing new." He ran a hand through his hair and unbuttoned his suit jacket before taking a seat in the chair behind the mahogany desk.

"Sometimes I wonder how someone related to me can be so evil. Anything else before I get the hell out of here?"

"I think that sums it up. I'll have our secretary introduce you tomorrow."

She put her empty glass on the desk, the tension in her stomach refusing to abate. More hoops to jump through. She should've never agreed to this bullshit, but desperate times called for desperate measures. "Got it. I was in theater in college, and I pulled off a convincing Abigail Williams."

"Who?"

"The Crucible. Salem Witch Trials, pretty well-known stuff if you paid attention in history class."

He shrugged his shoulders. "Can't say I've heard of it. Be here first thing in the morning. We open at nine."

"I do have a job, ya know. How long will this meeting take?" She grabbed her purse, sensing their conversation was at an end. If not, then she'd wrap things up for him.

"It will take however long it takes. If you want the money, you'll be here convincing my partner to help you. If your job is more important than grandma's crappy house, you'll be at work."

Asshole. "You know you're a dick."

"Not the first time I've heard that one either." He focused on his computer screen then, dismissing her without so much as a thanks or goodbye.

"Why am I not surprised?"

Less than two minutes later, she'd buckled herself into the front seat of her beat-up, not-so-dependable, silver Chevy Impala and turned the key in the ignition. For once karma was on her side. The engine roared to life, and she mentally prepared herself for the six thirty rat race traffic jams waiting for her on the too-small streets of Bentonville, Arkansas. Her reason for coming to Bona Fide, the lies she'd have to tell to reach the finish line, and the ridiculous idea that she'd actually be able to follow through with an image makeover would have to be dealt with tomorrow. Before then, she needed advice and a drink.

***

"Great job, ladies, your progress on your resumes has been fantastic. Our next session, if you want to come, will be on interviews. A lot of companies are doing virtual interviews via computers, and we'd like to do a demonstration so you know what to expect. We will also conduct mock ones for anyone interested."

Victoria cleared her throat. "Now if you still have time, ladies, I can take you into the donation room where you can pick out a brand-new outfit for interviews, shoes included."

Dev watched the women of all shapes, sizes, and ethnicities stand up from their chairs and follow his office manager out of the church Sunday school classroom toward the gym. The clothes and shoes were donations from local businesses, ones he'd forged good relationships with by bringing them business from clients.

"Thank you again for filling in and putting this pop up session on." Theresa, the shelter's Activities and Donations Coordinator, put a hand on his shoulder. "We really appreciate the donations too, but they weren't necessary."

"When I told a couple of businesses about the monetary contributions we give to the shelter, they asked what they could do. I had nothing to do with it, nor do I want any credit."

She scoffed, removing her hand and tossing her blond ponytail behind her shoulder. "I'm sure you said more than casually mentioning donations. Business aren't always forthcoming or eager to have it known they support shelters for woman. Plus, spending your evening working with women who've suffered violence, sexual exploitation, and drug abuse is not always easy. So, thank you."

He'd become interested in helping the shelter because of Pru. It had been their project, one supposedly close to her heart, but she'd stopped getting involved. Seeing women in this environment was "too much" for his ex. "I'm honored you thought of me to fill in, and I was a little bit nervous."

"When the college career center fell through, you were the first person I thought of, and Victoria is a familiar face. I think it reassured some of the ladies to see her here."

Speaking of the devil, she walked back into the room. "Hey boss, everyone is all finished and heading out. I'm going to pack the rest of the clothes and accessories up in Theresa's van."

Adjusting his suit jacket, he stood up a little straighter. "Sounds good."

"Really? You could just give those back to the businesses; we don't want to take more than what we need." Theresa sounded surprised. Her left eyebrow, metal ring piercing and all, arched.

"I believe the intent is for you to have nice things on hand for any incoming ladies, whether they are staying at the shelter or need something to get back on their feet." He looked over at Victoria. "Let me know when you're ready to load those boxes, and I'll help."

"We'll write some thank you notes," Theresa replied as Victoria left the room.

Another reason he loved working with Theresa and her team, they were always so grateful, never selfish, and humble. "Not necessary, unless they want to write them. Those women are going through enough as it is, and there are no expectations."

"You know, most people would expect it though. You're always surprising me."

To be honest, he'd never said out loud how much he had in common with the women here. He couldn't begin to understand the level of trauma they experienced, but he knew a bit about trusting the wrong person.

"I know what it's like to trust someone, love them, and have them use those feelings against you. For most of these ladies things are ten times worse, so thank you notes aren't nearly as important."

Theresa's lips went all sad and droopy, eyebrows falling in correlation too. "I'm sorry. We don't talk about personal things. Someone broke your heart?"

"Something like that."

"Why do you help then, if it might make you relive some of your own struggles?" She'd posed similar questions for him multiple times. He always had a different answer because the truth stuck a bit deep.

This time, he let it slip out. "Because teaching someone what I know is the most rewarding when I know those abilities will be used for good. These women have everything all locked up inside them, the tools waiting to be accessed. I only hope I can help them unlock a drawer on the toolbox."

"They appreciate it. I could tell by how the room felt. They started out nervous, quiet and by the end several were asking questions."

"Yes, things seemed to go really well. When do you want to hold the next session?"

"Probably within a month. I know you have a busy schedule. How about you email over a few dates that work for you? Maybe we can do something over the weekend, run two sessions so ladies who have other obligations won't have to miss it?"

He ran a hand through his hair before tucking chunks behind his ears. "We'll have to confirm the dates with the church. My mother says they are usually pretty open, but I want to make sure we have the facility to ourselves for the safety of those attending."

"Agreed and I'll run it by my director for final confirmation. Speaking of, Bona Fide is one of our biggest donors, and our Fall-Christmas fundraiser will be in a few months, right after Halloween. Can we expect another big contribution? Because Gary and the crew have big plans for this winter."

Theresa's advocacy talent came from her lack of shame in asking for money. She'd drawn him into the organization, first with contributions, now with time, thanks to her knowledge of facts and her no-nonsense approach. She genuinely cared about the well-being of the ladies they helped. Her passion had seeped into him, given him a sense of purpose with his newfound success in the business world; except success was fickle, like a good hair day.

Unlike previous years, he couldn't commit to a big monetary donation. How many other people and charitable groups would be affected by Bona Fide's falling sales numbers? *Too many.*

"I'm not sure where we sit on financials. Not my department. We've got a meeting tomorrow to review numbers. I'll let you know soon." He hated playing the non-committal-businessman card, but truthfully, he had no clue how much they could donate, if anything.

She smiled at him, a friendly gesture he didn't deserve. "Marvelous, as long as I can get an estimate from you, then I can figure out the number of donors I'll need to make up the rest. You almost make my job too easy."

The guilt found itself a home in the center of his chest, forming a firm lump that grew with each word out of her mouth. They'd be devastated if he couldn't deliver. "Don't give me credit where it's not due. You do a lot of work, and even taking my money doesn't come without challenges, like finding ways to make it last when so many need help."

"Truer words were never spoken," Victoria's voice came from the door.

Dev glanced in her direction. "Ready for my help?"

"I can help too." Theresa wasn't one to sit on the sidelines.

The hard work they'd done tonight, the future opportunities that would be missed—all of it hit home, the lump of guilt growing to a boulder. He needed a solution, some way to make sure he didn't let Theresa, Victoria, those women with hope in their eyes—any of them—down.

CHAPTER THREE

"She's your cousin?" Dev couldn't believe he'd allowed Mark to continue this conversation for the last fifteen minutes. He'd barely survived a similar conversation a day ago. Everyone wanted him back on the female client bandwagon, and he'd been trying to alert the masses that he'd jumped off ages ago. The message wasn't sinking in.

"Yes, and she's in desperate need of a makeover. Her finances are in a bad way, and I think the image makeover could help her get a leg up in the professional world so she'd start working a job worthy of her degree and making the money she deserves. You know how some of these ladies get undervalued because of appearance."

"I agree, but I don't take on female clients anymore. How many times do we have to debate this?"

Mark sighed. "As many times as it takes for you to say yes. We need it, Dev. I'm asking you to take this pro bono as a tryout. See if you're up for it? Because if you can't, we may as well close down now. That financial meeting tomorrow afternoon with the other investors is not going to be a pretty one. I've got a couple of people asking what we're planning to do because second quarter receipts are down. Theresa from the women's shelter called concerned as well."

Their conversation the day prior had never involved a mention of the company's finances, which struck him as odd. The straightforward woman never pulled punches, not when it came to concerns about where she'd be funding next year from.

"Where the hell did she hear about it?"

"She wouldn't say."

He knew they were down, the report being the reason he'd kicked back three stiff drinks last night and passed out without eating. Dev rubbed his face with his hands. "I know it looks bad."

"You've seen how worried Victoria is. The other consultants are whispering about looking for future employment at temp agencies, for god's sakes. I'm not asking you to give up the male clients or take time out of the workday. Work with her on the weekends, but use this as a chance to get back in the game. We can tell the investors you're going to be ready to assume a full workload soon, but they already know, without me saying anything, that you don't have female clients on the docket."

Mark's words were another stabbing reminder of how his bad choices had cost him his integrity with the board. Instead of allowing Dev to announce changing the direction of the company, Mark had privately passed on to the investors that Dev was working through some personal issues and reducing his caseload. Investors didn't want to hear about gender exclusivity, not when Bona Fide had led the charge in co-ed image consulting.

"How about you help her?"

Mark laughed. "Dev, you know the only way I help women is by assisting them in getting their clothes off, and I may live in Arkansas, but I'm a firm believer in carnal relations outside the family."

"You're so crude."

"And you wouldn't want me any other way. Now say you'll do this. For Victoria or for me or for the shelter, I don't care, but do it."

He didn't want to. Lord, he didn't want to. He was still trying to recover from the last disaster of a client—his ex—and how his own bad judgment had started a debacle that was still wreaking havoc.

"I don't know, Mark."

"For Maggie then?" The words were spoken softly, given the proper homage they deserved.

His best friend knew how to get him. Every. Time. Bring up the woman who got him started in this business. Her very name invoked a heart-clutching squeeze in his chest. The words came out easily. "Let me meet her first."

Mark clapped his hands together. "Good deal. She's coming today for a meeting."

"*Dulce Madre*, you already had this planned didn't you?"

"I told her to come and meet you, yes. But I never told her you'd agree to it. In fact, I told her there was a good chance you wouldn't want anything to do with her."

This would be a damn mess. He rubbed his temples and silently prayed for strength. "You're an asshole, Mark." Before he opened his eyes, a knock sounded on the office door. "Yes?"

Victoria poked her head in the door. "I have a Kathleen Baum in the waiting room to see you?"

He looked at Mark and raised an eyebrow.

"She's not quite in line with the whole image makeover idea."

His friend could be a real idiot sometimes. "Then let's not try to lead an unwilling horse to water. Why didn't you just give her some money or refer her to one of our competitors?"

"You'll understand when you see her, and I don't think we need to give those competitors any more business, do you?" His partner stood up and buttoned his suit jacket, then smoothed his hands across the polyester blend; the gray was always a good color for him. "Whatever you do, don't let her back out. She's going to try and avoid change at all costs, but I'm telling you, she needs this."

Mark's instincts were pretty dead-on when it came to reading potential client's needs, male or female. Sometimes Dev wondered what stopped him from becoming a consultant. The man possessed as much natural talent for this type of business as he did, when he chose to deploy it.

"Fine. We'll see what happens." Dev looked over at Victoria and nodded.

Mark jumped out of his seat with a clap of his hands and a victorious smile as he headed to the door. Dev caught Victoria's narrowed, suspicious look leveled at Mark and her mouthing the words "I'm on to you" as he walked past her.

Dev wouldn't begin to analyze the dynamic between those two. Though they set aside their mutual dislike for his sake, there were several times he'd expected to walk out in the hall and find them verbally duking it out to see who'd draw first blood.

"I'll bring her right in." Victoria came forward and set Kathleen's folder on his desk. She left, thankfully, without further comment.

No picture or physical assessment had been completed, but she'd signed all the appropriate release forms. The folder, her name, and the woman were all a mystery—a covered canvas that would be revealed as a potential Picasso, Rembrandt, Monet, or O'Keefe after a little restoration. Or she could simply be a work of art by an unknown artist. He didn't want to be excited about the prospect, but instinct and the love for his job naturally took over.

When he looked up from his desk next, the mystery had arrived... and he'd seen her before. Before him stood the angry brunette from last night in another poor-fitting ensemble, but her face captured him. He took a more detailed look this time. Full lips, high cheek bones, a defined nose— not petite, but not elongated—and a diamond-shaped facial structure he'd only seen a handful of times. For a moment he couldn't speak. A woman rarely left him speechless.

"Devid Esposito?" Her question revealed a smoky, alto voice capable of both an attack like their first meeting and a seduction. She stopped a step or two in front of the desk.

He nodded his head in agreement, stood, and extended his hand. "That's me, but you called me Metro Man last night. Do you prefer Kathleen or...?"

"Kat. I'm only called Kathleen when I'm in trouble."

"Now I know what I should have called you last night when you almost ran into me. Would you care to sit down?"

She eyed him with skepticism. "Is this all you plan on talking about? A mistake I made?"

A tough crowd.

Kat took a seat in the walnut-colored chair.

Victoria chuckled from the doorway. "Let me know if you need anything."

Dev had honestly forgotten she'd been there; he'd forgotten nearly everything since his potential weekend project had walked into the room. As his secretary shut the office door behind her, the room became small; Kat's presence became larger than life compared to his. "Not at all, but an apology wouldn't be too much of an ask would it?"

"Fine, I apologize. Can we move on?" The words were spouted like venom from a cobra ready to strike. He'd been ready to offer her a drink. Not now.

"Apology accepted. Let's move on. Why the brash, rude attitude?"

She laughed, and the melodic sound broke something loose in Dev. Something yearning. And the fact that she laughed at him added to his growing frustration. "I'm sorry, I'm a bit... hesitant with new people."

"Then let's work on breaking the ice. Mark already told me why you're here."

She nodded in agreement, draping her arms over the top of the chair. The oversized armrests gave her body a waif-like appearance, especially in the bulky slacks and her disaster of a blouse. "Okay."

"How tall are you?"

"Five foot four, why?" Her face screwed up in annoyance. From happy to angry to pacified and then, in a split second, gone again. Hesitant wouldn't be the word he'd use to describe her with anyone. Instead, he'd go with *rough* or *unapproachable*.

"I tend to ask a lot of questions. As a consultant, it's in my nature. And, the answers you give are never right or wrong nor do I judge you for them. For me to assist someone, I have to know facts, thoughts, preferences, and any number of things, so when I think of a question, I tend to blurt it out right away."

The indents on her forehead smoothed, and she relaxed into the cushioned chair a bit. "Okay. I'm just here to talk about the possibility of a makeover. I'm not even sure I want one."

Dev shook his head. "Then why bother coming?"

"Really?" Her sapphire blue eyes went wide, and she glanced around the room. "You just said Mark told you why I'm here, so it's not a question worth answering."

"Yes. You need some financial help, but he feels an image makeover would help you more in the future with securing a better job and ensuring you get paid what you're worth. We'd all like to believe appearance discrimination_doesn't exist in the world, but unfortunately, it does."

She didn't respond, her expression unchanged with lips pursed.

"I tend to agree with him, and if you're willing, I may be willing to help. All you have to do is answer one question: What do you hate about yourself?"

Knowing previous clients, she'd never answer honestly. Most barely contained themselves before becoming outraged at him. Pru had suckered him because she'd provided a completely unbiased, blunt assessment of her dislikes, and he'd believed that made her different—someone willing to be brutally honest about herself. He'd been wrong. Judging from Kat's hunched eyebrows and the pout of her lips, the next words out of her mouth would end Mark's experiment before it began.

***

"Nothing. Absolutely nothing." Kat sat up straight and stared him down, trying not to waver or give in to the whispers in her mind. Her gran had always told her to love herself no matter what. She'd keep to herself the deep, secret longings about fixing the gap between her two front teeth and wanting to do something with her hair besides pulling it back every day. A little voice inside cried out *there's more*, but he wasn't a priest to hear her confession.

"Then I can't help you." Devlin got up from his chair and walked over to a small refrigerator against the wall. "Feel free to show yourself out."

Wait a minute. He'd made it that easy to secure him as her consultant, and she'd blown it. When she'd walked into Bona Fide that morning, she'd been trying to figure out how she'd convince him to help. Dev had appeared ready and willing at the start of this whole awkward meeting. Kat hadn't expected her cousin to do her any favors, but he'd talked to Dev beforehand, smoothed a path. *That's what I get for thinking.* When he'd wanted to know what she didn't like about her body, she'd been unprepared. Then there was his appearance.

Devid made Hollywood heartthrobs look like chopped liver; she'd thought the same last night when she almost knocked into him. Shoulder-length, dark brown hair, matching goatee, and piercing, amber eyes paired with a gray suit. Add in his accent, the rolling Rs, and she nearly melted into a puddle. He defined sex appeal. The suit he wore today gave away no hints to the physique underneath at first glance, but as he bent over to reach into the mini fridge, she couldn't help the little whimper accidentally escaping her lips thanks to the fine outline of his ass.

He turned with a bottle of water in his hand. "You can leave."

Idiot! He'd kicked her out, and she still sat there ogling him. "Can I have a drink?" Anything to prevent the moment ending. She needed a few seconds to gather her courage. He'd probably tell her to get lost. "My throat's dry."

He reached back into the refrigerator and grabbed another water bottle. Something squeezed her chest tightly, like being at a higher elevation. Maybe telling him a few things wouldn't hurt, especially since she'd hit level desperate.

She grasped the bottle of cold water he'd handed her, opened it, and took a big gulp. "I don't like my hair or my teeth."

"Hair and teeth, okay. Anything else?" His sexy, tan-skinned face remained impassive and unimpressed, like a well-trained poker player.

Putting the cap back on the water bottle, she stared down at Devid's tie, a black-colored fabric with a nearly invisible embroidered pattern. She needed the courage to let go of her thoughts. She allowed her vision to blur, similar to shifting a picture within a picture. The words spilled forth like they used to when she'd found herself confessing to her gran about all her troubles over a cup of tea.

"I feel awkward in my clothes sometimes. I'm not good at conversations. Around my friends things are fine, but with other people or crowds I've no clue what to say or how to act. It makes company parties or social gatherings strange, and in ways, I don't think I'm connecting with other people. Is that what you're looking for?"

"Like I mentioned before, there are no wrong or right answers. I'm not looking for anything specific beyond your thoughts and feelings."

"It's that easy?"

He smiled, and she realized he needed a sign reading "Caution: a Predator Lives Here." "Not a lot of people would call what you did easy."

"Well, will you help?" Another drink of water and she mentally cursed at how easily he kept all his emotions under control. A gift she wouldn't mind possessing.

"I don't think I will."

What the hell? "Excuse me? You said if I told you what I didn't like about myself, you'd help."

Propping himself against his desk, his body stretched out a mere foot from hers, her mouth went dry again. "I said I may help. So far you've given me no real reason. Awkward at social gatherings, hair, and teeth? These are—trivial thoughts, not deep and not from someone who's looking to make a life change." No man should have that much charisma while being rude.

"But you said there were no right or wrong answers."

"There aren't. You gave me all the shallow ones, which means no commitment. I don't take on clients unwilling to give this process everything." The way he said "everything" made her want to shiver. He sounded sinful, and she needed to maintain some perspective.

"My boss can tell you how committed I am to any project I take on. I'm pretty sure I can handle this." Her tone may have come across too strong. Dev stared her down. That gaze from his chocolate eyes sent her own darting around the room. His office didn't have all the fancy shine or the bar set up. No, he'd settled for his degrees framed on the walls, pictures of family, and a few paintings that she didn't recognize.

A shadow crossed the room. Refocusing meant acknowledging the fact he'd moved in front of her. Still staring. "You're stubborn aren't you?"

"Like a mule, at least my family has always said so, and I like the trait."

He smiled. "It's beneficial at times and no good in others. Tell me what you'd want from this experience."

More questions. Obviously he asked more than he gave answers. No surprise the girls in the lobby were gossiping about the state of the business and rumors about the company being steps away from closing their doors. If she wanted to secure his help and get the money, she had to indulge him. "I want to have..."

"Yes?"

"Give me a minute." Ideas rattled through her brain about the shows she'd seen, the movies, even a couple musicals. Makeovers meant getting respect, gaining sexual appeal, lighting up the room, and having confidence. Usually the woman in question always got the guy they wanted, too. There were also new clothes and makeup, not her thing. Maybe she just wanted— "People to take me seriously."

"If you're acing work projects, I'd think you already have people doing that."

"You'd think so, but not really."

Devid moved away and took a seat behind his desk. "Let's talk more about this. I'm familiar with women, well known for doing a good job, not being taken seriously. But at first glance you appear confident and sure of yourself."

Maybe she should have gone for looking more drowntrodden? Truth be told, confidence in her abilities earned her varying results. Time and again her co-workers made jokes, Mark made jabs, and even Royce, her boss, changed the subject when she broached certain topics. "I get your assessment, but when I try to imply I'd like a management position or that I'm serious about pursuing a relationship, people make comments trying to discourage me from the goal. Being sure of myself falls flat." The reasoning sounded a bit messy, but she had no other way to explain it. Her friends were all supportive and kind.

"I think you'd benefit from simply being more assertive with the people closest to you."

"How do you suggest that? I have a hard time keeping curse words out of my normal speech."

"You haven't used any here."

"That's because I'm trying really hard." The fucks and the damns were breaths away if she'd wanted to call on them. Everyone got used to the sailor part of her, yet it didn't make good impressions. Her goals required her to curb those words until he committed to helping her. "Will you help me?"

The room went quiet except for the ticking of a grandfather clock in the far corner. Seconds drained away, signaled by the constant tick and tock. She crossed fingers on both hands and tried her best not to let the negativity in her brain take over.

Finally something happened; he started flipping through her papers again. "You didn't fill out all the paperwork."

"I can." She pushed herself to the edge of the seat. Her toes tapped on the floor. "Right now, in fact."

"Don't bother because I'm really not seeing how I can help you." He pushed away from the desk, rising to walk over and water a plant. "Your willingness to commit and troubles notwithstanding, I don't think you're serious about this."

"I think you're starting to rank up there with my cousin... in other words, you're an asshole."

He turned, one eyebrow raised in that condescending manner. "Really? And that's how you continue to plead your case."

The fucking nerve. "Pleading isn't my style, and I won't beg. No, I'll leave the job to your fan club in the lobby. You're a cocky sonuvabitch, and it's no surprise your business is failing. If I had my nose in the air at every potential client, believing they weren't worthy of my precious time, I'd be out of work too."

Grabbing her purse at her feet, she stood, ready to march out that door and straight to her cousin's office to tell him to fuck off. He could take his money and shove it, but then she'd never save the house. *Damn!*

Stalking towards her, his face filled with anger, Dev stopped inches short from her. "And that's why I wouldn't help you. Too headstrong and unwilling to see when anything is your fault. You lie and then offer false platitudes instead of just being yourself. I wouldn't have confidence in you either. Get out."

"Really? You're a piece of work. I wish you the best in the unemployment office." A little over the top? Maybe, but he'd hurt her feelings, and she stomped out of the office. Men could go to the devil, especially the ones at Bona Fide. She'd take her chances with a payday loan or personal loan service company. There had to be options. It'd be a cold day in hell before she accepted her cousin's help without an apology from Devid.

CHAPTER FOUR

Dev scowled at the retreating backside of Mark and the last investor as they headed for the exit. He followed them out the doors but made a left toward the north end of the parking lot. The meeting had been brutal and predictable, the blame of Bona Fide's red balance sheet being laid at his feet. Claims and evidence were presented for his inability to bring in new business. Then there was a survey showing how the majority of female clients didn't want to work with a female consultant because "they found them untrustworthy."

Dev found the board's proof prejudiced and far from impartial, which is what he'd said. Mark had quieted him down and then told the board Dev would begin taking on new clients— preferably female, once a trial run was executed. Corporate consultations would be reassigned, etc. The words were everything they'd rehearsed, except he'd told his partner's cousin no. He shook his head, climbed into his BMW, and fired up the engine.

She came with too much baggage and was clearly hiding something— what that could be bothered him. Sure, he could work around those issues, focus on the glaring problems like how she dressed in poorly fitted trousers and blouses old women wore. She needed help, badly. A closet clean-out and shopping excursion might open her eyes, but who's to say a guiding hand wouldn't exchange her sailor's mouth for passive-aggressive verbal barbs. If anything, their interview proved clothes were the least of her problems. As Victoria would say, the girl embodied a hot mess. He'd always enjoyed messes.

Except when they use your tools against you and convince you to sell controlling interest in your company to a group of investors.

Kat wasn't Pru in a lot of ways. From the moan she'd let out while he'd retrieved the water, a sultry sound etched into his mind, to her refusal to be cowed by his comments, she radiated a subtle beauty and appeal. She stood

25

her ground, and he admired her for it. Paired with her wishy-washy confidence, he'd been drawn to her like a siren sending out a call. He wanted to help, to fix. To guide her on the path by bolstering her confidence, restoring her self-image, and awaking her to her own strengths.

He pulled into his favorite bar and grill, Jimmy's, determined to put all the wayward thoughts behind him with a stiff drink, a good meal, and plenty of alone time to brainstorm a better plan.

Jimmy's was one part sports aficionado mixed with a hint of dive bar and a splash of man cave. The small hole in the wall, positioned in a strip mall in the city of Rogers near the commonly known "restaurant row," proved a wonderful place to get away from the corporate crowd and blend in with the blue-collar folks. The hostesses, bartenders, and waitstaff knew him. They gave him the same booth, which magically never had customers in it, and positioned him at the back of the restaurant, far away from the door. He liked eating with a small bit of privacy. Once seated, his drink of choice, scotch on the rocks appeared.

Jenna, his waitress for the evening, received his nod of appreciation. She wore the standard jean skirt and tight T-shirt top with Jimmy's emblazoned across the front in black Comic Sans letters. He recalled her mentioning she was in business school and this job, while not ideal, worked with her class schedule. "The usual, Mr. Esposito?"

"What's the special tonight?"

"The Swiss and mushroom burger with steak fries and a side salad." She grabbed her notepad and waited patiently.

He stroked his goatee and gave a smile, before shaking his head.

"The usual then."

"Yes, but add some extra honey mustard." The meeting from earlier required extra dipping, and he'd happily "eat his feelings" as Victoria often called it.

"You got it."

He gave her backside a glance, but any appreciation was replaced with a question about Kat's opinion of miniskirts—more precisely, had she ever worn one. He frowned at the random thought and threw back the drink—no sipping tonight.

"I knew you'd come here to pout after the meeting." His ex's voice cut through the rush of relief from the scotch and dropped a stone in his belly. She'd been one of the loudest voices at the investors meeting, a constant reminder of his failure, smirks and sultry eyes be damned.

Pru still looked flawless in her pinstripe skirt and white blouse, the matching jacket hanging from the crook of her arm and a daiquiri in her hand. "Won't you invite me to sit?"

How had he missed her when he arrived? The decisive moment, yes or no. His mama had raised a gentleman, but this woman instinctively drove away those habits. Her downturned lips and puppy-plea look reminded him of the arguments, her inability to see when her words hurt. *Screw it*. He'd have Jenna pack up his dinner. "No, I'm just getting ready to leave."

"That's all right. I only need a few minutes." Pru gently slid into the seat across from him. Obviously, the phrase "no means no" didn't do anything for her. It never had. "So… it's been a while since I've been here."

Her smile of white teeth flashed in the light from the Mason jar lamps hovering over the table.

He'd taught her to never relent, to own the conversation, direct it, and experience success. Most men enjoyed women who knew how to make a man feel important and handle tense situations. She'd become a pro. He could get up and walk out, but it would only mean she'd accost him somewhere else. Better to let this play out. Fast.

Dev signaled Jenna for another drink. "Why are you here? If I recall, this place is too lowbrow for you."

"We didn't get a chance to speak one-on-one, and I wanted to apologize for the lambasting at the meeting." Another smile, a sip of her drink, and the slide of her fingers along the stem were the subtle invitation signs of a future sexual encounter. He'd taught her that too, but as something fun between them and not as a trick to be deployed on anyone, even himself.

Before he could disabuse her of the belief they'd be jumping into bed together anytime soon, Jenna appeared with the second drink. "Your dinner will be right out, Dev. Anything for you, Ms. Stone?"

Damn. Jenna had been working at Jimmy's too long if she still recalled his ex's name. Hopefully this little conversation didn't give the impression they were back together.

Pru gasped, eyes narrowing on his all-too-innocent waitress.

Jenna jerked back, eyes darting around the table and floor. "Is something wrong? Something on my clothes, in my teeth?"

"No, nothing in your teeth." Pru leaned forward on the table. "It's just the makeup you're wearing. Not for you for sure. Wouldn't you agree, Dev?"

Dulce Madre. The final ax in their relationship had been Pru's insistence on playing the image game wherever they went. She'd have Dev make image suggestions for everyone—waitresses, cashiers, department store clerks, even her mother. It had been embarrassing, especially when Pru made suggestions to his sister at the family Christmas party. The embarrassed flush of Juanita's face, a murmured *"puta"* comment, and then Pru had *accidently* tripped, spilling her wine all over his sister's sweater, a gift from a fellow teacher. He'd caused all of it, and that had been the official beginning of the end.

Jenna still stood there looking at him imploringly, desperate for him to tell her something. So he did.

"Honestly, you should wear what you like to wear, regardless of anyone else's opinion. Can I get my dinner boxed up, to go?"

Pru's expression held a glimmer of satisfaction and pride. Her little games cheapened his abilities. "See Jenna, he always has the best advice for everything tasteful, and I don't need anything."

How did she ever convince me to sell out to a group of investors?

Dev noticed the waitress walked away briskly, her face a mask. He couldn't tell if what he said had ruined her night, but she'd definitely be winding her way to the bathroom any second.

Pru cleared her throat. "Now, back to business."

"To be clear, my mind hasn't changed about us."

"I know, you need space and time. I'm willing to give you that, but it's not the reason I came to talk."

Dev couldn't help but chuckle. "Then what did you want to talk about?"

"I have an idea for how to put Bona Fide on the map and help all the ones who really need help. It's about image consulting at reduced costs for college graduates, single mothers fighting the system, and waitresses like Jenna." She looked surprisingly staid, hands in a steeple setting, eyes locked on his.

Here she went again, using her position on his board of investors to try and wrest control of his vision, his company from him. "So, you want to change Bona Fide?"

Her smile re-appeared. "Of course not, just add life preparation courses. The idea is minimal fees, low-cost classes, with corporate sponsors for job training, conversational training, fashion, business acumen, computers, and a host of other ideas. We'd start with image consulting and branch out. It wouldn't be about helping elite people with money. It'd be about bringing services like yours to those who can't afford the high-dollar treatment Bona Fide offers. My idea is for you to turn over the managing of the paying clients to one of your other consultants and head up this new concept."

Dev took a sip of his scotch to let Pru sweat for a minute. The hypocrisy present in her statements about his previous and current efforts was apparent. Whether blunt or not, she wanted him to give up his position as head consultant and CEO, allowing him to still be a part of the company, but at her direction. And leaving the company under her thumb for longer. "How would we pay for this?"

"An additional loan. One that myself and the other investors would supply of course."

At that rate, Bona Fide would never be able to pay off their investors and eventually own the business themselves. The original idea had always been to only use the investors as a temporary crutch, not a permanent one.

"First, you were part of those elite people with money whom I helped. Second, I'm not giving up the main reason I started this company. Third, I planned to offer all those things, for free to the shelter and other nonprofits in the area. I regret listening to you about selling interest in the company for a chance at money to expand. I certainly won't listen to you spout my own ideas back to me as if they were your own. I want this to be the last time we sit across from each other, outside of investors meetings."

"You can't possibly mean that." Pru's voice cracked with each word, and moisture pooled around her eyes. He felt like an ass, but she brought out the worst in him, especially when she wanted to pervert his dream even further.

"Yes, I do."

Her face turned into a menacing scowl. There was the vengeful woman he'd become acquainted with in the last days before they'd separated. "You asshole, I gave you all of me. I'm still willing to give you everything. I'm supportive and much better than most of the trash in this area. Maybe the rumors are right. You like to fix them, bang 'em, and leave 'em."

Dev tossed his glass back and let the last vestiges of alcohol slide down his throat. *Time to go.* "There you have it. That's me in a nutshell, even though you're the only client I ever broke my rules for. A mistake I can't fix."

The attack dog expression of hers mellowed, barely. "Oh, baby. I'm sorry. My temper. You know I didn't mean anything I said, right? I want to fix us so badly, and this life preparation idea would be perfect for you. The shelter has your monetary support; they don't need more of your time. If you'd give me—"

"Feel free to eat my dinner." He placed a twenty on the table and tucked his wallet into his back pocket as he stood. "One other thing, don't stop seeing your therapist. No man, even a rebound one, wants someone who rages at the drop of a dime. Anger doesn't suit a pretty face."

And he left before she could respond. Most men would've been happy to get the last word in, even a cruel one, but he didn't find satisfaction in acting like a jerk. Not now, not ever. *Fuck.* He'd let the senseless thoughts slip out, revenge words for the way she'd made him feel—helpless.

No sense in denying it any longer. He needed to get back to doing what he always wanted to do… and it started by taking on Mark's cousin as a client. This was his dream job, and he needed to stop treating it like an enemy. He'd show Pru, Mark, and all the other investors why he was born to run Bona Fide. To make it through the trial run with Kat, he'd need to be more detached, as distanced as he'd been with Pru.

I'm learning from past mistakes.

Give the facts, hard and cold without the nice and sweet he usually peppered in, the glimmer of attraction kept locked up tight.

***

"Goodbye"—Kat shut the front door and then, for added measure—"and good riddance." The paper clenched in her hand, she walked back into the living room, stamping her feet the entire way. Now she wished she had convinced Devid to help her.

She'd been so sure she'd make it without his commitment, without Mark's money. The ten thousand dollar estimate in her hand proved otherwise, and this one was the electrical only. She'd need a couple of bottles of wine before it was all over. The doorbell chimed, echoing through the house. Immediate dread clenched in her chest, reminding her of what Betty said heart attacks felt like—tightness in the lungs, difficulty breathing. She was losing it.

Opening the door, she half expected to see the contractor back to tell her the price had doubled. Instead, the very friend she'd been thinking of stood there looking out at her poor excuse for a front yard. When she turned, she smiled, so damnably cute. Blond hair and blue eyes, the woman could've been a model, especially with her pencil skirt and blouse. The woman dressed to the nines with a late 50s or early 60s style. Few could pull it off.

Then the unbidden thought of Dev's eyes, face, and his arms crossed at the elbows came forth, all wrapped up in the power suit he wore. He wouldn't have looked at Betty with as much disdain. Thinking of him brought unwanted attraction-based thoughts, along with an urge to lick her lips. Anything besides a professional relationship would be completely wrong, and a man that good looking and educated had flaws. They all did. Regardless, she'd officially joined the fringe ranks of his lust club from limited association only. The thought made her stomach curdle.

"Wow, show me how you feel."

She jerked her head back, blasting away all the inappropriate thoughts. "What?"

"You looked at me like I was one of those clean-carpet salesmen looking for a chance to sell you the latest product."

"Sorry, long day and not the greatest news. Speaking of, what are you doing here?" Last time she'd checked, co-workers, even those within her circle of friends, didn't make house calls in the middle of the day.

She grinned and held up Kat's laptop charger. "Someone forgot her necessary wall plug and called to see if our boss could send someone. I'm the lucky winner and got to cut out of work early."

"Lucky you, for sure. Come in then." She stepped back, motioning for Betty to step inside. The house wasn't its usual mess and disaster zone. No scrapbooking stuff lying everywhere and all that nonsense—not with contractors in and out. She dreaded the arrival of the next one, in another hour according to her cell phone.

"So..." Betty moved past her, and Kat closed the entrance to the outside world. "Here's the charger. Now, give me the lowdown. Everyone is worried about you, especially since you called in and you never take a sick day. Ever."

Kat took the outstretched computer cord and threw it on the couch, contemplating how much she should tell her friend. When it came to personal problems, she'd always fallen under the heading of listener. Sharing didn't come naturally to her, not with anyone besides her gran.

"Ouch, is that how you treat all your stuff?"

"No, I have a care for the *stuff* I appreciate." Like the boxes of family photos, clippings, and info she'd been organizing since before her gran had passed. A firm reminder that the one person she confessed her problems to could no longer listen. Maybe it was time to put a little faith in the friendships she'd cultivated, starting with the woman standing beside her.

"I'm in a little bit of a pickle, and I don't know what the hell to do."

Betty walked right by her and into the living room, taking up a seat on her tan sofa next to the discarded charger. "I'm all ears."

"Remember when I told you about the lady wanting to buy my house?"

Her friend nodded before leaning forward to reach into the candy bowl on the coffee table. One of her gran's traditions was keeping chocolate for visitors; like the house, it was something Kat wanted to live on forever, passing it down to her children, if she ever had any.

"Well, the Purple People Eater sicced the city's code enforcement department on me, paired with building inspection. It appears my grandmother's home is breaking multiple codes, including plumbing and electric. I don't have carbon monoxide detectors, and my refrigerator has to be on its own circuit. Staying home was the only way I could make time for all the contractors to come over and give estimates on the work I need completed."

Betty didn't say anything right away. Nope, she chewed on the chocolate caramel in her mouth. "Why didn't you tell us?"

"Tell who?"

"Any of us. You have friends, Kat. I can count us on one hand, but still, we're your friends."

Betty was right. Somehow over the years of being employed at Ying and Yang Marketing she'd become a group of five. Betty, Royce, Natalie, and Ana made up her inner circle, and they spent plenty of days after work tossing back a few cold ones at a local bar. Dragging them into her issues wouldn't have done anything though.

"What can you do? None of you are rolling in the dough last time I checked. It's silly to whine about my problems."

"We may not be able to do anything physically about it, but emotional support never hurt anyone. You're supposed to whine about your problems to us. Bottling stuff up doesn't help you; take it from the girl with experience in such things."

"I don't want to burden you guys with this crap." The last thing she wanted was for someone else to resent her presence, to want to put as many miles between her and them as possible.

Pushing herself to a standing position, Betty walked over and wrapped Kat up in a hug. Her friend wasn't big on encroaching personal space and touching, which made this display of emotion a bit surprising.

When the embrace came to an end, Betty's face was scrunched up as if she was in pain. "See, I even hugged you. Something friends do, even germ-a-phobic, anti-intimacy friends like me. Now, how bad is the damage?"

Kat frowned. The other problem was talking about her whole mess made her skin crawl and gave a real quality to her predicament. If she spoke about it out loud to someone close to her, it made the whole thing tangible, a nightmare no longer confined to the slim possibility of it being a hallucination.

"That look on your face tells me the news is not good."

She held out the paper from earlier, now wrinkled thanks to her death grip. "Ten grand, that's only electrical. I'm still waiting on the construction contractor. He's supposed to deal with the foundation cracks. This shit makes my head spin, and the thing is, I asked my cousin, Mark, to help me out, but the situation turned out a bust."

"How so?" Her question got muffled around the second dark chocolate caramel in her mouth.

"He agreed to give me the money but wanted a favor in return. I'm not good with favors."

"Seems if it's not sexually related or something illegal, then the favor is probably worth it. Almost anything is worth saving your security and safety. This home is your safety."

If only it were that easy.

"Remind me why a refinance loan or home improvement loan is out of the question?" The third piece of chocolate disappeared from the bowl, the most sweets she'd ever seen Betty eat in one sitting, outside of watermelon daiquiris.

"Yes, a big fat rejection story there. The ex-boyfriend, douche-a-million racked up a credit card in my name, which I'm still trying to get written off as identity theft. In the meantime, the banks don't want me, my car is too old for a title loan, and payday loans don't come in increments of ten thousand."

"This favor to your cousin is looking better and better. No help from Mom and Dad?"

Oh, not from them. They were useless when it came to anything involving money, family, or responsibilities in general. "I've no clue where they are or where to start searching for them. After Gran's funeral, they mentioned backpacking through Asia, and they haven't been in contact. Besides, at the reading of the will, my mother told me I should sell the house and use the money to go on an adventure, like them. She doesn't give a shit about the home any more than my cousin does. You'd think there would be a familial bond there between mother and daughter, but no dice. I'll have to take on Purple People Eater all by myself."

Betty started laughing, which quickly turned into coughing. "Where—" More hacking ensued, and Kat stepped up, patting her on her back. When Betty had things under control, Kat dashed into the kitchen for a bottle of water.

Betty took a drink. "Thank you. Chocolate down the wrong pipe."

"Yeah, glad you didn't die. The last thing I need is an accidental death lawsuit."

"I know and sorry. Those chocolates are delicious."

"The devil's own, but you can't stop at just one."

Betty lifted her water bottle, toasting the air. "Damn, straight. Where did you come up with that nickname for the house buyer?"

"The devil-woman had worn these ridiculous purple pumps when I first met her and the other day. Now the name keeps popping up without a second thought. I should stop saying it because it will get worse, but I can't." She failed to add that the only way to keep herself from breaking down involved making jokes any chance she got. Gran always said to make sure every day involved a reason to laugh. There'd been little to laugh about since she passed, and now with the house issues, laughter came at a premium.

"You're awful sometimes, but that's why we love you. I've got to get back, but I'll cross my fingers that a solution will pop up. If anything, maybe re-think the favor. It can't be that bad. Also, if you do decide you want someone to complain to, my phone is on, and my ears are ready to listen whenever."

Letting an outside party play *My Fair Lady* with her life sounded pretty awful to her, especially if she had to analyze her personal feelings and shit. She walked Betty out, and once inside the living room again, her phone buzzed in her hand. A number she didn't recognize popped up, most likely the construction contractor. "Hello, this is Kat."

"Ms. Baum?" The familiar male voice, all low and smoky, sent a shiver through her.

Somehow she willed her vocal cords to produce the automated response. "This is she."

"Devid Esposito. We met Wednesday at Bona Fide." He paused, and she wasn't sure if she needed to respond, but as she opened her mouth, he continued. "I wanted to apologize for my rudeness the other day. In fact, I think we both got off on the wrong foot."

Surprise. "No feet involved, and I don't regret what I said. You were extremely rude." *Fuck.* Where the hell did her attitude come from? She'd been relieved to hear his voice, hope blooming for a second chance, and then her mouth went and ruined it.

"I admit, not my finest first impression, and your follow-ups were a product of my reactions."

"Thanks for the apology? But what do you want now?" The hope, like a tulip bulb emerging from the ground, still grew inside her.

He sighed. She could picture his shoulders heaving in the process. "Against my better judgment, I've decided to help you."

Fuck, if the regretful tone of his voice didn't shrivel her tulip bulb in a blast of frigid cold. "I don't want to put you out, Mr. Esposito."

"If we're going to work together, I think you need to call me Dev." He acted like her last sentence, outside of his name, didn't exist. "We'll also need to discuss some parameters for the upcoming sessions."

"Mr.—"

"Dev."

She stuck her tongue out at her phone. "Dev, as I said before, I don't want this to be something you're doing out of pity for poor little me."

"It's far worse than that; I think I can help you."

Dread pooled in her belly, low and spreading out like a slowly stretched slinky. She wanted to run, hide, anything to escape being transformed into some cookie cutter, materialistic, calorie-counting woman. "I don't—"

"Right now, stop thinking I'm going to change your whole identity or make you into someone you're not. The process doesn't work that way." How the hell did he know she'd been thinking that?

"I can't help it, damn it. 'Image makeover' implies taking away the parts of me that are me." She'd seen the shows, the movies, and skimmed through a few books. Changing your image meant getting rid of all the unwanted and undesirable bits to be replaced with palate pleasers. Natural instinct rallied her to fight against replacing her quirks for socially acceptable norms. She liked being the weird one at times because it forced her to be happy in her own skin. *But you're not happy.*

Another heavy exhale sounded in her ear before Dev spoke. "I don't operate that way. I discover your preferences and find new things you like but haven't experienced before, and we bring the two together to create a classy and socially acceptable fashion—at least with clothing and shoes. Each consultation is unique, and you still emerge your own person, even more familiar with yourself. Now, how free are your Saturdays and Sundays?"

"My social life isn't very active at the moment." She wouldn't mention Nick, the ex-boyfriend-who-deserved-to-be-castrated. No sense in wasting her breath. With the need for money to pay for all the work on the house, any other fancy, fun adventures—even ordering pizza—were on hold.

"All right then, we'll meet for our first session this Saturday morning at eight a.m. Wear running attire and meet me at Compton Park." He said everything matter-of-factly like there wouldn't be any objection. "The number I called you from is my personal cell number. If something comes up or you're running late, feel free to text. If you don't know if you have appropriate running clothes, snap a photo and send it to me. I'll text a reminder of the appointment time and location."

"I don't run." As a general rule, Kat didn't exercise at all. There were other things to be done— scrapbooking, household chores, or television to catch up on. She was a sucker for any foodie reality show, which could be why she'd gained five pounds in the last six months. Not like she counted the weight, but there were a few pairs of pants she'd found a little tighter around the middle.

"We won't be running. We'll be jogging and walking alternately. Part of improving your image involves improving your health. If this doesn't work for you, we'll find something else, but since this whole consultation is on my time and completely pro bono, then I'll need you to be flexible with my schedule."

"Asshole." Kat coughed, pulling the phone an inch away from her face.

"Excuse me?"

"See you there." Those three words sounded nothing like the one she'd originally delivered, but too late to take back the lie now.

She put her finger to the end call button and barely heard his, "Saturday at eight."

"Yep." A quick reply, but an attempt to stay polite, even with the doorbell ringing in the background. She tucked the phone into her jeans pocket and couldn't stop the smile, nor the fear bug burrowing in her belly. As long as the next contractor didn't go over twenty thousand, she'd be in business. The only hiccup? Attraction and business didn't mix. So those wild, wandering thoughts about Dev's voice, his body, and even the way she liked how he gave as much as he took, needed to take a hike. He'd help her get a leg up and her money from Mark, but physical legs would stay firmly on the ground and closed.

CHAPTER FIVE

Kat got out of the car, longing for her bed and a couple more hours of sleep. Last night had been a title bout of tossing and turning, involving thousands of scenarios on how to convince Dev to go all in on the makeover. His previous commitment echoed in her mind like one of those too-good-to-be-true infomercials her Gran called "devil's traps." The best solution in her sleep-deprived mind involved telling him about her ex and the issues leading to her move to Arkansas in the first place. The latter being a last-resort case only, but a good possibility for a sympathy wager.

As she trudged across the parking lot and onto the trail entrance, the crisp September air hit her nostrils. The sensation triggered favorite fall memories—football, apple cider, pumpkin pie—not exercise. The Compton Garden Conference Center loomed in front of her. Once a house, it had been remodeled in honor of the doctor who'd lived there as a meeting center. Another historical piece of downtown Bentonville transformed for public use. If Pru got her hands on Kat's house, a similar fate would occur. The idea congealed the soda pop in her stomach. Reminded of her purpose, the Herculean task she needed to undertake to save her future, she marched forward with a bit more resolve.

And the man she needed to convince to help her stood on the sidewalk in front of the building, bent over touching his toes. She stopped and watched, mesmerized, as he stretched and moved. Compared to Nick, who'd been all lanky, gangly limbs with little tone, her image consultant had enough muscle to spare. Shame Dev hid his body inside a suit all day.

He finished his last stretch, released the foot in his hand, and turned to face her. "Good morning."

"That could be left up to interpretation." Her response garnered a raised eyebrow. She came to a stop next to him. He appeared awake and alert, and yes, she believed eight o'clock on Saturdays was too damn early for greeting

36

the weekend. "I'm more for stumbling out of bed around ten for brunch."

"Is this how you usually respond to people who offer you greetings?" Dev's grumpy tone sounded as sexy as any other tonality he'd used with her.

Get a hold of yourself. "You're not an early riser either, are you?"

He crossed his arms and entered full glowering stance. "I am an early riser, and notice how I was polite enough to answer your question, whereas you didn't answer mine."

"No, I don't usually greet people like that, but my mouth tends to get the best of me sometimes." Her statements at their first meeting were no lie. She kept the lid on most of the smart stuff in the office, but outside those hallowed walls was a whole different story of sarcastic remarks to servers and thoughts blurted out in the heat of the moment.

"You need to warm up before we get started." He treated her statement as if it was a logical explanation instead of an excuse. Then he looked at her legs, covered in the stretchy spandex-blend capris. She'd bought them last year with every intention of working out but never did it. His perusal made all her woman parts tingle, and her nipples tightened. Even if he was looking at her for a reason completely non-sexual, her body wanted the opposite. Deprived libidos were a bitch.

"Stretch, sure." She bent over, half-heartedly reaching for her toes. The awkward position sent signals of discomfort through her legs, up her back, and to her middle. "Is it supposed to hurt?"

This time, he ignored her question. "Your form is all wrong, and you're going to sprain something that way. You need to bring your feet in line with your shoulders."

Kat stood up and took a couple of small steps to widen her stance. "What makes you the expert?" She bent forward once more. Instead of success, she hung there, not even bothering to stretch her fingers forward. Her thighs burned in agony, and her calves sent a blatant white flag of surrender.

"Track team for ten years, football for six. I know all about pulled muscles, stretching, and calisthenics. My clients get the privilege of my expertise as well."

She rolled her eyes. "Congrats to them."

"Including you." She couldn't see him but heard the annoyance in his voice. "Now, are you ready to warm up?"

"I thought that's what I was doing?"

"No, you're doing static stretches that will lower productivity. You do those after the workout. The warm up is coupled with the jogging."

Kat pointed at him in annoyance. "Then what was all the stretching crap you were doing when I walked up?"

He chuckled. "The wind down from my earlier run. I already put in two miles this morning. I need to warm up again before we do your routine. Let's get started."

She wanted to punch him for the laugh, for his overinflated ego, and his sheer determination. Damn show off, up at the crack of dawn running and then doing a bit extra just for her.

"Bet you think I'm impressed."

Instead of responding to her comment, he pointed at the start of the trail. "We're going to jog south. As we go, watch me, and I'll demonstrate a couple of warm-up techniques."

He took off, and Kat had no choice but to follow, especially if she wanted to ensure he didn't change his mind about assisting her. Her previous experiences with people and verbal commitments had resulted in rapidly changing minds and broken promises, too many to count. They entered the trail, and he glanced back at her, motioning with his arms to catch up. She put a little effort into her speed, but within minutes her calves abandoned the white flag and screamed in surrender.

"Now we're going to do butt kicks."

"I don't want to get my butt kicked." She wanted to kick his.

Dev shook his head. "It's a warm-up technique to stretch your quads. Watch."

He kept jogging, but with each step kicked one foot behind him until the heel touched a butt cheek. The limited impact of his heel to his firm cheek spun around in her head like a record on her antique turntable. "Now, you try it."

She had to struggle for the first couple, but after a few more steps she was pretty sure there'd be a twin pair of bruises on her ass later. "Achievement unlocked. What's next?"

"Knee lifts." Dev changed his jogging style, bringing alternating knees up to touch his chest. "Try to bring your knee as close to your chest as possible, and if you can, twist your left side a bit to the right or the right a bit to the left as they come up."

"What does this workout?"

"A lot of things. Flexors in your hips, lower back and abdominal muscles, and your glutes."

She did those and one other weird, march-like step that made her feel like an idiot, especially when a group of gals on bikes giggled as they road past them. Officially, the warm up wore her out, and they had to have jogged half a mile by now. She waved her hand in front of her throat signaling to Dev she needed to stop, even if for a minute.

"Why the slashing motions? Are you hurt?"

"It's a good signal for stop. How far have we jogged?" She needed water and a chair.

"Not even one-eighth of a mile."

Kat frowned. "Bullshit, it feels like at least a half. I can't go any farther. If I do, I may throw up." She probably wouldn't, but saying it made her want to.

"This is just a warm up." Dev looked at her intently like he was willing her to keep going. "I honestly didn't believe a woman like you would give up this easily."

"You'd be surprised, and you barely know me. I give up all the time." Not quite the whole truth. She gave up on things that wouldn't end in happiness, like wanting a man who'd put her in debt to come back, or seeking approval and attention from people who never intended to give it.

The look of exasperation and a muttered, *"Dulce Madre,"* from Dev told her now was the time to present her proposal. "I know you don't want to do this."

"Do what?"

"This." She motioned between the two of them. "The makeover, or 'life change process' as you call it, and everything. Hell, I've no idea why you even called agreeing to it in the first place. Mark does want to help me out, but I can sense your reservations. So, how about we figure out a way to make this process quick and painless? A couple of makeover sessions with some tips and pointers like this morning. I can now do a proper warm up to a running workout, thanks to you. You sign off on my makeover success, and we're done. I come out with a little bit of knowledge, and you don't have to put up with me."

Dev cocked his head to the side, like that first day in his office, the look on his face reminiscent of someone trying to puzzle their way through a problem. "Image makeovers are completely different than what you describe, and how do you know I don't want to be here?"

"It's obvious I'm annoying and slowing you down. I get it. I annoy most people. I've accepted that fact. We can wrap all this—"

"Who told you that?"

Kat raised an eyebrow. "Who told me what?"

"That you annoy them."

"Ex-boyfriends, co-workers, classmates in college. People." She shrugged. Folks she worked with didn't seek her out for discussion unless they needed something related to the job. No one called her to hang out on the weekends for fun, except the occasional phone call from Betty or her close circle. She'd accepted her lack of companionship and the human population's obvious indifference toward her.

"All right, I want you to put the word *annoy* out of your vocabulary in regards to anything to do with you. I'm more concerned about the word *motivate* because we need to get up and around the next part of the trail and back before the place where I like to enjoy brunch closes. If you're game, I'll even pay for yours." Dev smiled, and she immediately looked at the ground.

He was attempting to cheer her up, make her come out of the small raincloud she'd cast over herself with one of his made-to-make-women-wobbly-kneed smiles.

She placed her hands on those knees to steady them before making eye contact; thankfully the smile had reduced in size. "For free breakfast, I'm in, but what about the makeover—"

"Jog first. The conversation can wait until breakfast."

She nodded, and they both took off again. No full-on commitment, but he'd been more considerate about her first admission. Her good luck wouldn't last, though. It never did.

***

"Table for two, Susan." He glanced at Kat. The woman was out of breath, bent at the waist, and with her hands on her knees. Maybe he'd pushed her too hard for their first round of exercise, but he'd wanted to see what she was made of. "Are you okay?"

Kat lifted her head, cheeks still flushed. "Talking to me?"

Dev nodded. For a beginner at running she'd wowed him. Showing up in appropriate attire, reluctantly cooperating, and showcasing a competitive streak once she'd caught her stride.

"Yeah, fine." She stood up straight and took some more deep breaths, slowing her racing pulse. "I've never eaten here before."

The hostess flashed a bright smile at them both. "Then, welcome to the Blue Dove Café. It's good to see you again, Dev. It's been a while."

For good reason. This was another place he'd frequented with Pru and then avoided out of fear she'd appear. There had been a plethora of random encounters in those first few weeks after the split. The favorite dishes outside his door or dropped off at the office, *surprise* meetings at the park or the store—she'd made his home a war zone and he'd become an effective guerilla. No more. His ability to walk away on Wednesday night proved he could withstand her games. He had developed immunity to her simpering apologies, too.

"That's going to change in the future. Can we get patio seating, please?" He glanced at Kat to see if she agreed, but her attention was focused on everything else about the place. Another trait to admire and explore: curiosity.

"Sure thing." Susan escorted them through the main dining room and out a side door to the patio. Wrought iron tables and chairs dotted the brick paved enclosure. Blue and white umbrellas rose from the center of each table, providing shade from the sun, which was already on a nice climb into the morning sky. "The second from the end will give you a perfect view of the courthouse and the fountain in the square."

Susan set the menus and silverware on the table. "Your server will be right with you. And, Dev?"

"Yes?"

"I'm so happy you're back." She left whistling some song Dev had heard her echo a dozen times.

He sat down, and one look at Kat told him she was thinking all the wrong thoughts. "No, I've never dated her or been involved with her in any way."

"I didn't say anything, and I'm not judging." The sheepish expression crossing her face said otherwise.

"Do you lie often?"

Her face flushed, and she started to flip the single page menu back and forth. "This can't possibly be the menu. I know fast food joints with a bigger selection." The question obviously bothered her, and her hesitancy bothered him. Image consulting required trust and honesty; his previous experiences with female clientele proved it. If she couldn't provide both to him, then this experiment ended before he placed his order.

"So?" Yes, he'd push for an answer on this. Kat already displayed a lack of self-esteem, which most likely contributed to her lack of caring when it came to her clothes. He'd worked with a lot clients with the same tactics, attempting to rebel against their hurt feelings by dressing without caring. The effort didn't have the effect they wanted.

"I'm not a fan of lying, though I'm good at getting used by liars." She stayed focused on the menu, the tension lines in her forehead making an appearance. "Maybe their crap rubbed off on me a bit."

The part of him desperate to understand, to help and fix her issues, wanted to ask about the liars. Before he could, the waiter appeared with a basket of biscuits and offered to get their drink order. Dev stuck to the usual, water and green tea. Kat asked for a Dr. Pepper.

"Is that something you drink all the time?"

She shrugged. "Usually, why?"

"As I mentioned before, this makeover process isn't simply focused on clothes and basic business tips. This encompasses your eating habits, lifestyle habits, and mental health, if needed. The idea is to enhance the person sitting at this table into someone with the skills for longevity in all life's aspects, personal and professional."

"What does that have to do with my choice of soft drinks?"

This would be the part where she'd rebel, of course. Changing clothes was tolerated by most clients. Changing food and beverage choices always raised eyebrows and voices.

"It means you give up the high sugar, high calorie selections." He sat back in his chair as a look of horror crept over her face. An animated facial structure could be added to her list of talents. He tried not to laugh as he watched her lips pucker out in dislike and her eyebrows narrow in some laser-esque stare. Maybe he possessed a bit of a sadistic streak because he enjoyed getting those reactions. He recognized his pleasure as an early sign of attraction, something he couldn't afford.

"That wasn't in the paperwork or mentioned before. I signed up for the first bit you mentioned. Changing my diet is not included. Adding exercise, I'm okay with that. I've always wanted to be more active. The mental health bit... I'm perfectly sane, so no need to dive into that issue. Essentially, I want basic makeover services, nothing fancy or extraordinary."

The drinks arrived at the end of her little speech. She propped the straw between her lips, and for a split moment the small seed of attraction he'd thought of before sprouted. Those lush lips looked so soft and puckered in such a way that reminded him of a kiss and many other sexual things he hadn't experienced in too long. Add in the look of ecstasy her face embodied, eyes fluttering toward the sky as if the mere taste of her drink stimulated more than her taste buds and pleasure endorphins, and he found himself with a semi-hard dick.

"Are you ready to order?" The waiter's question brought his focus back.

"I am," Kat replied pushing her glass away. "I'll have the eggs benedict over country potatoes, with bacon."

No surprise she'd choose a meal with nearly eight hundred calories. He'd chosen to live life a bit on the safe side. "I'll have the egg white spinach omelet, turkey sausage links, and a fruit cup on the side."

Once the waiter had disappeared again, Dev knew it was time to awaken Kat to the realities of their partnership. "To recap your little pronouncement, you want the basic makeover service. How long do you think that takes?"

She took a minute to think about it, chewing on the end of her straw. He found the motion of her teeth distracting, like her lips earlier, and took a moment to readjust his position in the chair. This was business; his neglected sex drive and her attractive tics be damned.

"I'd say no more than two weeks at most. A couple days for clothing sessions and a few more for business professional and conversational pointers, including maybe an excursion in a business setting to try some of the stuff out."

"What if I told you the basic service would take two months?"

She choked. Dev jumped from his chair and had one hand on her shoulders and the other on her back in less than two seconds, patting gently.

"I'm fine," she croaked.

He rubbed two spots on her back over her shoulder blades, and her breathing evened out. "Are you sure?"

He alternated between soft pats and rubs on her back with one hand, while the other massaged her shoulder. There was a knot hidden in the muscle, and he kneaded it with his fingertips. The contact became intimate, and why the hell he kept it going he didn't know, except he liked the way she seemed to trust herself within his hands. Maybe she'd be willing to trust him with everything else.

Then she moaned. One of those moans that touched a man's sexual center and awakened everything. *Remember she's a client.*

He let go of her, and she nearly fell forward against the table. "I know the number is a surprise."

"I don't have that kind of time to commit." Where a sound of pleasure had existed a minute prior, panic replaced it. "And what could possibly take two months?"

"First off, time constraints should never be put on personal image success. Most of my consultants set their own time expectations based on an extended interview with their clients. We haven't even gotten to that portion yet. If you don't mind my asking, though, why don't you have time?"

Another pause and he used the momentary silence to sit back down in his chair. He needed to see her face, get a glimpse of her eyes.

Those blue depths showed fear of something, possibly him. "There are personal things in my life I have to take care of. Spending a lengthy amount of time on a makeover will—"

"Put a damper on your social life? I thought you said you didn't have one?" He sighed, gripping the bridge of his nose before inhaling again. "This is why I didn't want to agree to this in the first place, your obvious inability to commit to anything."

She gripped the table with one hand, knuckles going white, lips thinned in a firm line. "I can commit. I'm super good at committing. If I wasn't, I wouldn't have stayed with my ex-asshole of a boyfriend for three months after he got a credit card in my name and racked it up. The error right there proves I'm committed."

"Or rather, that you should be committed," Dev replied.

There'd been only one other female he'd ever seen so determined to go through with a consultation, and she'd invested in expanding his business and turned into the very thing she'd escaped from. In equal measure, Kat's short, impassioned rant made him consider breaking his rules on time constraints if merely to reduce the chance of getting emotionally wrapped up in this one. She'd already proved dangerous with her looks and strong demeanor. That paired with her being used by someone of his sex tugged at the protector in him. If he discovered anything else to endear her, he might do something he'd later regret.

The food arrived, and Dev used the meal as a welcomed timeout under the guise of eating versus the reality of replaying their conversation and interaction thus far. Professionally, Kat needed more services than what she wanted. He didn't operate under client's wants. When they submitted to his expertise, they subjected themselves to his decision-making. That was why, discounting Pru, he had the best success rate in the industry. No one was as thorough or as devoted.

Working on a compressed timeline would allow him to keep his distance. If he refused to help now, he'd be breaking his core principle: never turn his back on someone who needed him. Whether she'd use those exact words or not, Kat needed him to help her for reasons she didn't want to reveal yet. Those reasons always came out over time.

The biggest hurdle would be working with someone who'd fight him every step of the way. She may not want to, but she would. He could tell during the exercises earlier. After she'd overcome her initial aversion to the process, everything changed. Each task would require a saint's amount of patience. After six months of working with men, who typically preferred blunt speech over kind, constructive feedback, he was unsure if he could handle the job.

"Fine, the arrangement continues."

She halted her potato and egg-covered fork. "But? I sense a side note to this."

"Yes, there is. If I'm going to help, you have to agree to follow my lead. No objections to my suggestions, no matter how much you want to. No more hesitating with my questions or asking a question in response to one of mine. Also, I need to know right now if you're the type that needs gentle words or if you appreciate the truth, regardless of how ugly it may get."

She looked hesitant, which was expected. He was asking her to basically give up her say in this whole process, trust him with the direction of their sessions. He would be lying to himself if he said those words didn't conjure up the sounds of her moan once more.

He would need to focus everything on work—the tips and pointers. Maybe it was also time to have Mark set him up on a date with one of his many female friends. If it would get his mind out of the gutter and away from desperate territory, he'd sign up.

"So?" Dev asked again and then took a bite from the fruit bowl.

"I'll do it."

The look of determination told him she would try. Obviously, her goal meant that much to her, and Dev would work just as hard to help her achieve it, even if the process caused him some pain. "Then let's discuss your homework for the next week."

CHAPTER SIX

"I'm impressed that you convinced him to say yes."

Shrugging her shoulders, Kat stepped into her cousin's office and headed straight for a chair. "I didn't convince him; he came to the decision mostly on his own."

"Then I was right; you're his type." Mark detoured to his bar and poured himself a drink. "A female in the wrong clothing with a desperate need for an intervention, and he can't help but help you."

"Misogyny at its finest." At least that's the excuse she'd go with. To be honest, Dev turned out to be really understanding and patient, more so than she would've expected, but telling her cousin such a thing gave him more power. She'd keep those internal thoughts to herself.

The sound of scotch in a glass echoed in the room. "Can I get you a drink?"

The idea teased her. She wanted a drink, but not when she needed all senses focused on her snake of a cousin. "No, I'm good."

He wagged a finger at her, like his mom used to do to them when they were getting into something they shouldn't. "First rule of business meetings, you always accept a drink, even if you don't like it or don't plan on drinking it. Makes you appear more malleable. So, drink?"

"Fine, pour me one of whatever you're having. Now, I called you; you said to come here to sign a few things, so... let's get this over with."

Mark set his glass down on his desk and grabbed a small stack of stapled papers. "Paperwork is essential. Provides protection for us both, all nice and tidy, and makes our arrangement official."

"What do we need that for?"

"Standard business deal things. The top one says you won't go back on your deal to do the makeover and that you have to complete the process in full to receive all compensation. I'll give you five thousand dollars to start and the remaining amount after you complete everything."

"That's not what you said before." And not what she needed. Five thousand would only get both contractors started, not take care of the plumbing work. She mentally tallied everything up. "Let's settle with eight thousand."

Mark shook his head. "You're not very familiar with business practices, are you? What college did you graduate from again?"

"You're an asshole." Childhood memories of him at random family gatherings flitted through her head and ended with the same conclusion. Like the times he'd pulled her pigtails and when he'd pushed her off the playground swing or when he'd cheated her and his brother out of a hard-earned snack by dropping a cup of worms on top.

"That's not the first time I've heard that and probably won't be the last. The deal is simple, five thousand now and the rest later. Expense money for wardrobe and other items will be dispersed as needed; we can meet up for an exchange, whatever."

"You've been an asshole for far longer then you've been called it." After being screwed over by one person too many, she should've known better than to expect him to be kind. Just because a gal had some lemons didn't mean she'd get delicious lemonade, sugar being a crucial ingredient. "The other papers?"

He extended the small pile and a pen toward her. "Read through them. Basic non-disclosure agreements about our company's methods and practices, a liability waiver, and of course, there's an indemnity clause in case you decide to back out. I already told Dev I'd have you fill these out."

She accepted the stack and leafed through them. Her patience for reading through things sat at record lows after putting in eight painful hours going through every single line of three marketing briefs. Skimming, she got the gist of things. Signing the documents took another few minutes, with her chicken scratch signature practically illegible, except for the "K" and "B."

Mark still sat there nursing his now-watered-down drink, an amused expression on his face.

"What's so funny?" Kat plopped the signed papers back on the desk.

"Nothing, but some folks like to have lawyers look over documents prior to signing them."

"The fact I need money would probably imply that I don't have a lawyer on retainer. I'm also hoping you won't screw me over since we're family. Make sure I get copies of those."

Her statement got a laugh out of him. "Sure thing, and being a blood relation has never stopped people from screwing others over before. Lucky for you, I believe in helping those who are somehow connected to me and mine. The agreement is solid and beneficial to us both."

He took the papers, and they disappeared into a folder on his desk. When he faced her again, his hands clutched a single, recognizable, rectangle-shaped paper. "I'll have Victoria mail the copies. This check is good for immediate deposit. Five thousand dollars."

She reached for it, but the butthead pulled it out of her range at the last second.

"Before I turn this over, a couple of things."

The muscle in her eyebrow twitched— again. Something possibly associated with annoying cousins or men in general. A reminder she needed sleep and to make a deposit at the bank's ATM posthaste, assuming he turned the check over. "What?"

"First, no discussing the fact that I'm paying you to do this, with anyone—especially Dev. Our agreement is between us, and the money direct from me. I don't need this tied back to Bona Fide's books in any way. Second, this is strictly professional. Don't get all gooey-eyed on my business partner."

An unladylike snort burst out. "Yes, that's exactly my plan, to fawn all over his egotistical, snobbish self. I'd like to think I have better taste in men than that."

"Not according to my mother and her opinion of that Nick guy, but whatever. You're not attracted to him, right?"

The truth stood on the tip of her tongue, but she didn't want him to know. Didn't need another thing to be used against her. She'd become familiar with that; the more information shared, the more likely people would direct it to benefit them. Mark possessed the talent to prey on those he thought were weak. So she settled with a misdirect, jumping up and reaching for the check. "Give me the damn thing. I've got meetings tomorrow and need to get to bed early."

He rolled his chair back, dodging her move. "It's only after six. Besides that's not an answer."

"I'm not attracted to narcissism, better?"

"I'll accept it." He handed over her momentary saving grace, and she immediately tucked it into her purse. "You might ask Dev to get you some new accessories, too. That brown corduroy handbag is hideous."

She looked at her faithful bag with its half-a-dozen quote buttons pinned into various places, the frayed shoulder strap, and blue-ink-stained front pocket. "It's a representation of me."

"Okay, Hobo Jane, tell me what's next?"

"Fuck off."

He laughed again, a common occurrence now. "You need better comeback lines. Tell me the current steps he's put in place for your makeover."

"Why is it any of your business?" She didn't want to talk or discuss the obstacles in front of her.

"My business could go up in flames if my partner doesn't complete this makeover process with you. You truly are a Hail Mary pass in the fourth quarter. I've got no other solutions."

"You don't treat me like a precious football sailing through the air."

"Bad analogy. Please, tell me what the plan is." The please got her since Mark's manners were largely non-existent. To pull a simple, polite word from the bowels of his crude vocabulary meant the request was important.

"Fine." She sighed and sat back down, the leather seat letting out a small pocket of air as she landed. "We're meeting on the weekends only, mainly Saturdays, which works best around our actual jobs. He's going to give me homework that I have to work on during the week."

"The first assignment?"

She'd halfway hoped her brief explanation would be enough, but not with her luck. Choking down her urge to say screw it and leave, she forced out the words. "I have to select four outfits, two for work and two for a date, out of my current wardrobe."

"That's not hard."

If she hadn't immediately believed the assignment was a test. "He didn't provide parameters. I'm going to fail with a big capital 'F' in red lettering."

"You can't fail." Mark went to make himself another drink while he talked. "Having you choose your clothes is a way to assess your fashion style, your comfort zones. There's no right or wrong. No pass or fail."

"See, that shit right there. I'm not used to it, and I sure as hell don't want to deal with challenges or assignments I can't win." Things were easier in black and white. The idea of accomplishing something without a clear path to success screwed with her brain.

"Haven't you ever taken a Rorschach test?" The question blended with the cracking of ice as he poured himself another Scotch.

"Yes, and hated every damn minute of it. Tell me there's an endgame like a Rorschach though, like some solution he's building toward."

Mark sipped his drink and then shook his head. "I can't. Honestly, every client is different. I've seen him push folks out of their comfort zones when it comes to clothing, and I've seen him allow them to keep their current styles, or at least elements of it. Just depends on what he feels you need."

Words she didn't want to hear. The need for money put her image, confidence, and sense of being at the mercy of a man she hardly knew. One who looked like a magazine model and made her weak-kneed as much as he pissed her off. "Crap."

"Any other assignments?"

"Just to select a venue or social event where I can show off my skills at the end of the makeover, which is incredibly hard to do since he won't set a deadline for when we'll be done."

"Then don't follow up on that one until he asks you again. Dev's an honest guy, Kat. Be honest with him, and he'll do the same. From what I can tell, he's taking the same steps he would be with any other client, so you're in good hands."

"I hope you're right."

"I wouldn't be doing this if I didn't have confidence in him. He's my best friend." Another moment where her cousin acted more like a human with a heart, a rare sighting at best—and he'd already demonstrated at least two instances this evening.

"I don't think I can stand to see you this in touch with your emotions."

He leaned back in his office chair. The spring creaked with his weight. "Then get the hell out."

***

One word to describe Kat's house—tiny. She occupied what had to be a two-bedroom, one-bathroom cottage with an ancient terra cotta roof and orange-and-tan-toned bricks. The front walkway was in desperate need of weed eating and a gardener's care. He'd driven by this house more than a dozen times and believed the place to be inhabited by a hermit or elderly lady. Not a woman in her prime, perfectly capable of at least basic home maintenance with a little elbow grease.

He grabbed the brass knocker on the door and tapped twice. The sound against the wood reminded him of scary movies and white-haired witches. The door even joined in on the farce by creaking slowly open. Kat's emerging figure nearly rivaled the horror shows, hair standing on end, eyes puffy, and shoulders slumped.

"Whose grandma died?"

That question started a fresh round of moisture welling in her eyes and her lower lip quivered. Like being targeted by a heat-seeking missile, he couldn't back away now.

"Don't cry." Dev stepped forward and pushed the door open the rest of the way as Kat shuffled backward.

Tears were already tracking down her cheeks, but no sobs had burst forth. He moved to shut the door behind him and simultaneously grab her arm. He pulled her forward into a loose and gentle embrace. Her hiccups and sniffles were muffled against his suit coat. Regardless of how inappropriate it may be, his body recognized how perfectly her body fit against his, soft in so many places where he no longer allowed softness. He needed to have Mark set him up on a date with one of the many girls Mark seemed to have on retainer for such things.

Dev pulled back to see her face while he talked to her—at least that's the lie he'd tell himself. "Did your grandmother really die?"

Kat shook her head no and wiped her nose with her sleeve.

He withdrew his handkerchief and extended it to her. "Then what's going on?"

She bit her lower lip then, gaze darting around the room at everything except him. He'd become familiar with contemplation on a woman's face, the internal debate.

He should've cancelled everything. No sense giving his free time to something she appeared less than interested in every time they talked. She ran gung-ho one minute and detached the next. They'd agreed she would be dressed and have the four outfits ready at nine a.m. Judging from her present appearance of sweatpants and an "I Love Pie" T-shirt, she'd rolled out of bed sometime in the last fifteen minutes.

"My gran died over four years ago, but this house was hers and yesterday was the anniversary of her death." Kat blew her nose, and Dev tried to give her privacy by looking away.

I'm an ass. "I'm sorry. Mark's never mentioned it before to me, but I know he's not a fan of remembering sad things."

She shook her head. "No, and I'm sorry for crying and all the feelings and crap."

"You've got nothing to apologize for. I'm here if you want to talk."

She rubbed her nose with his handkerchief, sniffling.

"If you'd rather keep them to yourself, then I'll leave you to those 'feelings and crap.'" He wouldn't stay where we wasn't wanted.

Dev had barely opened the door an inch before Kat said, "Wait. I'll talk. I mean, I want to talk to someone."

He shut the door again and followed her. The entryway expanded into a narrow hallway leading to what appeared to be the bedroom and another small room. Off to his right was the living room and beyond that the kitchen. The furniture pieces were mismatched, and the floorboards warped in some areas—a house in desperate need of a makeover itself.

If the personality of a person was based on their home, then Kat would be labeled a disorganized disaster. Papers were stacked on every bare surface except the floor. The spare couch acted as a throne for piles of clothes, which he assumed were clean. Coffee table clutter included an array of plastic cups, empty soda pop cans, and a few pens and pencils.

She scuffed her slipper-covered feet against the floor and scrunched the handkerchief between her fisted hands before plopping onto her couch and motioning for him to take a seat.

He did, albeit hesitantly, and only after looking to make sure he wouldn't sit on a half-eaten plate of last night's dinner or a pile of used tissues. The urge to judge her and the state of her house came unbidden, and every wayward glance at another section of the room reaffirmed his unfair prejudice. So instead of focusing on the location, he turned his attention to her.

"You said you'd talk?"

She sighed, slow and long as if attempting to delay the inevitable a few moments longer. "I look like this because I spent yesterday wallowing with ice cream and old romance movies. We used to do that together. Movie days with Yul Brynner, Cary Grant, and Audrey Hepburn paired with comfort foods. I stayed up way too late and woke up with this headache.

"I mean, up until about this time yesterday I was fine—would've made it through work with no problem—and then my mother shared some photo of me and my gran on Facebook. I checked it because most of the time it's an actual update about my parents, a where-in-the-world check-in. I broke down in the office and left early. So, hello again. Kat Baum, notorious fuck up, and I suck at this shit."

"Feels good doesn't it?"

"What? Being a giant disaster?" Kat looked at him like he was crazy, but he could see the tension releasing from her shoulders. She judged herself harsher than others, a trait common to his clients. They took on the weight of their personal reactions as if they were Atlas and bound to hold everything up for eternity.

"Talking to someone about what's bothering you instead of leaving it all bottled up inside. Don't beat yourself up for having an off day. You have emotions, you're human, and we're all vulnerable from time to time."

"I hate looking weak, and I failed your first assignment." She pointed to her clothes mountain on the couch. "Those are all my choices for outfits, and I planned to go through them last night, which in theory would've been a great plan."

He let out a small cough. "You were a procrastinator in school, weren't you?"

"Maybe a little." The chuckle and small smile she gave surprised him. Kat wasn't all rough and tumble or doom and gloom. "And I know Mark means well, or at least I think he means well, with this makeover deal, but it's stressing me out a bit. I feel like a wild animal rattling around in a cage."

He could relate. The urge to prove he could help a member of the opposite sex and have her turn into a success nagged at him. He didn't need the money, but their employees and Victoria did. No, his need lay in wanting to be the person he'd been before. Before negativity and fear latched on to him, similar to how it did now. What if he steered her wrong? What if his advice made her a bully instead of a woman who empowered others?

He shook his head in equal amounts to her statement and the emerging anxiousness his own thoughts brought. "Trust me; you're not the only one. But I will say from experience that greater rewards are found when you have to work harder for the win, even if that means working through your stress and fear."

"Is that personal experience talking or advice from an old coach? Because I'll tell you, experience has proven to me that the best rewards come from taking what you can when you can. Eventually, things always go from good to worse and people always let you down."

"I guess it depends on what you want in life." Standing up, he moved toward the clothing mountain. "The dynamics of living in the present versus preparing for the future are always up for debate. I tend to prepare for both."

"How in the hell do you do that?" The glint in her eyes held a challenge, one he couldn't resist.

"I'll teach you, but first let's find your outfits."

***

When she'd asked him how he did that, Kat had failed to prepare herself for the smirk, coupled with the confidence and raw sex appeal Dev radiated. Her female parts went tingly until he used the word "but" simply because the next words paired her imagination of his body without the suit he wore, an image she did not need. "You and the word *but* should've never met. And who wears a suit on a Saturday?"

The smile disappeared, but amusement still sparked in his brown eyes. "I'm working, and suits help me when I work. Clothes are an extension of oneself. They determine our mood for the day. Stand up."

She did as he asked, steeling herself for the initial stage of arousal that coursed through her body like a thousand butterflies let loose inside an enclosed space with no escape route. He crooked a finger at her, and the fluttering sensation got worse. Horribly worse and marvelous all at the same time.

"This outfit you have on." The same finger pointed at her favorite t-shirt and sweatpants. "It speaks of being comfortable and staying inside. Lounge clothing. Why do you wear it?"

Kat shrugged. "It's not restricting and soft on my skin."

"Exactly, but you wouldn't wear it to work?"

"Hell, no. It's against dress code, but also because no one else wears it." She liked it when his smile returned, this one not as big and blinding, yet still devastating. Liking him, wanting to make him look like that over and over, didn't qualify as part of the plan or the makeover process.

"For me, all my clothing fits the purpose of empowering me. Lounge clothes at home, suits for working hours, polos and slacks for visits with family—each selection prepares me for my task ahead, builds my confidence. The goal is to build your confidence through what you wear." Dev glanced down at her collection of tops and bottoms. "I hope you're not attached to any of this stuff." The last word sounded like he'd found something disgusting in her pile. The way he inspected her favorite, comfortable, gray-and-orange-striped sweater reminded her of how Betty looked whenever she saw any crustacean— completely grossed out.

"Is this everything?" He asked the question with a hint of hope, and all those fuzzy feelings were replaced with apathy toward his snobbish attitude about clothes.

Empowering oneself with clothing, who really believed that shit? "Yes," she growled. "Everything I've worn over the last week. There're some other outfits, the ones for a date, but I haven't gotten them out yet."

"Go and get them, and I'll start looking through these." He'd already started sorting through the clothes, breaking them up into piles, classifying them like a librarian did books.

Her stomach roiled at someone judging her clothes. "Maybe I'm not ready to start today."

"Nope," he clucked while picking up a gray blouse she usually wore with matching slacks. "You don't get to back out now. This is the tough part, sorting through the options. You put your clothing at my mercy when you didn't have outfits ready."

"Bullshit." She huffed.

He paused, hand already in motion to take three pieces from her pile and toss them onto the floor. "I understand this process is outside of your normal comfort zone. I understand you won't like my choices, but I won't use the same language choices with you. I recommend you go to your room and get your date night outfits instead."

Guilt, coupled with embarrassment, made her hot all over. He set her down like some rude employee, but he did it without raising his voice or using profanity. "I'll be right back."

She walked away, quelling some childish need to stomp her feet or at least flip up a bird back toward the living room once she was out of sight. He drove her crazy, up one side of an emotional roller coaster and down again. That was the only way she could describe this urge to cuss him out and kiss him at the same time. *Hot Jesus on a pogo stick*! That particular thought could get lost in a dark hole somewhere. Yanking open her closet door, she started shoving hangers around. She'd win round two and do her best to stay sane even if it killed her.

***

When Kat walked back in, he'd successfully rummaged through everything with little hope for whatever she'd brought with her. He prayed they'd have a civil conversation, at the least. Her arms laden with two colorful choices, Dev dreaded seeing the outfits in their entirety, if her other wardrobe collection proved any example.

"I've got my selections."

"Perfect timing. I'm all done." He stepped back, allowing her to admire the small assembly of three pairs of slacks and four tops remaining. "The good news, everything on the couch you can keep."

She jostled the clothes in her arms onto one shoulder and motioned to the pile on the floor. "And these?"

"Donate to Goodwill, Salvation Army, or any of the dozen clothing donation stores in the area."

If someone had asked if he expected Kat to smile happily and agree, he'd have told them he wouldn't bet on it, and those words were correct.

"You can't expect me to get rid of all those clothes. That's crazy!" Her voice cried out in panic and anger. She tossed the clothes to the couch and crossed her arms. She'd completely locked her frame and closed herself off. Those locked arms meant nothing would get through.

"All of the items will be replaced with other clothing, and only things you and I both agree on. You can't honestly tell me you enjoy wearing a puce-colored top with ruffles?"

The clothes he'd sorted through were hideous. Either they were too big for her frame and in colors not even his *abuela* would wear, or they had something wrong with them. A tear here, a stain there, or the article had been worn and washed so many times the color had faded into muted territory.

"The clothes are comfortable, and my job isn't to impress people."

"It is if you want a better one at some point." He ran his fingers through his hair, and then tucked the edges behind his ears so he'd be able to connect with this frustrating woman visually. Her blazing blues told him she still didn't get it. "Most of the women I know would rather walk around in the nude than be caught dead in some of these outfits."

He grabbed the closest offensive piece.

"This is a tank dress, navy blue with white straps, ankle length." He waved the dress in the air, turning it side to side in an attempt to find a good angle, but there wasn't one. "It's designed to hide baby bumps and potentially slim down a size. It's also made of heavier cotton, perfect for teachers of small children who can expect to get dirty. Professional women don't wear something like this in the corporate business world."

She looked at the dress and dropped her arms to her sides. "I didn't really like that dress anyway and only wore it once."

Score one for the under-appreciated image consultant. Maybe he'd make a second goal.

"At least that's one piece. How much will you fight me for the rest of them? "He was used to dealing with a little resistance. Clients typically bent to his expertise—they'd shown up on his doorstep in the first place. She had to know how horrible these clothes made her look, how they gave off the impression she possessed very little sense and didn't belong in corporate buildings.

She thumbed through a few of the pieces at the top of the pile and nodded her head. "You're right; half this shit is ugly as all get out. Most of these are cast-offs from family or friends, and I kept them because I found something to like in the pieces."

"When it's free, you can find at least one thing to appreciate about an item, but it doesn't mean it's right for you."

"Guess I have to stop being so willing to take the free stuff."

He couldn't stand to see her frame slump or for her face take on that disappointed look like she'd somehow made a mistake. The protective part of him roared to life, and he reached for the clothes on her shoulder, putting them onto the love seat next to the keepers. "No, you just have to learn to be pickier, and I can help with that. Let's look at the dating outfits."

Grabbing her first choice—an ankle-length skirt, no ruffles, and an ombre-style coloring that moved from yellow to red—he held it up. The colors went well with her eyes and hair, but the look centered on her top... a cream-colored pirate blouse that again hid her upper half from the world. The flowing sleeves drew attention to themselves in the worst way. "The skirt is good; let's keep it for now, but this top. Tell me why."

"I like it." She gazed at the blouse and gave a small smile. Her expression drifted into a euphoric state, one he was a little jealous of. How she coveted this blouse made him long for a similar look, directed at him. To be seen as a hero and not a villain.

"This shirt makes me think of far-off places and adventure. I don't have the money to venture into parts unknown, but this outfit can make me feel like I'm there."

To throw the top in the donation pile meant breaking her heart, and he wanted to find a way to make the blouse work for her. "Okay, we keep it. But these two pieces don't go together. We'll have to find separate articles to fit them. Next."

Basic jeans and a tank top–blouse combo—a pastel blue over spring green. Surprisingly, he liked this pairing; even the rhinestones on the back of the jean pockets worked in her favor. It was a country type outfit, and if paired with ankle boots, she'd kill. "What shoes do you wear with this?"

She shrugged. "Tennis shoes?"

He groaned. "I worry about you... but we'll deal with the shoes next week. We need to head out to the store immediately."

"Why?"

"There's approximately enough clothing for four days of work on that couch. You could use this jean number as day five, but I'd recommend you have a few more choices available to you since naked is not an option." He didn't mean to let the word slip, but it had. Then he followed up one bad sentence with several. "You go get ready. I'd suggest comfortable clothes, something like those workout pants and T-shirt from last Saturday, as well as some slip-ons if you have them. You'll be in and out of them all day."

Inappropriate images flooded his brain, and before she could respond, he moved toward the living room entrance, edging around the pile of donation clothes. "I'll swing out and grab a couple of breakfast sandwiches. Be back in thirty minutes."

"I'll be dressed and ready," she replied.

Once safely outside, he straightened his suit jacket and kept a steady pace to the car. His hand shook as he clicked the button on the key fob. No getting around it, this makeover might kill him.

CHAPTER SEVEN

Kat walked out of her front door dressed in a pair of cotton capris, a plain black T-shirt, and a pair of flip-flops. Dev wanted simple, easy-to-get-out-of clothing, and this was what she'd come up with. The way he'd rushed out of her house had made her less likely to give a crap if he did care what she had on. He'd lost his say in things the moment he rushed out her door, the jerk.

He leaned against his car with a paper sack in his hand. "Breakfast?"

"Yes, please." Maybe he wasn't so bad after all.

She reached for the sack as she came to a halt in front of him, and he easily relinquished her prize.

"I realize you're spoon-shaped."

She paused her movements, breakfast sandwich already released from its packaging and on a one-way collision with her mouth. "What's that mean?"

"Nothing. Forget I said it." Dev opened the passenger-side door of his BMW car. *A fancy car.*

"It's not nothing. What kind of spoon are we talking about?" She slid into the leather seat before taking the next bite of her sandwich— a delicious egg and cheese concoction on a perfectly toasted English muffin.

"Doesn't matter," he replied before he shut her door and walked around to the driver's side. He acted like a gentleman and reminded her of one of those heroes she'd watched from her movies yesterday. The little gestures, breakfast, opening and shutting doors. What was next? Would he dab any cheese that got on her face?

Once he'd gotten settled into his seat, she lit in again. "Matters to me. Are you a spoon?"

Dev chuckled. "No."

The car roared to life beneath them, and she set the sandwich in her lap to get her seatbelt on and then resumed eating. She took another bite of heaven before continuing with the conversation. The silence brought even more worries to her mind. "And if we're on the subject of spoons, I would rather be a teaspoon than, say, a soup spoon. I'd be horrified if someone called me a serving spoon."

"Forget the spoon." Dev glanced over his shoulder before turning the wheel to guide the car into the street. "You can be a teaspoon... Well, no maybe you're a soup spoon."

Kat swallowed her latest bite rather harshly, and it hurt as much as his comment. "Excuse me, did you just call me fat?"

His eyes were on the road. The only signal he had any guilt or concern about his last sentence was the way a finger slipped beneath his shirt collar and tugged it away from his neck. "No, not fat, but more proportioned, like the beauties of Italy. It means I have something to work with."

"Nice save. I'll take it, but if you were anyone else I'd have kicked you in the nuts, presuming we weren't in a moving car. Now, where are you taking me?"

"We're going to Stripped Down Chic, a clothing boutique in downtown Rogers."

She chewed and contemplated in silence the idea of spending money she didn't have on clothes. Sure, Mark had said he'd reimburse the expense, but she'd been hoping to limit the shopping excursions. After finishing her sandwich, she asked, "What are we looking for?"

"Replacements for everything we tossed out. You need a new wardrobe and, no doubt, the undergarments to match." The mention of clothing beneath her clothes sent a shiver down her spine. Today she'd settled for some simple cotton ones, nothing fancy or sexy. His words made her think about him taking the cotton underwear off, slipping them down her legs and doing whatever he wanted to her after he did.

Why in the hell did her mind go there? A natural thing? Besides, those things couldn't exist between them, never would.

Ten minutes later, they walked through the doors of a brick, building storefront sandwiched between a bar and a restaurant. The scented air teased her nostrils with the fall smells of apples and spices. Bright colors were everywhere. Clothes weren't arranged in a color format but spread across the room like a mismatched rainbow. Patterns, fancy designs, dresses, skirts, pants, tops, and an array of everything possible spread before her.

Kat couldn't picture wearing these types of styles. She stuck to muted tones—blacks, grays, browns, and the occasional navy blue. Pastels were her closest foray into adventurous, but typically landed her in a heap of trouble—like the blouse she'd worn when she'd met Dev. A glance at a couple of price tags and the sandwich she'd eaten transfigured into a rock of anxiety. "Dev, how is this going to work? I don't exactly have a crap ton of funds for this."

"Nothing to worry about; we can figure that out later. Hold on a minute." He stepped in front of her to greet a woman approaching them. A handshake turned into a hug with air kisses to each cheek. She reminded Kat of a pixie with her short and spiky brunette hair, her whitewashed jeans, and a bright orange top with sleeves that revealed the tops of her shoulders and draped around her elbows.

A few verbal exchanges and she approached Kat, green eyes sparkling with excitement. "Hi, Kat. I'm Sam, and I'll be helping you today."

Dev smiled. "More than helping—Sam is the owner of this fine establishment and a personal friend."

The statement earned him a slap on the arm from said owner. "Quit with the flowery words and bullshit. He thinks that will make me want to help his consulting clients, but I do this because putting women in clothes that are comfortable, professional, and sexy all at the same time is what I do. Now tell me your favorite colors."

Sam didn't know the meaning of personal space and wrapped one arm around Kat's like they were long lost friends, edging Dev out of the picture. Kat saw something of a kindred spirit in the designer and decided to open up and see what happened. "Red, black, white, purple, dark green, royal blue, gray, and sunset orange."

"I've got plenty of items that you will love then." Sam clasped her hand. "Come with me and tell me, have you ever tried on a jumpsuit?"

"No, but I love overalls."

"A jumpsuit is similar but better. What about textures? Cotton, silk, chiffon, polyester, do any of those irritate your skin?"

Kat glanced at Dev. He stood there with an amused look on his face, obviously enjoying the whole exchange. She couldn't have been more out of her depth. "I have no clue, but I don't like turtlenecks. The idea of cloth constraining my neck messes with me, makes me itchy."

"No turtlenecks, got it. Anything else?"

She shrugged her shoulders.

"She wants items that are comfortable, not constricting. Modest but still feminine, and with the ability to be worn in different combinations."

Kat scoffed. "How do you know that?"

"It's my job to know." He stepped in next to her. "I can also learn a lot by the contents of a woman's closet."

The heat in his eyes made her want to squirm. Pure sensuality and all sorts of bad promises were hidden in those depths, tempting her to dive in for a closer look. It had to be her imagination that he was flirting with her, but just in case. "You don't know all my secrets."

"Not yet."

Sam laughed while placing her hands on Kat's shoulders and pointing her in the direction of a rack of clothing. "Let's get started, you two. We've got a lot of ground to cover."

Within two hours, she'd tallied up over a thousand dollars in clothes, and that was even with the Bona Fide client discount. Kat wasn't sure if such a thing really existed, but Sam protested that not a single one of Dev's past clients was allowed to pay full price for her clothing. Not when the female designer believed the discount encouraged return business and new clientele.

Sam had proven to be a miracle worker with seams, lines, and style. She suggested colors and types of blouses Kat had never considered, like empire-waisted and low-banded waist tops, and waist-flair jackets paired with dark colored jeans. For the first time, Kat found herself enjoying the shopping experience, even if the price tags were more than she'd ever spent on clothes.

The part that made her cheeks flush was when Dev suggested that sleeveless and wrap-around tops showed off her bosom. And when he suggested a skirt far shorter than anything she was comfortable with. Some things were better off keeping covered, her legs being one of them. Dev argued fiercely against her beliefs.

"Your legs are an asset," he'd said after taking a drink from his water bottle. "You need to be daring and show them off. Allow them to display your sophistication and confidence. Besides, in the right outfit, bare legs make a woman appear taller than she is."

She twirled around in the burnt-orange top with three shades of yellow on the layered fabric near her breasts. A strapless thing, which surprisingly held up against gravity and her boobs. "You're insane."

He gave her a raised eyebrow. "Sam can back me up on this."

The designer whistled in response and walked off to help another customer.

"She doesn't want to get in the middle of this, which shows how smart she is." Kat glanced at herself again in the mirror, trying not to enjoy how she looked. "I like her."

"Good, but you'll need a different bra with that top."

"I'll wear one of those cardigans Sam added to my pile. It will cover the straps."

Dev groaned his disapproval. "Strapless bras, like sleeveless tops, are a necessity to every female wardrobe."

Kat wanted to call bullshit. "Never needed one before."

"Well, you'll need one now."

"Yes," Sam piped in. "Especially if you're going to wear this."

Kat's hands flew to her mouth to hide her unladylike jaw drop. Gran had always said shock should never show on the outside lest the devil find a way in. But Sam's idea of a little black dress nearly floored her. The material and cut were fancy and refined from the empire waist flowing into a miniskirt with varying lengths of layered black chiffon and mesh fabrics. The top was sleeveless with a mesh covering that went around the neck and tied into a bow with long black ribbons.

"No one I know will be impressed if they see bra straps peeking out of this number, and I refuse to let you have it unless you promise me you won't do it an injustice." Sam held the garment out to her.

"It wouldn't work on me." She'd seen dresses like that one before her and never considered them. Ever. They were worn by skinny, size-four women who didn't have fleshy behinds or thighs with more flab than muscle. She'd been a size twelve since freshman year of high school and accepted her fate long ago.

"I beg to differ," Dev chimed in this time. "You'll look perfect, and the layers of the skirt will prevent any immodesty. If you're super worried, the lingerie store has some other undergarments that will keep things where you want them."

He made it sound so simple and easy, but she'd found dresses to be anything but. They were breezy and made her feel self-conscience more often than sexy.

"Do I have to try it on right now?"

"No." He glanced at his watch. "We have to get going if we're going to make the next stop."

"Where?" She asked, stepping into the dressing room once more. There wasn't much left to purchase; they'd replenished her wardrobe. The only thing that came to mind—shoe shopping. She'd rather walk around naked than go shopping for shoes she'd never wear. Especially if Dev thought she might be willing to give heels a try. She hoped he'd say lunch. Her stomach growled at the prospect as she whipped the top over her head.

Right as it got past her breasts he replied, his voice a whisper on the other side of the curtain, "Knickers in a Twist."

***

Dev didn't feel guilty for making Kat jump behind her changing room curtain. He did it to put a little blush on her cheeks when she walked back out dressed in her simple ensemble. That's the very male, bullshit lie he told himself—she deserved to be momentarily flustered because her outfits continuously one-upped themselves, making him notice things about her that stoked his latent libido.

He doused those musings with reminders of the board's threats, of the disastrous relationship with Pru, and the fact that Sam kept giving him the you-are-full-of-crap look.

She was another not-quite-native to the area. He'd met the fledgling designer at a local small business owners' meeting hosted by the Chamber of Commerce several years back. He'd hit on her, and she'd dressed him down, calling his suit for the evening a cheap, Hugo Boss knock-off. They'd been friends ever since.

Once Bona Fide was off the ground, he'd started using her store as one of his go-to spots. Sam not only made beautiful clothing, but she designed for every size. Whether small, short, tall, or plus-size, anyone could find something flattering in her store. She was even known for her side business designing costumes for local drag queens.

"I'll put it all on my card," he replied, pulling out his company plastic. Kat's growing stiffness as the total climbed higher and higher on the machine had him covering the expense. He'd bill it back to her.

The raised eyebrow Sam flashed at him showed her suspicion. He didn't give in to the bait and kept his expression neutral, while Sam flashed her smiles for Kat. "Thank you for shopping with us, and be sure to come back. Especially when he's done with you. He may finish helping you, but I'm always here to assist if you need something for a special date or an important meeting. Any occasion important to you is important to me."

"Thank you, Sam. It was a pleasure meeting you." Kat picked up two of the bags and headed for the door.

Before Dev could follow, Sam snagged his jacket sleeve and growled at him. "What the hell is going on?"

"She's a client."

Sam gave her familiar, sarcastic smile. "Yep, but I've never seen you drop fifteen hundred on the company card when clothing a client. Maybe a single top or one outfit, something to try out. A whole set to keep her in fashion until spring? Nope."

"Money is tight for her, and she's Mark's cousin. I'm doing nothing nefarious. This is pro bono work."

"I-wanna-bone-ya is what you mean. Don't even try to give me that innocent, emotionless response. I saw the heated stares and hooded expressions you flashed her way when she wasn't looking." She pulled tighter and put his card into his hand.

He chuckled, trying to keep himself calm, to school himself in the ways he taught his clients. "The gazes were my appreciation for how the clothes look on her. I'd look the same way at any beautifully dressed woman."

"Cut the crap. You better not get involved with this one." Sam let go of his sleeve and shoved the remaining bags across the counter toward him. "I like her, and you don't need another relationship with a woman who's a project. The last one didn't turn out so well for you. I always said it's bad luck mixing business with pleasure, and that's my own personal experience talking."

Dev tucked the loops of the bags into his palms, enjoying the weight of the packages as he lifted them. A burden, one he could bear. Much like this damning attraction he had to a woman he couldn't be with, a woman he didn't necessarily like. "I'm perfectly capable of maintaining a professional work balance with someone I find attractive. We're friends, aren't we?"

"Only because I bat for the other team," she replied with a wink. "Stay safe."

"I will, and thank you again for your donation to the shelter. Those women were over the moon the other night, and the outfits cheered them up immensely."

"Glad I could help. Make sure you keep your pants zipped."

He walked out of the shop a little off-kilter by his friend's deep and correct assessment of his interest in Kat, but determined to stay strong. Kat waited for him at his car. The trunk popped open as he pressed the key fob. Once all the bags were in and the garment bag containing her dress hung from a hook in his backseat, they were off.

"Thank you." She said this as he came to the first stoplight, the sentence a near whisper, as if she didn't want to say two words defining gratitude of any kind.

Naturally, he needed to know why she bothered. "What for?"

"The clothes. I don't have that kind of money sitting around. In fact, I'm embarrassed for spending so much."

"Don't be embarrassed for purchasing good quality, flattering clothing. You're tamer than half of my clients. Most spend twice as much on the first visit." He gripped the steering wheel tighter, memories of Pru and her need to try each style in every color. His ex wanted to have everything.

"Do they actually wear it all?"

Pru never did. "In most cases, I'd guess not. They just get eager. I think you showed admirable restraint."

"Well, I'm exhausted and ready to go home."

"We're not done yet."

"How is that possible? You just helped me locate and purchase a new business wardrobe. I'd say that's a full day's work."

"Not until we go to Knickers in a Twist."

She laughed a day-brightening, jolly sound that transformed her entire face in a youthful, refreshing way. Another light turned, and he glanced back at the street. "It's a store?"

"Lingerie store, yes. You need a few things to get ready for your clothing selections."

She sighed, loud enough he didn't even have to look. "I don't need strapless bras."

"You say that now, but you'll thank me for this when you have them in your possession." He made a left turn. Only a few more blocks and they'd be there. "Patience is a virtue, and so far you've been marvelous. Give me one more hour, and I promise you won't regret it."

He waited, hoping she'd let the stubborn wall fall. She'd taken some jabs, made some objections at the clothing store, but overall, she'd listened to his advice. The fact that she'd looked fantastic in every blouse, top, slacks, and skirt she tried on had to mean something. If anything, he still possessed some semblance of talent when it came to dressing others. The art of clothing hadn't abandoned him.

When it came to lingerie, he let the experts in the store handle that part. Though clients often offered him a chance to view bra and panty sets, he always declined. Bras and panties were a horrible thing to think about.

"All right, one hour." He saw her sit up straight out of his peripheral vision before starting in again. "Thank you for the clothing advice. You were right."

Seconds ticked by. Another intersection marked the approaching conclusion to their time alone. No way would she get out of this. "About?"

"I do look good in certain colors if the cut, shape, and execution of the outfit are right. I still can't believe I agreed to several skirts above the knee."

"Trust me, whatever horrible thoughts you have about your legs, they are not true. Even Sam agreed with me; those skirts"—he paused mid-sentence to parallel park the car on the street. Once successfully maneuvered, he started up again—"will enhance your entire appearance and give your frame upward volume. Are you ready to trust me again?"

"Lead the way." She motioned with her hands toward the building.

The logo for Knickers, what he called the store for short, possessed a pair of boy shorts waving from a pole like a flag and each letter of the first word in a different print/fabric style. He knew the owners, who operated a flagship store out of Eureka Springs and were never in town. This second shop catered to a client base he'd helped create. A sense of pride filled him at the idea he was introducing another person to their brand of under-care. They called it that. Clothing underneath the clothes was the owner's passion. Once introduced to a pair of American-produced, cotton-blend undergarments, one didn't go back.

They walked in and the bell over the door rang. The employee behind the counter, Riona, smiled at him. "Welcome back to Knickers. I can get those twists out."

Her heavy Scottish accent was rare in this part of the state, but the owners loved employing exchange students from the local college, and she was the lucky winner for the semester. The last time he'd been in here was with a couple of male clients, since the boutique catered to all genders.

"Riona, this is Kat." Dev touched Kat's shoulder, ignoring the heat and the instinctive reaction to squeeze and stroke his way around her frame. "She's looking for a few particular things. Mainly some No Peeky's, a strapless, and Hug 'em Bottoms."

"Oy, and you know the lady's mind, do ya?" Riona's wink reminded him she joked, but her demeanor said the opposite. "Come with me, fair one. I'll let the man who knows everything stay here. Unless you want input on colors?"

Kat gave him a side eye. "Do you want to help choose colors?"

"Stick with nudes and black. Maybe white, but I wouldn't try anything with color or patterns. We're looking at business attire; best to keep it simple."

"Do you know yer size?" Riona motioned to her own bust.

The look on Kat's face had him coughing to cover the laugh that tried to escape.

Both eyebrows up, she glanced back at him once more.

"Is she for real?" she mouthed.

He nodded and motioned with both hands to answer, otherwise, this would get even more awkward. Kat appeared to be more modest about her body than he'd expected. At some point someone had given this beautiful woman the idea her body was ugly.

"36B."

Riona shook her head. "If you're a 36B, I'm next in line for the throne. Come on. I'll measure ya."

They walked off, disappearing behind a changing room curtain. He heard Kat yip and yelp as if being poked and prodded unfairly. The noises made him curious, but he tamped the wayward thoughts down.

When Riona came back she grinned at him. "I was right. She's definitely no 36B."

The measurement sounded like an offensive swear word.

"She isn't?"

"No, any woman with sense can see that. She's a 36C. I'll fetch the garments. You may want to stand nearby and give her moral support. She's a bit feisty and shy, but nothing like my sister Molly." Riona marched off toward the women's section.

Dev headed to the back wall of the store where all the changing rooms were housed. Thick, burgundy velvet curtains hung over each entrance, reminding him of the old school curtains at his college theater house. "Doing okay in there?"

"Okay except for my ladies being shoved around and cinched by a measuring tape. I think she pinched me on purpose."

"Well, she mentioned you were feisty."

"Me? She expected me just to peel my top and bra off in front of her."

"They don't have the same prudish nature in Europe as we do in America, or so I've heard from her lips. She's gathering the items for you to try on now and should be back in a minute."

"Great." The sarcasm elongated the word, and he could picture her shoulders slumped, like a dejected cartoon character.

"Don't slouch," he called out.

"Fine, but tell me what the hell are No Peeky's and Hug 'em Bottoms?"

"No Peeky's are a type of underwear without a panty line. They are perfect for business casual and dating clothes. I wasn't one hundred percent sure, but I took the liberty of assuming you don't like thongs. These are the next best thing, full coverage and no worry about people seeing exactly where they end or begin, depending on how you look at it. Hug 'em Bottoms are Knickers's version of Spanx. I mentioned you getting a pair for the dress or at least trying them on. These would work for the skirts you selected, too."

She peeked her head out the curtain. "Does it bother you to know so much about women's fashion and their undergarments?"

"Does it bother you?"

A blush stole over her cheeks, giving her a nice, rosy glow. "A little."

"Why?"

Kat opened her mouth to answer, but never got a word out because Riona hip-checked him. "Out of the way, silver-tongued devil; we've got undercare to deal with."

Kat moved back out of sight, and Riona disappeared into the room with her. Dev decided to browse the men's section, especially the latest fall styles of socks. He had a collection of socks, from favorite television shows to patterns for the seasons. A guilty pleasure to take away from the singularity in his dress code of suits.

He was deep in thought considering the socks and the next steps in Kat's makeover. He didn't care that the bell over the front door rang out. Nor did he care to look up and see who walked in.

"Fancy seeing you here on a Saturday." Pru's voice cut through his musing and made him regret his false sense of security. "I remember times when I'd never catch you in here on the weekend."

"You're right. Normally I wouldn't be." He wanted to call out he was working with a female client, wanted to verbalize he'd done what he promised he'd do. Fear slithered its coiling body around his stomach. She'd tear him apart, pry into his work, and it wasn't ready, wasn't complete. To have her know, left room for her to taint his process. "But I was out and about and thought I'd see if they had the fall collection of socks in."

He picked up a black pair with jack-o'-lanterns wearing lacy underwear. "And I was right."

"Yes." Pru grinned. "I forgot about your stash of non-business-like socks. That's why we fell apart, wasn't it? I didn't pay attention to those little things as much as I should have."

As usual, it always came back to her bringing up their past and making up new reasons for why things fell apart. "If you want to call it that, fine.

I'm just here to do some personal shopping, not get into this again."

She held her hands up in surrender. "All right. I won't bring it up. But I will ask, have you given any more thought to my idea of a second branch at Bona Fide?"

"No, I haven't, and I'm not going to. Maybe in another year or two when we've secured our consulting piece."

Someone tapped him on the shoulder then, snuck up when he didn't expect it, and he turned around abruptly, fearful Kat stood there. Instead, it was Riona. "I'm done. Do you want to buy those?" She pointed at the socks in his hand.

"Yes, along with my other selections."

"Sure thing. Anything I can do for you, ma'am?" She turned her attention to Pru, who eyed the both of them skeptically for a moment.

Pru stood straight and haughty, as only years of practice could have done. "I had an order that came in under the name Pru Stone."

"Aye, I have that behind the counter for you. One moment." Riona rushed over, grabbing a hanging plaid garment bag and brought it back. "You're welcome to try it on here if you'd like."

"No, I'll save it for later." The words were inflected with plenty of innuendoes. If Dev was interested, he'd only need to express said interest to be invited to her unveiling of the outfit in the bag. "Have a nice day."

Dev nodded in agreement and didn't bother watching her walk off. No, he needed to keep his focus on the end game and to secure his place at his company.

CHAPTER EIGHT

Kat sat on her couch sipping a Dr. Pepper in defiance. Dev was scheduled to arrive in the next thirty minutes, and she'd been warring with herself all week about what to do. She'd seen him talking with her enemy. In fact, the pair appeared to know each other well. Maybe they were in cahoots, and he was helping Pru in her nefarious plot to take her childhood home. Regardless of their connection, it had made her throw a fit and act a little childish about her homework assignment from Dev. In fact, she'd basically given him a middle finger sandwich with an extra side of fuck-you sauce by not responding to his texts. If he showed up at all, she'd be surprised. But it was better to light the Trojan Horse on fire before he got past her defensive perimeter. *And just when I started to trust him too.*

Outside of contemplating her next steps with the image consultant, an electrician had come by today to begin redoing her breaker box and fix the power distribution between the master bedroom, the bathroom, and the kitchen, including the separate circuit for the refrigerator. This, according to the electrician, must have been wired by a crack addict on LSD. Since he'd started working, the repeated flickering of lights gave the impression her house was rented to a family of ghosts.

Somewhere between thinking about the electrician and wondering if she should check on him, someone pounded on her front door. It appeared the electric work had done something to the doorbell. *Gran, make sure Mr. Sparky hooks everything back up right.*

She dragged herself off the couch, ready to tell the unwanted door-to-door seller-of-goods that she'd found God and enjoyed all her television on the Netflix subscription she got through her internet. Instead, she opened the door to a stern looking Dev. Somehow his frustrated face made her want to cuddle up next to him with attempts to placate, possibly arouse. *Traitorous, deprived body.*

"Hello?"

"You say the word like you're surprised to see me. When a person makes a business appointment based in good faith, they keep it unless an act of God, vehicle accident, or death prevents it." He sounded a little ticked, and with good reason, but he didn't get room to judge.

"Agreed, but..." But she couldn't reveal her ace in the hole yet. Giving away the one piece of intel—that she knew he had a relationship with Pru Stone, Queen of the Purple People Eaters—could ruin her chance at the money from Mark. No, she'd play this out. "I told you I was difficult, and I don't like being bossed around."

"*Dulce Madre*. Get me off this doorstep and let me once again implore that my advice and my assignments are for your benefit alone. Not mine. I could have spent my Saturday doing a million things besides wasting my time with you."

"Yes, all valid points, and I'm sorry. Come on in." God, it was hard to drag out a sorry when she wanted to scream at him. The memory of how he'd purchased her a dozen outfits and a dress, one she'd tried on once she got home but stubbornly refused to take a photo of, served as a good reminder to play nice. So far Mark hadn't mentioned a single word about paying him back for those clothes, and she did relish the idea of the look on his face when he'd seen the receipt.

Once they were both in the living room, she resumed her seat on the couch. This time, the love seat was clothing free, so he took a spot on it. With him across the room from her, providing distance, she took in his suit. All black with a gray button down. He'd gone dark for a bright, sunny-with-a-hint-of-chill, fall day. She liked it. The same way she found too many other things to like about him.

"Your assignment for the week was to wear at least two new outfits to work and send photos of them to me. Also, you were supposed to try on the dress, but I never saw a single picture."

"I'm self-conscious." A true point. She didn't get excited about sharing photos of herself.

"And full of shit."

Wow. Her mouth even mimicked the word, in shock that he'd cursed. She didn't think he'd cursed since they'd met. Nope, pretty sure his vocabulary rarely reflected negativity, let alone profanity.

"Why do you look like you're in shock?"

"You said 'shit.'"

He shook his head, out of exasperation rather than disgust, at least she hoped. "I can be as profane as the next person when the situation calls for it. This particular situation may require a few more vulgar words if it helps you let go of your excuses and whatever ridiculous notions you have in your head. Help is here for you to take, free help with no strings, and you freeze up when asked to do something outside the comfort zone."

"I took the pictures," she said, before draining the rest of her Dr. Pepper can.

"Excuse me?"

"The photos, the homework? I have them on my phone. I just couldn't hit send." She wanted to make him sweat. To make him think she'd discovered his dirty little secret. Instead, he appeared the exact opposite—pissed, riled, and frustrated after spending a Saturday with her, spending money on her, only to have her slip him the old bite-me-sign. Maybe he wasn't planning anything nefarious.

"Let's see them, then."

Kat unlocked her phone, stood, and handed it over once she got to the photo album.

He perused each photo, taking a minute or so to review the selection, even zoom in. "The outfits flatter your figure well, and the dress is perfect for your body shape. Were you wearing the undercare from Knickers?"

"Of course, otherwise there would be bra straps all over two of those photos."

"Then that's all I need to see." He handed the phone back and looked up at her. "Did you feel comfortable in those clothes?"

"Yes."

"What else did you feel?"

He asked the hard questions. His dark brown hair was down today, not swept back in a low ponytail like usual, and his goatee was a bit unkempt and longer than usual. She wanted to touch his hair and see how it felt, not examine her innermost dwellings on the clothing selections. "To be honest, I felt like me. There didn't seem to be a difference between those clothes and the ones I wore, except I received several compliments from co-workers."

Natalie, Betty, and even Ana had told her she looked fabulous. Not that she'd never looked good before, but they really noticed her this week. The styles she'd chosen had even gotten her boss's attention, with a side helping of concern when he'd asked if she had interviews for other jobs. His relief was clearly visible when she'd told him she was only updating her wardrobe.

"Excellent. That's what I like to hear."

"That I don't feel different?"

"You shouldn't." He stood, putting himself mere inches from her. She meant to step back, but her body locked in place. His scent, the bergamot and citrus smell, toyed with her senses, made her want things off limits and out of reach. "The goal is to find clothes that make you still feel like you. Otherwise, you won't want to wear them."

"Then you succeeded."

Why did he have to smell so good?

"Meaning you're ready for the next step."

She leaned in closer, and his head came down. Was she horrible for licking her lips? Probably. Heat flared in his eyes; maybe she wasn't the only one affected by their proximity. "What's next?"

"Ms. Baum?" Mr. Sparky's voice called out to her from the living room entry.

Closing her eyes, she counted to three and silently prayed he would go away, except he didn't.

"Ms. Baum, I need to speak with you for a moment."

Dev chuckled. "I don't think praying he'll disappear will make it so. You may as well face the music."

"How do you do that? How do you know what I'm thinking when I haven't said anything?" When she opened her eyes, his brown gaze twinkled.

"I'm magic, or it could be you have a horrible poker face," he replied with a shrug of his shoulders.

His analysis scared the crap out of her because if he could read her displeasure, then did he pick up on her attraction? She walked over to Mr. Sparky, eager to get away from Dev for a quick second—if anything to practice schooling her thoughts and expressions. "What's up?"

"This whole hallway and the front entry will need to be re-wired. Our crack addict installer connected them to your bedroom, and I missed it before."

Another setback, another expense. "How long and how much?"

"I can still get this all done today, but you're looking at at least another three hundred dollars for the cabling and supplies. Probably another two hours on labor. That is, assuming everything is easy to rip out, but I'll have to put holes in the walls everywhere I need to go."

More money down the drain, and patching walls wouldn't be cheap, either. "Do what you have to."

"Yes, ma'am. But..."

"What else?" She couldn't stop the sigh and heave of her shoulders in response to the word "but." A word she generally disliked because it meant she was about to receive news she'd rather not hear. Bad news seemed to be all she heard lately.

"If you want your furniture and items to stay relatively clean, you'll need to cover everything with the plastic sheeting I have with me. There's a roll on your kitchen table."

"Where are we talking?"

"The master, the bathroom, this hallway. Maybe put some down over the floors as well. I'd hate to muck up the wood. It won't stay perfect, but the clean-up won't be as bad."

She nodded in agreement. "Give me five, and I'll get started."

"I need to finish marking everything. I'll start with the box first."

She didn't respond to his statement and decided no more talking was required. She'd gotten exhausted by his mere mention of covering everything to protect it. If she didn't hate cleaning house so much and didn't fear for the quality of those fine wood floors, then she would've left everything be.

Dev still stood in front of the love seat, taking in the room, not on his phone. "Everything okay?"

"Yes, now what's next?" Whatever momentary attraction they'd shared minutes before had dissipated, replaced with her business mind. She needed to stay focused, lock in this makeover. The initial money Mark provided would dwindle quickly, especially with the latest electric snafu. No more wayward thoughts about the scent, sight, or touch of her meal ticket.

"Heels."

Oh, hell no.

***

Kat's facial features struck him as animated and ever-changing. The word "heels" produced such a vehement and sour expression of down-turned lips and hunched eyebrows he had to cover his mouth to stifle a laugh, which came out more like a burst of sound. His addition to the moment failed to help endear her to his idea of a shoe-shopping trip.

"I don't wear heels." The sentence came out through gritted teeth.

"Ever?" Surely not, every princess and rock-goth beauty possessed them.

"Never. They're uncomfortable restraining and I've been told they can ruin your posture."

He shook his head. "I'll have to disagree. They can ruin your posture if you're wearing above a two-inch heel for over four hours a day. That's based on a podiatrist's research. Proper stretching techniques can help prevent damage, and I always recommend that my clients have a pair of neutral flats with them everywhere, in case the heels need to come off."

Arms crossed, she'd closed herself off to the conversation. He needed to break the barrier, anyway and anyhow. "Let's talk about it. I get you have a pretty set opinion on the subject, but like the clothing, I wouldn't steer you wrong. What can I do to convince you to hear me out?"

The disturbing part about putting himself out in the open like this meant opening up to an infinite number of possible reactions. Though judging by the emerging smile on her face, he wouldn't like it. "I'll go with you and I'll try on one pair of heels if you help me cover up my furniture."

"This furniture?" He pointed to the couch.

"No, my bedroom and hallway. I've got to move things away from the walls and cover everything with plastic so the electrician can get access to all the outlets and switches. Also so drywall doesn't get all over everything or ruin the antique floor in the hallway."

The idea of entering her private space appealed to him, both as her consultant and because he wanted to know her. He'd be lying if he didn't admit he'd experience a few daydreams about her during his working hours. He'd thought about her wearing the black dress and wondered if it would hit her curves in all the right ways. These were thoughts he couldn't act on, but helping her move stuff and viewing her personal belongings without invading her privacy might quell those thoughts. Maybe she was a mess, a genuine, straight up mess, like her love seat the previous Saturday. If so...

"Well?" Her question brought him out of his tunnel vision.

"Sorry, just wondering how much damage this work could do to my suit."

She scoffed. "Really? If it means so much to you, don't bother. I won't bother with any heels."

"I'm joking, and of course I'm going to help. If this gets us out the door quicker and to the shoe store where I need you to be, then lead the way."

The journey to her bedroom started with a detour to the kitchen, a quaint, cozy space, all bright red with rooster-patterned curtains for the window over the sink and matching tiles for the splashboard. The counter tops were a faded tan surrounding oakwood cabinets that had seen better days. An old sixties refrigerator stood in the corner, and an even older oven in the wall with a stove top sat beside it. A small eating nook was off to the side with a kitchen table and four chairs. He liked the room even though it could use as much updating as the electrical Kat had mentioned.

Grabbing the rolls of plastic covering and masking tape from the kitchen table, Kat motioned for him to follow her. "This way. We can cut through here."

The dining area had a nice archway, similar to the living room, which went into a laundry room. The electrician stood at the far end, neck deep in wiring the breaker box. The white-overalls-dressed fellow already had a huge chunk of drywall torn out above the box.

Kat didn't say a word, merely moved forward and propelled them through another door to their left, which opened up into the main hallway. A few more steps and a quick right turn and they were in her room. The walls were green, a dark hunter's green with gold brocade curtains hanging from the only window. He naturally went toward the window, the one source of light in an otherwise dark space. A sheer cover separated the room from the glass, but he could make out the fenced backyard of her vista. The grass had started to brown and die in preparation for winter.

"We have to start by covering the furniture in plastic and taping it sealed so drywall dust and pieces don't invade."

Dev turned at the sound of her voice to get a full view of her backside as she bent over to grab a pair of scissors on the floor. He swallowed but couldn't erase the image being implanted in his brain of her bottom in yoga pants. *¡Ay Dios mio!* "Where do you want me to start?"

She stood up and faced him with a pair scissors, pointy ends faced in his direction. "You can start by unrolling the plastic over the bed. Then we can each secure either side of the bed with the tape."

He tore the tape holding the sheeting in place and walked to the far side of the bed. He'd hoped for messy. A ramble in shambles room with clothes piled everywhere, stockings hanging from drawers, maybe a bra strewn over a blade on the ceiling fan. Instead, the drawers were neatly closed, nightstands orderly. The dresser top possessed one pile of papers, and the only thing that looked out of place was her carpet, which needed a good vacuuming.

"Dev?"

"Hmm?" His little thought about her carpet took a turn for the gutter.

"Pull the plastic over the headboard and down to the bed legs. Make sure to wrap the cover around the leg, and then I'll tape it."

"Got it."

A few minutes later the bed was sufficiently covered and pulled away from the wall toward the center of the room. They repeated similar steps with her pair of oak nightstands. Natural wood seemed to be her preference of choice.

"So where are you hiding it?"

She raised an eyebrow while tearing off another piece of tape for the cover they'd begun to hang over her dresser. "What?"

"The mess."

"Excuse me?" She leaned down, and he glanced at her backside once more.

Damn. Pathetic creature that he was, he needed to keep his visuals to above the waistline. "No bedroom is this perfect, even my own."

When Kat straightened, her face held a little more color, and she looked guilty as hell. "I don't know what you're talking about."

"I will happily disagree. I think you do know and are afraid to admit it. It's just me." He held the other side of the plastic tight so she could secure the tape on the other side of the dresser. "I'm no one who can tattle on you, but honesty is a problem spot for you. So go on, tell me your naughty secrets about this room."

If anything, her blush deepened. Confession was good for the soul, at least it would be for him. He needed this as much as her—a silly, childish way to try to erase some of the unwanted desire.

"I'd like to add that my mother used to call me *el toro*. It means the bull. My reputation for discovering truths and hunting them down like a bull seeing red is practically world-renowned, at least in my family."

His confession earned him a small smile and a shake of her head. "Fine, I shoved everything in the closet, as much as I could get in there, before my company came. The rest I shoved into my dresser drawers. I'll be afraid to open them tonight. Probably a job for tomorrow."

Relief flood his entire body he was so thankful she wasn't neater than him. He needed things to set them apart from one another. A way to dampen his growing attraction to a woman he shouldn't—strike that— couldn't want, for the sake of his company and the future he planned to have with said company. The admission allowed him to shove her back into the client space, gorgeous backside and diamond-shaped face and all. They would be horrible together. He liked things clean and tidy and had no time for disorganization.

"There will be time. This will also be a way to know if your electrician— "

"Mr. Sparky."

"Who?"

"The electrician. His name is Mr. Sparky. At least that's what I'm calling him in my mind. I forgot his real name."

Unbelievable. "Do you do that often, assign people random names when you forget theirs?"

She shrugged her shoulders. "Maybe."

"What's my name?"

"Dev, and don't worry, you've always been 'Dev.' Though I also assign names to people I don't like sometimes."

The idea at first horrified him, and then as she talked unabashedly about her habit, he found he liked it. Something unique and endearing. *Dulce Madre.* "I'm not on the list of unlikeable people?"

"Not yet."

That didn't bode well for him. He didn't mind the idea of having a nickname, something personal assigned by her, which meant he was an idiot. Regardless, goading words came out of his mouth. "I'll endeavor to work harder."

With all the furniture covered in the bedroom, they moved to the hallway. At that point, he had to ask. "Why all the electrical work?"

Wrapping a piece of tape around a plastic-covered hallway table leg, she sighed. "I recently found out my house wasn't to code. So I have to get it fixed by order of the city."

"Not cheap."

"Nope, this is eating up everything I have. So you can hopefully understand why I need to ask you to help me cover the floor."

The wood panels underneath them were oak, shined to a polish and old, most likely as old as the house. He couldn't imagine the cost to replace something so fine, even if the panels had been laid over a concrete slab. "I wouldn't want to repair this if something went wrong, either."

"Exactly." She gave him a smile, a big one, one that spoke of friendship, understanding. They were forming bonds slowly between helping her with clothing selections to covering furniture. A relationship built on aiding one another gave him pride as well as fear. He didn't need to care, but his damned protective nature made him susceptible.

Once the last piece of tape was secured against the baseboard, Kat went off to tell Mr. Sparky he could begin whenever he wanted to. Dev stayed behind checking his phone and going over the plan for his trip with Kat. The only thing to accomplish today involved shoes. In particular, ones that got her away from the flip-flops she wore now and the other disasters she kept choosing with her other attire. The clothes he'd outfitted her with required more than combat boots and the latest on-sale cross-trainers.

When she came back, ponytail swinging as she walked, he got a mental image of her in the dress, black, slinky, and with a low enough neckline to see her cleavage.

"All ready?" His question came with him shoving his phone back into his pocket and jamming his middle finger against his keys. An accident but much appreciated. He wouldn't deny the current situation was just about how things had unfolded with Pru. A latent attraction, which grew to ungodly proportions as they got to know each other, to trust each other. Only after he'd throw his chips all in had she revealed herself to be nothing like the woman he'd thought her to be.

"Yes. Mr. Sparky claims he'll be working on this until five tonight. Enough time to get me to my fairy godmother for my glass slippers, right?"

"Indeed."

His answer must have been a little off-beat or distracted because he was, but she put a hand on his forearm. Her body heat bled through two layers of fabric, and he beat back the urge to shrug her off. "Are you all right?"

"Fine."

She let go. "Just looked like something was bothering you."

Maybe it was her proximity. Maybe he'd finally lost it. Regardless he blurted out. "Something is bothering me—images of you in a black dress."

They'd been slowly taking steps toward the front door, and she stopped—paused, eyes wide like a doe in headlights. "Excuse me?"

"Images of you ruining the dress by wearing one of the three pairs of shoes you own. Tell me you have shoes worthy of a dress like that?"

Way to cover yourself.

She shook her head.

"Exactly what I thought. Let's go then."

"Where?"

"Nude."

CHAPTER NINE

Five minutes later they were back in Dev's car and en route to the shoe store whose name made her think of hot bodies, one hot body in particular. "What kind of shoe store is this?"

"A boutique. The only place I trust with my client's feet. Greg, the designer, is poised to take over the entire shoe fashion industry within the next two years. Think the next Jimmy Choo or Manolo Blahnik."

She heard the names and vaguely remembered seeing logos for one of the brands. Those types of shoes were always out of her price range and didn't fit her style. No, simple and relaxed summed up her preferences quite nicely. Like the pair of flip flops on her feet today. "Besides a pair of dress flats, I don't need any shoes. And if your designer buddy is anything like those other Mr. Fancy Shoes, then I'm not sure I want to try those shoes on."

He flipped on his left blinker, pulled into the left-hand lane, and came to a stop before turning a focused gaze on her. "Those combat boots you wore the other day, your Saturday sneakers, and those flip-flops won't cut it with all these new clothes. You need some fresh kicks to go with the new digs."

"I will happily go if you refrain from using the words *kicks* and *digs* in the future." Kat still didn't know if she could trust him, but he'd said some pretty funny things at the house, disarming her about her hidden mess and helping her with the furniture. There were elements to him that made her think maybe he wasn't sleeping with the enemy or in the art of abandoning people he said he'd help.

"Alright," he said chuckling. "I'll keep the slang terms to a minimum." His laugh acted as a balm and didn't grate against her skin like her ex's had. She'd been single for a while; maybe she suffered from sexual deprivation. Had to be the answer for why she wanted him near, why her skin heated when he made comments sounding more like innuendo than mere advice on her appearance. Like the dress bit... the words came out more like a confession, not a comment about her ruining anything with her shoes.

She kept quiet about her other fears as they got on the highway and headed south a couple of exits. She didn't know how to broach the topic of Purple People Eater and his connection to the woman ruining her life. Between that elephant and her growing attraction to the man who'd started to become a regular part of her weekends, she went mute. At least until they pulled into Village on the Creeks, a small shopping complex not far from the major mall in the area.

"Not an ideal location for your friend."

Dev parked the car and turned off the engine. "No, it's not. But he got in here on a good deal, and the lease will be up next year. This was a decent place to start, and his business keeps growing."

They both exited the car and began to cross through the parking lot when a car honked at them. Kat stood a few steps behind Dev, and he reached back, pulling her in close to him. His firm body seemed to fit against her soft one perfectly. She exhaled sharply and took a few steps to the side, providing a gap, but the tension still remained, stretching between them like a rubber band, more present now than at her place.

"What kind of shoes do you enjoy?" He asked as if nothing had occurred.

She moved forward with the same attitude. "The kind that don't hurt my feet."

"What about heels, what's your big aversion to them?" Dev stopped outside the store door, and she stopped with him. Their eyes connected, and the thread of tension between them flexed again.

"I wouldn't say I'm a fan. My last experience with heels put me flat on my face, and not because I wanted to be there." It sounded like a bad sex innuendo but needed to be admitted. Heat flared in his eyes momentarily, as if the amber sparks around his irises came to life.

They'd reached the doors of Nude, which gave no hint as to what was inside. The glass in a textured, old-style format told you something or someone existed beyond but offered no clarity about the person or object.

Dev pulled open one of the doors. "Then I'm going to ask you to keep an open mind."

She didn't move, frozen on the sidewalk. The answer to what scared her was located dead center—a pair of red, spiked stilettos on a rotating, nude-colored display platform.

He glanced inside. "I'd never suggest those for a beginner. Now, come on." He took one step toward her, balancing the door against his right leg, and wrapped his arm around her back. The proximity triggered unwanted desire, which was incredibly difficult to fight against as she let him usher her forward.

He finally removed his arm when she was through the door, and walked in beside her.

"What would *you* suggest?" Her voice sounded timid against the techno music playing over the speakers.

Nude shocked the senses. Between the music and the rows of stilettos she saw upon entering, she would've turned around and left.

"Don't get freaked out. Follow me," Dev said with a smile. He cut a path past the rotating displays and flashing lights and around a wall to their right. The turn revealed a treasure trove of wedge heels, sandals, business casual shoes, and other fashions.

"These are the shoes I want you to look through."

She chortled. "All right, that's a relief. Because I thought you'd lost your mind when we walked in."

"Do you like being judged by your cover?"

"Not particularly, but it happens and pisses me off at the same time."

"And none of us are innocent from doing it. We all commit the crime, even when we don't want to. We assume something about a person or place based on outward appearance. Hence the reason behind the stiletto's when you walk in the door. The owners want people who aren't afraid to be daring as their customers and clients. Those who are tend to explore the whole store. If you walk in and see the stiletto heels and walk out, it's better for all parties involved. Are you ready to try on some shoes?"

She gulped and straightened her shoulders, like a warrior girding herself for battle. "I can do this."

He motioned for her to take a seat in one of the fitting chairs. She didn't argue or fight, just sat down, plain and simple, like she did this sort of thing all the time.

Dev nodded toward one of the store associates, who rushed over. A quick glance at the gentleman's name tag, and Dev motioned to Kat. "Bill, I wonder if you could assist us by taking the lovely lady's shoe size."

She sat patiently, feeling a bit like a doll on display, ready to be dressed up and marched around for everyone to look at.

Bill pulled out a metal contraption she'd seen a dozen times in shoe stores and never used. "Please remove your flip flop on your right foot."

She did as requested, unable to help comparing Bill's pale skin and skinny physique to Dev's tanned, and delectable form. There were other differences to appreciate as well. She liked how Dev's hairstyle bucked the common trend, he preferred his locks long and to his shoulders. Paired with his goatee, he looked masculine and virile. Bill had short hair and no facial hair whatsoever. He looked like a baby's bottom. In fact, she decided to call him that as he sized her feet and declared her a size eight to the entire room.

Dev, in the meantime, had taken to glancing at the shoe styles along the walls. Unlike other shoe stores she'd been to, there were no boxes from floor to ceiling, only shoes on display, and they had hundreds of varieties. He motioned to Baby's Bottom and handed him a shoe. One she couldn't see, thanks to Baby's Bottom's rump. Then said salesperson walked off to retrieve what had to be the shoes.

"What was that?"

"The first pair I'd like you to try on. Bill will get one in your size. Greg's partner, Zahir, believes having a bunch of boxes on the sales floor takes away from the experience. They want customers to enjoy personal treatment and be given adequate time. This also displays Greg's designs in every color and pattern they have."

"Yes, which is exactly why I'm scared because you were standing awfully close to the zebra-striped heels right there."

"You'll just have to wait and see." Dev focused back on the wall of shoes, picking up different ones and turning back to her as if comparing shoe to woman. How in the sweet summer he could determine if a shoe would look good on her by just a glance she had no clue. Then Baby's Bottom returned and placed a nude colored box in Dev's hands.

When he walked over to her, removing the box lid and pulling out a black shoe, her heart did a little irregular pitter-patter. Her gut swamped with butterflies, and she suddenly got an image of Cinderella and a glass slipper. "That will never work for me. The heel—"

" On the way here you said you would give me a chance. Trust me just a little bit longer."

He knelt in front of her, giving her a close-up of his warm chocolate eyes and the goatee, dark brown with flecks of red interwoven. He nodded toward her foot with a half smile.

Irresistible, which he probably knew. He put his empty hand out, waiting. She scrunched the toes of her left foot against its corresponding flip-flop to check for moisture. A sweaty appendage in his hands would embarrass her endlessly. But her luck held, and the dry air in the store had kept the worst from happening.

She slid her foot from the comfort of the rubber straps and gently set the pad against Dev's hand. Immediate warmth enveloped her cold toes. Fingers from his other hand slid a nude disposable sock over the extremity.

Every change in his contact with her produced a new undercurrent of intimacy, stoking the fires of desire. She couldn't turn the damn dial off. She closed her eyes to try and take the edge off. No luck, as the action elevated the sensations.

Then the shoe slid onto her foot, and all the magic disappeared. His hands on her foot were replaced with cold, encasing leather that didn't feel tight like it normally did in most of the shoes she purchased. A few seconds later, thanks to a brief magical interlude with Dev's warm hand, her other foot wore the matching partner.

"Time for the real test; stand up and take them for a spin."

"What are these?" She walked a few steps from the chair and fell in love with the way her feet were caressed versus pressed into service. How the fabric of the shoe moved with her, instead of against. Even the added heel on the back didn't bother her.

"Those are Nude's Stretch Low Wedges. It's a better version of a flat with support for your arch and specifically designed for those with wide feet. It's a little over two inches off the ground, but nothing super fancy, and notice it only elevates your heel by half an inch."

Who knew a small heel wouldn't kill you? She'd always stayed so far away from them, when in reality she'd never known other alternatives existed. *You never wanted to know.* The thought came as she tried to pivot on the shoes and ended with her legs tangled up. She started to fall, connection with the floor imminent. Then warmth and strong muscles grabbed hold of her. Dev's scent flooded her senses, a hint of citrus as his hair brushed against her neck.

"Whoa *hermosa*, you shouldn't try to take off so fast if you've never worn heels before."

"They were comfortable. I got over confident." Heat rose in her cheeks. Her feet went flat with the floor again, and Dev stepped away.

"Homework for next week, breaking these, and any other shoes we get today, in. Let's talk best ways to wear heels." His gaze took in her stance, and she hated being under the microscope again, wondering if she lacked something essential to make her a wanted woman.

***

Her foot in his hand had nearly undone him, and catching her when she fell had made it worse. Normally he'd call bullshit if anyone told him they felt sparks when touching someone else, but he swore there were sparks, or at least invisible tendrils of energy weaving through them when they connected. He'd look like an idiot if he asked her if she had the same experience. Then again, there would be no point in drawing attention to something he couldn't act on anyway.

So he gave her pointers instead, helping her find balance on the wedges with only a two-inch heel, like keeping her back straight and walking heel-to-toe to help her stay steady.

"You sure know a lot about heels. Are you a cross-dresser?" Forthright and blunt, she had the effectiveness of a sharp knife, killing his libido as she stilted her way a few steps forward before turning and walking back toward him. Praise be for small favors.

"No, I'm not a cross-dresser, but I'm paid a lot of money to understand all aspects of clothing and footwear as well as being able to tell what works best for each type of person."

"Hmm." Her only response as she gazed down at another pair of one-inch heels, these with a cork-like heel on it and a navy-blue canvas upper. "What about plain, regular flats?"

"They don't make them here."

She sat back down in the chair. "Why wouldn't they?"

"Because..." He paused, leaning down and sliding his fingers around the back of her ankle, caressing her Achilles tendon in a way no one would consider business professional, gently and softly. He'd done it again, no rhyme or reason, and he had to stop. Sliding the one shoe off, he continued speaking while moving to the next foot without actually touching her, just the shoe. A Herculean task, but he was determined. "For some reason, flats don't allow the shoe designer to put in the necessary adjustments for arch support and tendon support, There are a lot of extra things he can do with just an inch or so of a heel on the back end, at least that's what he tells me. Do you like these?"

Kat nodded.

He set the box to the side and opened up another one. "One down. Twenty to go."

She let her head fall back and sighed. "This is going to take forever."

"You'll be thankful you took time to try each pair on. Many of my clients used to shop for shoes by looks alone, which resulted in uncomfortable selections that wasted money."

Dev made it through nineteen pairs of shoes without a relapse of his momentary madness to hold Kat's ankle again. He let her put the shoes on and take them off. Their conversation since that moment were limited to the shoes, the styles, and how each pair held up when she walked in them. So far, three pairs had made the cut to go to the register with them. Now he'd attempt to convince her to try the last one.

Opening the box, he took out the three-inch-heeled nude pumps. "Last one."

"No way. I can't wear anything with a heel like that. I like the wedges."

"If you enjoyed the wedges, you'll enjoy this. It's only another quarter inch or so higher than the others, and can you honestly tell me I've steered you wrong so far today?"

She frowned. "No you haven't, but this is my line in the sand. I'm not really the heel type. They hurt my arch and cause Kat-ccidents."

The word was made up and unique but said with a matter-of-fact tone, like other types of shoes weren't meant to enter her realm of existence. A practical admission he also respected. Kat was simple, down-to-Earth, and different from nearly all of his previous clients. A tiny part of him jumped for joy at her rejection of the heels because on some level he knew if she found the courage to wear them, the beauty hiding beneath the surface would be visible to everyone.

"All right then." He put the pump back into the box as she sprang forward in her seat.

"Really? That's it; you gave up that easy?"

"You said you had a line. I won't cross it." At least he wouldn't bother attempting to right now. In a few days or another week, possibly. Clients always had lines they wouldn't cross until the little changes got recognition from fellow peers, and then they wanted to know about the other alterations that could be made, anything to garner them more high praise or recognition.

She scoffed. "My lines didn't stop you before. In fact, I've tried on clothes I would've never given a second thought to if you hadn't been there coaxing me along. So don't even go there. Hand 'em over." She extended her hands toward the pumps. The no-games expression she possessed had him doing a double take.

"You're joking, right?"

"No, I'm not."

"You've never backed down from a challenge before, have you?" He tried not to find that part of her cute as well. Where in the hell did the word *cute* come from anyway?

With no response, she merely slipped on the shoes and stood up. "Yes, I have, but I won't fail tests. I know you're testing me. So here I go."

Two steps forward proved the best she could muster before she exclaimed an expletive and started a sideways dive for the floor. Dev reached for her, attempting to get her upright, but somewhere in the motions, he found himself along for the ride. The last thing he thought before positioning himself underneath her was the horror of possibly having a broken bone or sprained ankle after everything they'd gone through today.

The impact against carpet and concrete jarred him, and he tucked his head like any seasoned football player would to avoid a potential concussion. The result connected his forehead with Kat's, and she let out an, "Ow!"

"Are you okay?" Only after the question did he realize his arms had embraced her. Her legs were cushioned between his; her hands clutched the lapels of his jacket. His mind wandered to the heat of her body in relation to his own.

"I'm fine." Her words were a thready whisper. Then she added, "Can I kiss you?"

He shook his head. "That would be a bad idea. You're a client."

She wiggled her hips against him, as if trying to find the perfect spot, yet to him any spot where their bodies met was perfect. The look in her eyes, mischief and desire, made him long to be another man in another world. Someone else capable of sliding his hands around either side of her face and pulling those plump, pink lips to his, lips that reminded him of when kissing could simply be the only pleasurable thing you did all afternoon.

"I'm not a client," she whispered. Leaning in even closer, he caught a hint of coconut and shea butter from her skin. "I'm a pro bono case, remember? It's completely different, off the books and under the table."

Her words were a pure temptation, and he'd already sinned in the past. So easy to fall right back down the rabbit hole. One taste, one moment to get lost in, and yet there would be no coming back. He knew giving in would be like an alcoholic accepting a beer. All it would take would be one moment and then another.

Before he could tell her no, she leaned down and joined those tempting lips to his. He tried to fight it, the urge to open to her. But when her sweet tongue tentatively touched him, seeking entry, he lost control and drowned under the onslaught she unleashed upon him.

His hand came up to her cheek, angling her face. He enjoyed the little whimper as her mouth opened to him. Entrance gained, their tongues danced in exploration and rising desire. Time and sound faded; all that existed was her body pressed against his, and the taste of her.

Something sweet and a scent he couldn't define—a maddening pheromone she possessed. She may have rubbed against him, and he wrapped one leg around hers to still her. Any more friction and the semi-erection he already possessed would get much larger. They continued to mix and mingle their tastes, like slow-sipping on some delicious, fine wine. She embodied the very thing he could sup on for hours.

She pulled back first, breaking the connection and, with it, the magic of the moment. A smile and she leaned back in.

He moved his head to the side, the reality of where they were coming back to him. "We can't. I'm sorry."

Kat removed her hands, which had slid down and fisted his suit jacket at some point, and placed them palm down on the floor beside each of his shoulders. "Don't be. It was a moment of insanity. I—"

"Mr. Esposito? Ms. Baum? Are you both okay? Let me help you up." Baby's Bottom's loud exclamations effectively killed the moment. He helped Kat stand up first. Dev took the salesman's offered hand a few moments later and rose, brushing off his suit jacket and pants. No amount of wiping away dirt specks on his pants would stop the replay of the kiss in his mind—nor prevent him from having to face Kat. Guilt gathered in every corner of his body, a cold-sweeping guilt capable of making his palms sweat in some cold, clammy fashion. He'd done the worst thing imaginable and broken the barrier separating them. Even worse, he didn't regret it.

"Well, floor adventures happen when you trip while wearing a pair of pumps." Kat brushed at her pants and carefully held onto the row of chairs as she walked back to hers. "Thankfully, no puncture wounds and I had someone to break my fall, so no broken bones."

"Right, I think we're good here, Bill. And even with the unfortunate fall, she'll take the shoes on her feet along with the other three boxes in the chair next to her. Anything on the floor we don't want."

He watched in silence as Kat slipped out of the heels and back into her flip flops, not wanting to meet her gaze again or see the injury he'd probably caused. *What a culo.* Mark would've slapped him across the head right now, and he certainly would've deserved it.

"Dev, I—"

A shake of his head and she stopped speaking. Any words out of his mouth now would no doubt make the situation worse. He needed a few minutes to collect himself and calm the storm inside him, the devil wanting him to grab her again to see if the second time would be as good as the first.

"Are you ready to check out then, Mr. Esposito?"

"Yes, we're ready." He had to let go of this moment, to tuck it away somehow and lump Kat into the group of women who only wanted him for one thing. Anything else was a figment of their imagination or his. He had to break the strange spell she'd started weaving around them. This was business, his future, not a game.

Kat caught up to him at the register, and as he handed over his card to Bill, she asked, "What scent do you wear?"

"Bergamot and orange." He didn't bother to add that it was specially made, nor that he'd come across it as the scent of a gentleman in some old school book he'd read. She didn't say anything else. Not while he signed the credit card slip or when they each grabbed a bag containing her new shoes and started toward the door.

Once on the sidewalk, he worked up the gumption to apologize. He could've stopped her at any time, prevented the whole incident by turning his head, but he'd fallen into the pit. "Kat, I'm sorry for my behavior in there. I shouldn't have taken advantage of you like that."

She shook her head before tossing her ponytail behind her shoulder. "What if I wanted you to?"

CHAPTER TEN

Kat had a big mouth. In fact, her mother had said the same thing to her on more than one occasion when she'd chose to criticize rather than offer her affection. Her dear mother may have also mentioned that having a big mouth is part of the reason her uncle had ended up in jail. Whereas her gran recalled plenty of times where Kat's penchant for being a bit too verbal about her wants and desires had worked in her favor. When she'd told Dev she wanted him to take advantage of her, those words were out of anger. He'd apologized as if he didn't enjoy or care that they'd both shared a kiss that was hotter than an egg in a frying pan. And she refused, no, viciously objected to him acting all chivalrous knight-like. The self-sacrifice on the pyre of guilty emotions could go without a burning.

Besides, he'd said no. If anyone needed to step up for being an eager, wanton, bergamot-induced fool, it was her. She'd gotten caught up in his scent and the soft feel of his suit jacket in her hands. The eagerness to see if the whiskers of his goatee were soft. Note to self, they were— *Jalapeño suppository*—so soft and didn't make her skin chafe when they'd kissed. His full lips were delicious to the touch and taste as well.

The kiss rated up there as the best in her lifetime. At the moment they'd fused their mouths together, the room had melted away. People didn't exist, only them. No other boyfriend or date had possessed the power to make people, locations, or fears disappear. She'd been musing over her clumsiness, her inability to walk in a pair of heels properly.

One kiss from Dev had swept the fear away. The inadequacy she experienced had disappeared and been replaced with a sense of power. She, in all her plain, simple ways, aroused him, evidenced by the hard ridge she'd felt against her thighs when she'd rubbed against him. But she'd broken his rule and Mark's. If anyone found out, no money for her. No saving Gran's house. An earth-shattering kiss didn't mean more than her house.

In his car was where she let the guilt in. Let guilt sweep away all those good emotions she'd been riding high on. "It's not your place to apologize. I need to be the one to do that. I took advantage of you, made you break a rule. You mentioned me being a client."

"Yes, but I took things further," he replied. Fists balled against the steering wheel, he navigated a turn before speaking again. "I'm an adult as well. I could have been firmer in my objection, stopped you or held you at bay."

She'd be going to hell for being relieved he hadn't. Maybe the environment played a role, the shoes. She noticed he'd enjoyed touching her feet. Dev might have a foot fetish, one she would not begrudge him because it had given her a chance at an experience she'd never expected. "It's the shoes. Those fancy heels made us both a little insane. By the way, thank you for paying for them. I'll reimburse you."

"Don't bother. And what makes you say that? It's the shoes?"

Because any other reason meant the arrangement between them wouldn't work. "I'm trying to find a logical explanation and make light of things."

"Or is it because you don't believe I could be attracted to you? An attempt to downplay your beauty?"

They were mere minutes from her house, and the air in the car seemed thinner. The conversation was turning rapidly towards scary territory, a place she'd rather avoid.

"No. I'm sure I have some positives about my figure."

"Positives? Try maddening. Your lips, the shape of your face, your body, and curves— words like delicious and divine come to mind. I can probably come up with more and be even more inappropriate."

She blushed, the heat spreading from her face to her neck. The car's interior was too hot. Backpedaling from her earlier actions seemed best. The house needed to come first, not her idiotic want to be desired, touched, or stripped physically. Her fingers tapped on the car door, a frantic, horse-racing sound echoing back into her ears. "Stop, please."

"No, I won't let you hide from yourself anymore. You're gorgeous when you don't shove your smiles away or hide your body behind billowing clothes and combat boots. It's like you're afraid to let anyone see you. I want you to know I see you. Who you are and the potential you have. It's not potential because I want to re-make you. It's the possibilities of what a few different style choices can do. Then the whole world will see who you are."

His words—each sentence—sent a rising tide of panic through her body. She relished and hated each phrase pointing out, as he put it, the possibilities. She wanted to hide, to shimmy away into herself to avoid being disappointed because people always found someone else. Each boyfriend had—her parents saw her for who she was and found no use for her. So instead of blossoming under Dev's praise, she yelled, "I don't want the world to see."

The car came to a halt at the stoplight, and she felt his gaze on her. She glanced up, allowed the look of concern he held to come into full view. She willed her body not to cry or start going into a meltdown. "What are you talking about?"

"Seeing means attention, and I don't want it. Attention brings feelings, which end in disappointment, being abandoned. I want to be forgettable—do my job, make the money, and go home each day. No praise, no effusive comments that bring notice from others or an inspiring style."

"You've been hurt."

"Too many times."

The light turned, and they both went silent as Dev navigated the remaining few blocks until they pulled up in front of her house.

He turned the engine off first and turned to her. She didn't want to face him or confess anymore, admitting her deep, dark fears about attention and abandonment, how she feared people getting to know her, caring for her, caring for them. There were things better left unsaid because he might stop helping her, might stop her chances at getting the rest of the money from Mark.

"Kat, could you look at me, please?"

She summoned her courage, the will to face him for the sake of her grandmother's house, and lifted her gaze from her lap.

He grabbed her hand. The warm, soothing heat made her feel comfortable and safe. Damn him. "I'm sorry your previous experiences with looking beautiful or dressing up may have ended with bad memories. My hope is that, with my help, we can make all the future ones good. That is, if you're still willing to give me a chance?"

The expression he held was so sincere and earnest. She wanted to believe, wanted to trust. It just never worked out for her. Not in her favor. Like at the homecoming dance, where she'd lost her virginity only to have her date ditch her the next day for someone with more experience. A sexy outfit for her prom had gotten her a boyfriend who didn't want anything but for her to put out and be arm candy. As soon as she'd refused, he was gone. Her college years and early twenties had yielded similar results. The last guy, the one who'd met her with her armor on, eventually had left because she'd never be all the things he wanted. He preferred his women with a lot of money, evidenced by the debt he'd saddled her with.

"I want to." Her musings brought a tear to her eye.

Dev reached up with a single thumb and wiped the drop away. "I want to make sure you don't cry when being told you're beautiful. You are." That single digit turned into a palm caressing her cheek. "Let's make sure no one ever makes you think otherwise. Together."

She leaned into his touch, craving it. No escape from the want he inspired. The riot roared to life inside her. Instinct ordered her to move closer, and logic screamed to stay away. They were a pairing of impossibility. Why did his touch feel right? Unable to stop herself, she turned and pressed a kiss to his palm.

He groaned. "You're a temptress, too."

"I'm sorry."

A shake of his head, and then he leaned in closer to her. Fire lit his chocolate eyes. "I want to break all my rules at this moment and am trying hard not to."

He sharply inhaled, as if scenting the tension in the air. "Tell me to back away," he whispered with force.

Breath hot against her skin, she only needed to inch a fraction closer, and they'd meet again. Forbidden fruit, indeed. Was she Eve or the serpent? "I can't."

Then a sharp rap on his car window had her springing away from him, the moment brought to an abrupt end, like two kids caught necking in a park by the cops or something. When she turned in her seat to find out who in the fresh hell had interrupted what would've been the second best kiss in her life ever, she came face to face with the wide smile of Purple People Eater herself.

"Just the two people I was looking for."

***

Dev tried not to be annoyed as he got out of the car first, but failed. He walked around the car and into Kat's front yard. "Were you following me?"

There had been times he'd considered reporting Pru and filing a restraining order, but the number of times he "ran into her" had started to become less frequent. Twice in one week and now outside Kat's house, though? She was pushing it.

A hand fluttered innocently to her neck. Her green eyes widened. "I can't believe you'd think that of me. No, I wasn't following you. I'm here to talk to Ms. Baum, who, conveniently, is in your car. I had no clue you knew her."

He heard the passenger car door shut and turned to look at Kat, who appeared dejected. She already had her bags from the back seat.

When he faced Pru again, she smiled at him and then sidestepped. "Hello, Ms. Baum. Gorgeous day, isn't it?"

"What do you need this time?" The sadness in Kat's voice made him want to step in, to come to the rescue. But letting Pru rattle on would get him more answers.

"The city has determined that your house is a danger to you and the community. They are concerned about you living here, unless the house is brought to code quickly. So they've changed the deadline. You have six weeks."

"That's half the time they originally told me." Kat trudged four steps forward, standing beside him. A glance showed her nostrils flared, chin high... she was pissed. "I'd like to see official paperwork. Why didn't the city call me?"

Pru reached into her Gucci shoulder bag and hauled out an envelope. "This just happened late Friday. They planned to call you on Monday with the letter going in the mail on Monday as well, but I asked for a copy to deliver personally. I wanted you to know as soon as possible."

Kat's ears were a bit red as she snatched the envelope and ripped it open. "Yeah, especially if it gives you an opportunity to gloat."

"Well..." Pru did her best to look offended, yet Dev caught the twinkle in her eye. "Don't kill the messenger. Besides this isn't personal. Just business. I had no direct influence on reducing the deadline until the next inspection."

They stood in silence as she read, but his ex decided the moment needed to get worse. "Also, since you're here, I won't have to call and ask—did you want to grab an early dinner? Talk about business."

Dev shook his head, trying to think of a nice set down. "I don't think—"

Papers ruffled in front of his face, cutting off his concentration.

"Are you kidding me? Have you two been dating this whole time? This is like a bad reality show. Where the hell is the camera?" The rant came out pained and high pitched. Kat shoved the city papers into one of the shoe bags. "I'll leave you two lovebirds to figure out your dinner plans."

She marched off then, slamming her front door behind her. Dev kept staring, wishing he'd had a chance to correct her misguided notion. He was still reeling from the fact that Pru somehow knew her.

"So, early dinner?"

"With you? I think 'it's never going to happen' are the appropriate words. How are you involved with her?"

Pru's gaze narrowed. "I think I asked you the same question a few minutes ago."

"She's Mark's cousin, and I'm helping her with some suggestions as she's building out a new wardrobe." Not entirely the truth, and not a lie either. The less ammunition the woman had, the better.

"Well, her house is the last one I need on this block for my beautification project. It's been here forever with no updates or work and is becoming an eyesore. She didn't want to negotiate to sell, nor did she want to fix things."

"I thought the project belonged to the city and they just appointed you as the head of their board."

"I'm entitled to consider it my baby; this has grown to be a big deal for me. Like a crown jewel to wipe away the stain of my husband's legacy involving all that shady contracting. You know the rest."

"Babies tend to be more personal than business."

"A metaphorical baby isn't the same as flesh and blood. Regardless, this house will soon belong to the city."

"So you lied. You worked around the rules and are going to steal her house from underneath her. She doesn't stand a chance, does she?"

Pru gave a dismissive swipe through the air. "You make it sound so ruthless, but I'm doing her a favor. You should have seen the write-up Tom had to do. The house is a fire hazard and a death trap waiting to kill her. She doesn't have the money to get everything fixed."

"She obviously has some. There was an electrical contractor re-wiring things all over the place today."

He liked how his statement gave her something to worry about. She cast a look at the electrician's van and back toward the door. Dev could've sworn he saw the living room curtain move a bit, but he didn't say anything.

"Yes, I see. But the damage is more than some simple electrical work. There are plumbing and heating and foundation violations, thousands of dollars of work. Updating her wardrobe should be the last worry on her list."

A good point, which made him happy he'd paid for everything so far. Happy to know that his little bit of chivalry had saved her a couple of thousand dollars to use on her house. But it raised other questions, ones he wouldn't get answers to right away.

"It bothers me, Dev, that you think I'm so cruel. I offered her a contract that would allow her to stay in the home."

"One that primarily benefits you?"

"The best contracts do. You know I have investors, including myself, to look out for with the project. Same as at the company."

"You are a cruel witch."

"If I am, I learned from the best." She stepped closer to him, trailing two fingers from his shoulder to his wrist. The contact repulsed him.

"Please take your hands off me, and I didn't teach you those things."

She stepped back, lips pursed. "Funny, you weren't pushing someone else away. In fact, I can't recall you ever refusing anyone who wanted to give you a little attention until now."

"I don't recall ever asking for any, especially when I told you we were done."

"But we're not. And we won't be. I own a stake in your business, sit on the board. We can be friends and try to make this work, or not. Either way,

I'm in your life unless you don't want to be in the image consultant business anymore."

Her words were a kick to his gut, like a well-placed football skimming past the goalie's outstretched arms and between the posts to take the lead in the game. Hurting her back meant stooping to her level, throwing her past at her. He wouldn't do something like that to his worst enemy. "I'm not done with my business, and you're not the only investor or the sole decision-maker."

The confrontation escalated his need to get everything in gear and continue his work with Kat. He'd started to make headway, had begun tasting the hints of success once more. Until Pru had showed.

"Why are you trying to take Kat's house out from under her?"

"Like I said before, she didn't want to agree to our terms."

He could hardly believe she'd refused a free renovation, especially with an electrician putting holes in her walls. "I'm a little surprised. That seems unlike her."

Pru's gaze narrowed. "Tips, huh? It looked like you were much more familiar with each other."

"I don't see how anything I'm doing with her is any of your business."

"Fine, not my business. Have a nice afternoon, Dev. Let me know if you change your mind about dinner and decide to play nice."

She didn't spare him a glance as she got into her car, started the engine, and drove off.

One problem vanquished, he still had to deal with the aftermath of Pru's little interruption. How could he get Kat to let him in again? He feared the worst based on his client's automatic shutdown after she'd gotten out of the car. The look of betrayal in her eyes played over in his head. He'd need to come clean, to talk about his past, and worst of all, admit his mistakes. *Dulce madre.*

CHAPTER ELEVEN

Her phone dinged, and she didn't want to look at it. No, not after yesterday's run-in with Purple People Eater and the confirmation of Dev's involvement with her. The papers, cutting her deadline for the housing evaluation in half, acted as the vomit icing on the manure cake. Since then, she'd stayed inside wearing sweat pants, a big T-shirt, and furry socks. There may have been a pizza involved, along with a package of cookie dough she'd found in the freezer.

Believing in people once again had bitten her in the ass. No matter how she replayed the events from yesterday, she couldn't get the smug look on Pru's face out of her mind. The woman gave the definition of vindictive a new meaning.

She retied her hair, pulling it back into a low ponytail, and sighed. Wallowing on a Sunday sounded like a brilliant idea. No more contracting work until later in the week, she'd made sure of that. The text alert sounded again, and this time, she decided to take a peek. Just one glance to see if maybe her friends wanted to get together and watch a game at their favorite watering hole. Instead, it was from *him*.

Sorry for yesterday. Care to meet me for a chat? I'd like to explain things.

The second message was more of the same.

I don't deserve it, but if you give me a shot, I think I can help make things right. Have I led you wrong so far?

No, he hadn't, but it only took once to get another piece of your fragile psyche ripped apart. She'd been left, abandoned more times than she cared to recount. The insanity of yesterday proved she needed to steer clear to protect herself and her future—Gran's house would be lost if she didn't complete the makeover. Maybe he wanted to give her that, to officially end their working relationship. If the makeover ended successfully, she got the cash.

She texted back, *where?*
Rogers West Side Baptist Church.
That's half a town away from me. What time?
As soon as you can get here.

Kat dressed, opting for jeans, a blouse, and the black wedges from yesterday. He'd wanted her to break them in, at least that's what she told herself. The outfit wasn't about showing what she'd learned or proving she'd completed the clothing portion of the makeover. She wanted to put her best foot forward, to show Dev his efforts were working.

The drive over didn't quell her thoughts—mainly fears. Her evil brain concocted ideas about Dev sidetracking her while Pru sabotaged her contractors. Maybe Mark was in on it, too. For all she knew, everyone stood in the background laughing, watching her fail. How her brain hated her, derived some sick, sadistic pleasure in twisting up her insides and creating a world of doubt. She hated it.

Then she pulled into the parking lot, recognizing Dev's BMW off to the side. There were a few other cars, but no big signs warning her of a trap. She got out and walked in the front door. A woman with blond hair pulled back in a ponytail stood with a clipboard reviewing some boxes of clothes at her feet. Her ears were covered in piercings, and she wore a shirt that said, "got pepper spray?"

Kat cleared her throat. "Hi, I'm looking for—"

"Mr. Esposito? You're here to help with his pop up interview session, aren't you?"

She didn't know how to respond to that question because, to be honest, she had no clue what she was here for besides the explanation he'd promised her via text.

"Oh, don't be nervous. My name is Theresa." The woman bent down and grabbed another clipboard from a big bag at her feet. She offered it to Kat, along with a pen. "All you need to do is fill out those two sheets and sign them. It's a standard confidentiality clause, understanding our rules, and permission to run a background check. While you do that, I'll go through the rules. When you're working with the ladies, do not ask about their circumstances or what brought them here. If they want to bring it up, they can, but you're not to inquire or ask personal questions. Second, you should refrain from making any promises about coming back for another visit or taking our ladies anywhere. Finally, if they ask for anything, refer them to me. Most of them will be shy and reserved, but asking for money, tobacco, a ride somewhere, or alcohol is something I need to be aware of. . These women have all gone through tough times, and the last thing they need is to be let down again or led down a path they've just escaped from. Sometimes that one thing can impact whether one of our ladies are successful moving forward. We want them all to be living on their own and keeping their lives on track."

Kat signed the paper and handed the clipboard back. "What if I mess up?"

She was out of her depth, way outside the realm of her normal life. The rules reminded her of a sanitized hospital room where you couldn't touch anything for fear of spreading dreadful germs. What the hell had Dev gotten her into now?

"It's okay. You won't mess up. There will be other people, like me, in the room to help you navigate the waters. You'll figure out the ins and outs pretty quickly. Also, don't be afraid to refer them back to me or Dev. We prefer that versus the 'ask forgiveness, not permission' philosophy. From what he's told me, you're here for the interview session as an example to the ladies of what they might face. I'm also sorry my little speech sounds so harsh; it's basically verbatim of what the instructions say, and we have an even stricter policy for those who volunteer at the shelter, along with mandatory training. If you follow me, I'll take you to where Dev is. He's already started reviewing resumes with the group. They are super excited."

Theresa led Kat down a hallway. The church was spacious; they passed a kitchen and eating area, the main worship room, a small gym area, and finally they arrived at one of the classrooms, probably Sunday school from the drawings and coloring sheets plastered along the wall. A group of ten women sat in small-ish, child-sized chairs, all of them with eyes focused on the man at the front of the room with a display screen behind him showing the elements of a resume.

"So, to review, name, address, and phone number are centered and in size fourteen font on the top of the page. Everything will be kept in Times New Roman. It's tempting to do fancy things, different font colors, but those are the bad ways of standing out. Your skills and the way you present yourself are the good ways." Dev turned his focus from his rapt classroom to her, and he smiled, nothing fancy or earth-shattering, more like a look of relief. "Ladies, I'd like you to look over the list of interview questions in front of you. I'm going to prep our mock interviewee real quick."

She couldn't move momentarily, not as he approached her. Attraction punched her in the gut, hard and deep, nearly wiping away any lingering frustration she had toward him. Today he'd dressed in another suit, obviously because he was working. His hair was pulled back, goatee freshly trimmed.

Before he could reach her, an older woman outstretched her hand and brushed his coat sleeve. "Mr. Esposito?"

"Yes, Rose?"

"What if I don't have a phone number?" The woman with coal-black hair and thinner-than-normal arms and hands looked genuinely fearful.

"Then put the number to the shelter. They can take a message for you when employers call to request an interview."

Rose scoffed at him. "Never happen."

"Kick those thoughts aside. We're here to believe in ourselves, not put ourselves down. Don't let someone else's crappy attitude become yours. Now, take a look at those interview questions."

He continued toward her, and Kat couldn't stop the wave of admiration washing over her at how he'd helped Rose, encouraged her. When he stopped in front of her, she wondered if this wasn't the first time he'd been misjudged.

"You found the place."

"Yep, I did." Jeez, she sounded like an idiot.

Theresa took the chance to chime in. "I'm super excited you have someone that's not me to demonstrate the interview Q&A. I suck at interviews."

"Then hopefully this little session will help you too," Dev replied.

Theresa laughed, turning away and walking towards another group of women on the other side of the room. "Good luck with that."

"No negative attitudes, remember?" Dev brought his focus back to Kat and flashed her the mega-watt smile. "Victoria was originally going to do the interview piece, but personal business kept her away. I'm so glad you could come instead, Kat."

"Do you do these types of things often?" She wanted to know more.

"Bona Fide makes donations to the local shelter often. We've also secured several donations from local businesses. I got roped into this because the previous person who was in charge of the job-skills sessions quit."

Interesting. And now Dev made her rethink where she stood. The man in front of her appeared to be an advocate for women when he wasn't getting paid for it. She couldn't reconcile this side of him with the man in an intimate conversation with Purple People Eater. Someone associated with a greedy, vicious woman like Pru wouldn't give his spare time to help a bunch of women who came from bad situations. Would he?

"Mr. Dev, are they really going to ask us how we handle confrontation?" a woman from the back row asked.

"We're going to cover that in just a minute," he replied before looking at Kat. "What do you say? Do you have time to help me with this? Afterward, I'll explain things."

She nodded in agreement.

"Great. Can you take a seat at the front of the room?"

"Sure." Kat walked to the front and sat down. "Hi, I'm here to interview for a job."

All eyes focused on her. Dev came up and took a seat across from her. The usual butterflies she'd get in an interview setting popped up in her stomach, fluttering like mad. She shouldn't have been nervous. He clicked a button on his computer and questions lit up a screen behind them. Kat glanced at it and immediately wished for some sort of impeccable wisdom.

"Are you nervous?" Dev leaned over toward her.

She peered at him and gave a sheepish smile. "A bit."

"That's okay. Remember, no wrong answer."

Then they began. The questions were typical, standard things. Tell him a little bit about herself. Why did she leave her previous place of employment?

"What if we don't have a previous place of employment," one attendee asked.

Kat immediately started her answer over, stating it how she would have right out of high school. That earned her a beaming smile from Theresa, who'd taken up a seat near the back of the group. Questions moved into skills, her best ones and her worst.

"Can I say cooking for a deadbeat as a skill?" one of the women asked jokingly.

"Cooking, yes. Leave the deadbeat out of it," Dev replied.

Everyone laughed, and the woman did too. The best part about this experience so far was the women. They could've fallen apart after being beaten down or, in some cases, abandoned. But based on the little bits they were sharing through questions, they were stronger than many people she knew. She silently thanked her parents for leaving her with her gran and giving her a chance at a positive future. It still hurt that they didn't want to be with her, didn't want to be responsible for shaping her into an adult.

Another half hour later and each attendee had either asked a question about the interview or volunteered to answer one of the questions.

"All right ladies. You've successfully gotten the interview basics. It's time to start applying for jobs. We'll be holding another session with some laptops for you to use to apply at a later date. Appreciate everyone who showed up and spoke up. Have a wonderful evening."

Then they filed out the door, one-by-one. Rose, the one without the phone number, approached Kat. "You mentioned in your answer on handling a confrontation that you'd record the incident in an email and send it to HR. I did that once and it got me fired; of course that was over ten years ago. Is it really different now in the corporate world?"

"I believe it depends on the people and the culture of the company. Remember it's okay to ask the interviewer what you just asked me. Things that are important to you and your safety should be the highest priority." Those were the best words she could muster, and she sent up a silent prayer to the universe that Rose got a shot with a good job. The small grin Kat earned for her response made her want to do this more, maybe take some training and help out in another capacity.

"Thank you both." Theresa pushed off from her position leaning against the wall at the back of the room. "This is going to keep the excitement rolling. When do you think we should do the job-applying session?"

Dev closed down his laptop and slid it into a brown leather briefcase. "I'm not sure. I'll check my calendar and have Victoria send you something, but we'll try to keep it to within two weeks from now. Don't want them to get cold feet applying for jobs; all those fancy descriptive words and dozens of application pages can make the process seem daunting."

Daunting was one word to describe it. It'd be easy to get a bit nervous and overwhelmed applying for jobs where no one met you in person beforehand and where your future relied on blind hope that someone would give you a chance. If she didn't get the money to fix the house, this could be her in a few months—without a home and relying on the kindness of strangers.

Theresa left them to drive a van with some of the women back to the shelter. Dev continued to pack up and get his things ready, and that's when Kat decided to start asking questions about this strange day and yesterday.

"How long have you been helping the shelter?"

He looked up and pulled the briefcase onto his shoulder by the shoulder strap. "At least eight months. I've been donating money to the charity for over a year."

"It's really sweet of you, what you're doing for them."

"I wish I could say I started it, but it was Pru who got the whole thing going."

She looked back up at Dev and contemplated giving him a chance to provide excuses, to take back those words. She couldn't believe a person willing to steal her house would want to help the women here.

"Hard to believe, I know. She wasn't always so ruthless or driven, but it makes no excuse for whatever trouble she is causing you now."

"It's not your job to excuse her or justify anything she does."

He shook his head. "But it's my fault."

The word "no" rested on the tip of her tongue because brown-eyed devils were no good. She shouldn't let him take the blame for someone else and try and defuse her anger. "Is that why you brought me here? To show me another one of her projects, to try to make me less upset with the idea of her stealing my house because at some point she was like me—like them?"

"No, not at all. I brought you here because I thought you'd enjoy helping out. That helpless feeling you have rolling around inside you, the part of you stuck in some limbo waiting for money, contractors, and inspections—I'm familiar with it. Right now, my company is in a similar state. The way to fight it, the helplessness, is to do something. Helping the women is one way. It's forward progress and lifts me up a bit. I figured maybe it would do the same for you."

Damn him for his instincts and ability to see she was struggling and needing something to get her refocused. How could she stay mad at him? The same way she could refuse to talk to her parents or encourage them to visit, by remembering the sting of being left behind and forgotten.

"You're right; helping today took my mind off things. I didn't have time to worry about me because they needed my focus, but that's not why I originally came down here. You said you'd explain things, and I'll give you five minutes before I head home."

Dev reached both hands up to tweak his ponytail. "That's not much time."

"Then I suggest you don't waste it."

***

Dev sent silent *gracias a Dios* for getting a chance to talk to Kat, to explain. He'd tossed and turned the night away. Nightmares of Kat's devastated face as she lost her house and handed over the keys to a grinning Pru. He'd gambled by inviting her to the pop-up, but his instincts had paid off. Now he had a chance to learn more, to figure out if his idea would benefit her, help her.

"Clock's ticking, start talking." She stood with arms crossed, giving her best impression of a hard ass. He believed she would stick to her limits. This was his one shot.

"Fine, do you mind if I sit?"

His request was met with a sigh and roll of her eyes. "Sure."

"Thank you, it's been a long day. Between my morning run and then this, I'm wiped."

"How many miles?" She sounded concerned, which shouldn't affect him at all, but it did.

"About five, it's the easiest way to organize my thoughts."

He didn't miss the twinkle in her eyes as she replied, "When I'm stressed, I eat. In fact, multiple donuts met their demise this morning, and the remnants of a large pizza suffered at my hands over lunch."

Maybe she expected him to be appalled, turned off. There were a multitude of responses he could probably hang himself with. Instead, he settled with, "To each their own. You wouldn't happen to like jelly-filled donuts, would you? I'd love to sink my teeth into one of those."

"I didn't think your altar of a body accepted fried pastry sacrifices?"

"There are a lot of things you don't know about me."

"You're running out of minutes. Wasting them with your megawatt smile isn't going to make me give you more time. I'd say you have three left."

"My megawatt what?" They were bordering on yesterday's territory, stolen kisses and attraction better left for dead like the road kill he'd seen on his jogging route that morning.

She swore some profanity under her breath then replied, "The smile, you turn it on and blow away any rational thought in the room."

"Sounds like some sort of superpower." Maybe he should use it all the time.

"Or you're a male siren. Is this really what you wanted to discuss with me?" A pink tint stole over her cheeks, reminding him of his desire to see if her blush spread to other parts of her body.

Except he needed to stay focused. "I want to talk about yesterday. To explain how Pru and I know each other."

"Why?"

He finally sat down in one of the chairs, keeping his rear on the edge of the seat. This whole conversation would be awkward as hell, but he had a plan and had spent too much time thinking it up to stop now. "Let me explain how we know each other, and then I'll give you the why."

Nodding in agreement, Kat took up a position in another chair one row away from him.

"Pru and I met when Bona Fide was renting out a storefront in the Fayetteville Mall. She'd recently become a widow, and at the recommendation of a close family friend she came to my business hoping for a makeover and some assistance in getting past some issues she had with image and self-esteem.

She was in a lot of pain then and skittish. Over a period of several months, I worked with her, found her some additional support—something we do for all our clients who need it—and fell for her."

Dev waited a moment to let his confession sink in, the truth of his feelings for a woman he'd grown to view with apathy and pity.

"You're a couple?" The question came laced with venom.

He held up his hands. "'Were' is the key word to describe our relationship. We aren't together anymore, haven't been for over half a year. Pru helped Bona Fide. She brought in investors to form a board and back our company. Success was finally in our grasp, and we were able to get a true office and more consultants. Business boomed. But our relationship became strained. She turned jealous, vicious, and ruthless, using the things I'd taught her with cruelty in a way that was against everything I believe in."

"Sounds like PPE."

"What?"

"Purple People Eater, my nickname for your ex. She wears those ridiculous purple heels—I've seen 'em twice—and she acts like a monster." Kat shrugged her shoulders. "It fits."

He laughed, loud and proudly. The sound helped clear away the sad and angry emotions invading his brain as he talked about Pru. There were situations he'd remembered, awkward conversations in front of the board, accusations that maybe his relationship with her affected his decision-making.

"So why tell me all this?"

"Because I don't like what she's doing to you." The confession came out readily, honestly.

"I appreciate that, but everyone knows she's doing something crappy. Problem is I don't have enough money to solve the problem."

That's where she was wrong; Dev had discovered the perfect solution in his Saturday mail.

"I don't think you need money to solve the problem."

One skeptical eyebrow went upward and became paired with her telltale frown. "Maybe you don't get it. My house has been evaluated and found not to code. I fix it, or I lose the house to the city. So cash, a huge influx of it, is the only thing solving this problem."

With the invite to his solution tucked in his pants pocket, he stood and slipped the glossy card out, extending it. "My idea involves no money and happens in the next two weeks. Take a look."

"Is it a shot at the lottery or a house makeover?" Kat walked over to him, but she didn't seem excited. Snatching the invite from his hand, she silently reviewed the contents. "Why would I want to go to a celebration for PPE's Beautification Board?"

"Because this puts you in front of other people of influence, gives you a chance to plead for your house. I guarantee it takes months to get a house written up for code violations without some pushing and prodding on the right people. Your house got special attention because she knew which people to lean on. I want to level your playing field."

She shook her head. "My time would be better spent on the work around here. Talking to a bunch of rich, stuck-up people won't get me anywhere."

"Have you tried?"

"No."

"Then you'll never know. I happen to be familiar with the majority of them since this project was in its initial stages back when Pru and I were dating. You'd have access to insider knowledge, and I know for certain several of them weren't always rich."

She didn't say anything for a minute or so, glancing between him and the invite. He wanted her to say yes, not only for herself, but for him. The whole thing smacked of a chance, a challenge. One he could win.

"I still don't understand why?"

"To right wrongs. Pru has put my hard work to action in ways I never intended. This is my chance to redeem myself and, hopefully, save your house."

She laughed. "Righting wrongs by sending me into a den of people with my blunt mouth. That's dangerous."

"I have confidence in you."

"You're the only one." She had to stop that, so he leaned in and put his index finger under her chin, coaxing her to look at him. She did.

"First, stop putting yourself down. I've seen proof over the last couple weeks that you can learn. You've got potential. This isn't about changing you; it's about taking the rough diamond and adding a little polish. Besides, you said I had superhero capabilities. This would be a way I could use those powers for good."

He liked peering into her blue eyes, getting lost in them. For half a second he forgot his message and smiled like a damn fool.

"Quit doing that." She took two steps backward, putting distance between them. Necessary, but he didn't want it.

"What?"

Her focus back on the invite, she mumbled, "Megawatt smile."

"What about this one?" He took a step closer and let his smile turn feral with all the heat and longing he had for her—dangerous, but worth it.

"Distracting," she replied, only glancing up for a millisecond.

Wet-panties distracting? He wanted to verbalize his thought, but it crossed over the invisible line of professionalism they needed to maintain, at least for now. Instead, he stood up and closed the gap between them, watching her flush. "I can teach you both of them and when to deploy each smile."

"What will they get me?" She whispered her question, intensifying the tension. He'd be a mess if they kept up this game.

"If everything goes according to plan, your house, and after that, you can use them whenever you want." His turn to put some distance between them. The steps stretched their connection but didn't break it, temporarily putting a stop to their ongoing game of cat and mouse. Too bad he didn't know which player he was. "Are you in?"

"It's two weeks away."

"Don't worry about time; we can make this work. I'll come over evenings if needed. We can also pull some lunch sessions at the office."

A shake of her head in the no direction. "If PPE is on your investor board, I'd prefer not to go anywhere that creates a chance we'll run into each other. As far as she knows, I'm done with you as of yesterday. Can we keep this between us?"

"If you'd prefer." Funny how this woman had a near-mercenary mind.

"Then I'm in." She stuck out her hand. "Shake on it?"

"Are you sure? I don't want you to feel like I forced you into this." He didn't want her to feel cheated or go crazy if this didn't work, so he had to ask.

He cringed when she replied.
"I'm sure. I'm going to trust you and your story... for now."

CHAPTER TWELVE

"I wouldn't step foot in there if you paid me to." Kat shook her head vehemently and took a step off the sidewalk, heading back to the passenger side of Dev's car.

It had been almost a week, and she'd followed all his other homework assignments. He'd promised to see her Saturday—today—and review things to strategize for the party coming up the following week. He'd mentioned grabbing lunch, and she'd agreed, but instead he led her into a trap. A big trap with the word "salon" involved.

"Why? What harm would a trim do?"

She shook her index finger back and forth. "No, that's what people tell you to get you in the door. We already discussed this. You're polishing a diamond, not cutting it into a new shape."

Dev came closer to her, something she didn't know if she wanted. Since the kiss and the PPE revelations, she'd warred with herself over the attraction to him. He wore another suit today, all clean cut, black, and sophisticated. No tie, though, so the collar button was left undone, gifting her with a hint of his chest and the smattering of dark hair there. "Have you ever heard of the word pamper?"

"Yes, add the letter S, and you've got an extremely popular diaper brand. Are you making a reference to me acting like a child?"

The megawatt smile made an appearance. She liked being able to make him happy, to give him an opportunity to showcase one of his winning features. When he looked at her like that, she felt cared about, important to him. Dangerous thoughts indeed.

"I'll take that as a yes, but I imagine you don't do much of it."

She could smell his scent again, swirling around her, tempting and exotic. "Rich women, like your ex, can afford it. I like to spend my money on other things."

"We're not talking about money or who's going to pay for it. I am talking about getting you some pampering. A quick trim of the hair, a blowout, something to show me the possibilities you hide in a ponytail all the time. Whether you like it or not, you'll have to put forth a little bit of effort for this event."

Red flags pinged in her brain, and she put a hand on the car door handle.

He reached for her, covering her hand with his. Warmth spread. She liked his touch too much. Enough to keep her from asking him to back off, to stay away and keep her from making a mistake by breaking her deal with Mark.

"I'm not saying makeup or jewelry. Don't think I'm going to put you out of your element. I'm trying to help you find the element."

"No hair color or fancy curling?"

He applied pressure to her hand, squeezing it as if to reassure with touch as much as his next words. "If you wanted something like that, I'm sure the stylists inside would be able to make you look fabulous. But you already have amazing color, and I know curlers are not your thing. This is about running through some ideas and giving you a chance to have yourself taken care of for once. Shampoo, a style—that's it, no pressure."

His explanation made it sound easy, simple. She let go of the door handle and stepped closer to him. "All right, I'll give it a shot."

Beauty Magicians, the salon he'd selected, stuck out like a carnival ride at a refined shopping center. Over the top colors of purple, red, and orange with dozens of framed posters recounting magician acts hung on the walls and in the display windows. She caught herself staring at them, reading the messages from "the amazing wonder" to "a disappearing act you won't forget." She wanted to do exactly that.

The main desk was decked out like a stage with red velvet pleated and hanging from both sides, revealing "Beauty Magicians" in fancy block letters. Behind it, a woman in a tuxedo shirt and jacket with a black bow tie stood typing away at a computer. Her long, black-and-white hair flowed around her shoulders, a top hat with a wand sat beside her, and her name tag said, "Ace."

Dev spoke first. "Good morning, an appointment for Kat Baum?"

Ace didn't look up or acknowledge them right away. The clickety-clack of the keyboard was the reigning sound amid stage music playing over the speaker system and a blow dryer somewhere in the distance. "A 10:30?"

"Correct."

She then graced them with a visual cue. "We have you booked with The Charming Chad. If you have a seat, he'll be right with you to work his magic." The last word was paired with her picking up the magic wand on the desk and waving it in the air.

Dev provided a thank you, and then they sat. Nerves bundled up in her gut like an angry swarm of bees. She didn't want to go through with this or hear about her ugly hair. A million and one insults flitted through her brain, and she started tapping her toes on the painted concrete floors. Twice she opened her mouth to tell Dev she'd changed her mind, that she'd realized her fragile self-esteem couldn't go through with this farce. Each time, a new reason stopped her. She got so wound up in her musings, the yes or no, that she failed to hear her name being called until Dev put a hand on her shoulder.

"We're up. It's time to meet your hairdresser."

She blinked a couple of times to clear the errant thoughts and stood. "Ready."

Chad was a blond with a mass of tight, spiral curls on the top of his head. He inclined said curly head before stating, "Prepare to experience wonder."

This came with a wink from one of his light blue eyes. He wore a tuxedo shirt with no sleeves and a bow tie around his neck, very Chippendale's. The biceps and wide shoulders demonstrated a gorgeous physique, and she realized this was a prank.

"You can't be serious."

The smile Chad gave her was wide and perfect. "I'm confident I work wonders."

"No, I'm not talking skills, I'm talking about the uniform. You look like a stripper." Kat knew she'd made a faux pas by Dev's wide eyes and throat clearing, but fuck it.

"Thank goodness; I thought I looked like a sexy magician. Now bring your mouth and follow me."

Thirty minutes later, her hair had been washed and rinsed and she sat in Chad's "magic hair chair," as he called it. He'd combed everything out and then looked at her from all angles. "So refresh me Dev, what do you want to do for her?"

"A basic trim and then some ideas on simple hairstyling she can do from home. Nothing that requires any fancy equipment or more than twenty minutes."

Chad whistled low. "You're not asking for miracles, are you?"

The sarcasm and way he eyed her hair were exactly what she didn't want or need.

"You said you're the Charming Chad, but right now you're the cruel, crusty Chad." Kat reached for the hair cloth covering her. As she began to tug and rip the damn thing off, Crusty spoke.

"That's a pretty nasty nickname."

"She's got one for anybody she doesn't like," Dev chimed in.

Ol' Crusty shrugged his shoulders. "I'm sorry for being cruel. You've got gorgeous hair, and I can trim it and show you a few things."

So he did as promised, a trim, and a dry with some round-brush-thing that he told Kat she could have.

"You need volume, sweetie. No slicking this hair back. Give it lift, and it will love you. Even using the brush and then putting half the hair back." He lifted up a top layer, where bangs would have been, and showed her a simple half ponytail. "Where do you plan on showing off these luscious locks, if you don't mind me asking?"

"We'll be attending the Bentonville Beautification Board's fundraiser dinner this coming Thursday night."

Chad dropped the curtain of her hair he'd been fondling. "Excuse me? A fundraiser and you're going with a simple ten-minute updo? Oh no, honey. Call me Crusty if you want, but you'll be sitting your sweet bottom in this chair come fundraiser day, and I will have you looking fabulous."

Kat shook her head. "No, not necessary."

The look he leveled at her made her feel like she'd gotten caught in a cage match with a wild animal. "It's not only necessary, it's essential. Those rich society folks don't pay attention to anyone who doesn't try to look like they fit in."

"The money."

"Beautiful, it will be taken care of. Right, Dev?"

She looked over at her partner to see him betray her with a nod.

"I don't like to spend money I don't have."

"If it accomplishes our goals, I don't care about the money, and Chad can help us do that. Besides, *hermosa*, he's the expert. If you can't trust him, then you can't trust anyone."

The two men carried on once more like she didn't exist. Deep down she loved the special treatment, the hair salon time, and having her locks at the mercy of a professional instead of her poor attempts at a blowout— that's what scared her.

***

From the beauty salon, Dev took her to lunch at some swanky Mexican place on the downtown square where the butternut squash enchiladas were to die for, according to him. She settled for something a little more red-meat-style with the beef enchiladas and a glass of sweet tea. Once the waiter walked off with their order, she decided to get some things off her mind.

"You knew he would do that, didn't you?"

"Hmm?" Dev glanced up from the beverage menu still on the table.

"The offer to do my hair, you knew he'd make it."

"It was a possibility."

She'd been played, and she'd fallen in line with his little trick. Even if she enjoyed him helping her past her comfort zones, letting him run the show equated to a risk. Each day they spent together, the getting-to-know-you pieces slipped into place and increased the risk.

"You could still cancel," he offered. "It wouldn't take much time to place a call."

"And throw away a chance to spend someone else's money? No way." She tried to make her voice sound as laissez-faire as she imagined Purple People Eater's might, without a care or consideration. Then she asked another burning question. "Did you help Pru start her downtown project?"

He took a sip of water and reacted slowly and coolly. For the first time she picked up on his tell— moving like molasses before opening his mouth to speak. He hoarded those seconds, a master at the long game. "We both loved this area of the city—the restaurants and the hiking trails. Naturally, we wanted a radius of four to six blocks surrounding the area to be restored to its former glory. The history of this area deserves to be preserved, to gain attention. It hurts to know she perverted our dream in such a way."

Kat wanted to reach out and take his hand, for comforting only. For a few seconds, she staved off the desire, and then she didn't. His hand was warm in hers, and if he'd asked, she would've confessed to experiencing a tingling sensation at the moment of contact. But he didn't ask, so she spoke instead. "I'm sorry too, and thank you for what you did with the salon, even if I did hate every minute. It's very kind of you to keep doing these things for me."

"They are the right things, so it's no problem. And your outfit today, the slacks and empire-waist top go well together. The little sweater works too."

"I'm learning from the best."

He took his free hand and held it to her forehead; she resisted the urge to lean into it. She also stopped herself from reading too much into how he'd created another excuse to touch her. "You're not running a fever. Maybe there is a positive, compliment-capable woman inside you after all."

"Don't get too excited; this is temporary because I'm empathetic."

The megawatt smile appeared. "Then I'll have to give you more reasons to be this way in the future, at least toward me."

She let go of his hand and pulled back. At that moment, she wanted to kiss him again, but she needed to keep her line drawn in the sand, for her own self-preservation at the very least.

"My turn to ask a question. Where are your parents?"

One inquiry and he'd effectively doused whatever lustful feelings she possessed. Her lunch was officially ruined.

***

Dev didn't expect the mood to sour with one little question, but it did. He'd wanted to make simple conversation, to get to know the woman he'd been working with for the last four weeks. She'd become part of his life in ways he hadn't expected. He looked forward to spending time with her and enjoyed their banter, their moments of conflict, and their moments of intimacy without physical actions. When her lips fold inward and she winced, he instantly regretted sullying their moment.

"What's wrong?"

"Nothing." She took a sip of water. The word sounded hollow, a farce.

"I thought we were past the lying. You can tell me whatever, and I'm not going to judge it."

"It's not that. Talking about my parents is uncomfortable for me. Most people have a lot of happy memories with their parents. In my case, not so much since they left me on my grandma's doorstep when I was ten years old."

"What do you mean they left you on her doorstep?" The concept sounded foreign to him, a man who'd grown up with loving parents, grandparents, a sibling, and plenty of family all around him. To hand someone over to another person, to give up the ability to guide them and raise them, the idea sounded ridiculous. Yet, she wasn't the only person who'd confessed stories of abandonment by parents in one capacity or another.

"They wanted to travel, to do things too dangerous for a child, according to them. My gran called them lots of names, mainly fools who couldn't see their greatest gift. She told me over and over again how thankful she was in the later years for having me around, for not losing me to my parents' stupid adventures in the wide world. I won't pretend I didn't feel anger at them, though. They'd remember to send birthday cards or Christmas presents sometimes."

"Was their reason really traveling?" His heart broke into a million pieces at the idea of being a child with only a grandmother to rely on for support and guidance.

"My Gran said her children were the product of bad blood, a dismissive father, and not enough goodness. My mother would say she'd never planned on having a kid. In fact, I was unplanned and a mistake. Of course, she followed it up with how adorable I looked, how they didn't believe in giving me up for adoption because of some horrible story they saw on the news around the time I was born, and how both her and my dad were not fit to be parents."

"I'm so sorry, Kat."

She covered his hand with hers, and he soaked in the contact once more. He loved how she trusted him enough with these small touches without him having to initiate them. Giving her comfort was as natural as breathing.

"It's fine. I've had a lot of years to think about things, and I really wouldn't want my life any other way. If I'd stayed with them, who know how I would've turned out. Gran helped me a lot, though I'll admit being there started my personal curse."

"What's that?"

"I'm not adept at keeping boyfriends or anyone around, except for Gran. Friends left me; boyfriends hung around until they got what they wanted or realized they wouldn't get it. Anyways, I think I see our waiter headed our way. Let's ditch the sad conversation and get back to business."

He nodded in agreement and kept his promise to help her save her house silent. Actions spoke louder than words, and so far the actions she'd seen from those who should've cared for her were less than stellar. There would be time for him to show her, to gift her with caring efforts, and to win her over. She needed true friends, and he could be one of them.

The remainder of their lunch, the trip back to Kat's house, and the early evening hours were spent in heavy training. They started with conversation skills and small talk, reviewed the names and photos of the board members, and ended with good topics of conversation versus bad topics. He wanted to make sure she got attention. He helped her with subtle cues on when to bring up her house or when to move on. Hard, devilish stuff, which, with their limited time, made it so important she nail as many details as possible.

He'd used the session to move away from their personal moments earlier in the day, the ones where they'd touched or where they'd asked each other questions equivalent to peeling back skin. It was hard admitting to himself the pains Pru had caused, but confessing them to someone else made him feel weak. Not even Mark knew all the deep details. The fact Kat, in turn, shared her deep-seated issues with her parents, an open wound he'd encouraged her to reveal, had brought them closer. Keeping grounded in work, like Kat suggested, by focusing on the current issue at hand and not personal aspects, seemed the best way to go. He'd been honest when he'd told her that helping others acted as a way to make up for his past mistakes. For letting his ex stay on her rampaging path without doing anything to temper the woman she'd turned into—fiercely independent, but with such a vicious streak.

Staring at her opposite, a woman who'd been taught beauty and worth rested within oneself, the choices he had made so far felt right. "Okay, let's review again. Pru's board consists of her and?"

Kat took a deep breath. "Richard Lessing, President of Starfish Marketing; his best friend and a big VP for that giant retailer, Hugh Miller; and the old philanthropist, rich dude Jimmy something."

"That's Jim Hunt. He's Pru's godfather and is happy to support her in just about any idea she has. And you missed one. Colton Kinyon, he's a bit of a wild card and the only one on this project who doesn't sit on my board of investors."

She hung her head. "I should be able to get all of this, but we've reviewed it for hours and I'm still not remembering their names or the details. I'm going to screw the pooch without fail."

"It's only nerves, and you've got days to get this figured out. We have the index cards you can continue combing over." The words didn't seem to help; her body locked rigid, and tension radiated off her frame. "All right. Head up and stand up. We need to shake this off."

She stood, the frown on her face even more prominent. The look shouldn't make his insides clench or trigger an immediate desire to help, but it did. Her frown could be wiped away easily, and he saw the way in a flash of images in his mind, from taking her into his arms to molding his lips to hers. Then she'd sigh, lean into him with her breasts against his chest, and he'd get to taste her again. He'd woken from a dream last night that involved her mouth and unique taste.

"All right, I'm standing here." Kat's annoyed outburst brought him back to the present.

"Stretching. Those warm-ups we did a few weeks ago?"

"What about them?" She looked adorable when perturbed, and it bothered him how easily he got distracted, how she disordered his thoughts with one angry look.

He spread his legs apart, his suit jacket no longer an impediment, as he'd taken it off a couple of hours before. "We're going to do some of them to loosen up."

"I'm not kicking my own butt, not for anything."

"Let's stick with trying to touch your toes and hold the pose for fifteen seconds."

Leaning over, he resisted the temptation to engage in more flirtation. The kiss he'd envisioned minutes before might change her mind. Dangerous ideas. When he stood straight once more, he got a marvelous view of the curvature of Kat's spine. It shouldn't have looked so appealing, but it did.

She'd changed into a pair of yoga pants and T-shirt as soon as they'd returned to her house. He didn't blame her and wished he'd dressed a little more casually for the day. But suits were armor and gave him a barrier, a persona to live behind of the professional image consultant. If he let go of that part of him, he'd be a regular guy, free to do what he wanted, ask for more when he shouldn't.

Kat arched upward and sighed as she came fully upright.

"It works doesn't it?"

"A bit," she replied with an emerging smile. "This whole party thing has me in knots. I'm so afraid I'm going to jam up, make myself look like a fool."

He could tell. "Stretch your arms over your head and reach for the ceiling."

They both followed his directions. When they put their arms down, she sighed a big, long breath of air. "It's no use. I'm wound up, and the stretching isn't helping."

"I'm no big fan of parties, and you're right. You could make yourself look foolish and silly, but you're putting a ton of fear into the worst case scenarios. Don't think about then, think about now."

"There's a lot to remember." She yawned, and he grabbed his phone from his pocket to check the time. After eight in the evening.

"Let's take a step back. Instead of trying to figure all this out at once, let's work on one person a day. Four guys, that's Sunday, Monday, Tuesday, Wednesday, and then the party. Little goals each day."

She nodded in agreement, processing his suggestion. "What about the conversation parts?"

"My job is to get that piece rolling. I'll introduce you to each member. The biggest thing is to make sure to compliment the work they've done and point out their latest accomplishment. It grounds you with them, allows them to know that you're aware of who they are. For Richard and Hugh, this will create instant respect. Jim will take such a thing as an ego shot. Colton, on the other hand, we'll talk about him before the party. He's a bit different."

"Rich, charity-giving men often are." This time, she wobbled a bit, and he reached for her on instinct. "I'm good, just tired."

They both looked at the point where his hand wrapped around her bicep. His grip was secure but gentle. Her muscle tensed and relaxed underneath his hold. When their gazes connected, he caught the flair of desire lingering, slowly spreading. He'd been getting tired too, but now he was wide awake.

"Are you sure?"

"Sure?" She repeated the word, letting it emerge slowly. Her other hand came up to wrap around a lock of his hair.

He may have shuddered; he wasn't sure, but his eyes closed as he momentarily savored the closeness, the indulgence. All he needed to do was tug her toward him, and they'd spiral into something. A hot mess. Which might be worth it.

"How do you get it so soft?" Her question brought his eyes open, and he watched the pulse at the base of her neck start to pound. He wanted to feel it, and so he did.

Releasing his grasp, he trailed his fingertips up her arm. "It's a special conditioner. Nothing fancy." A few more seconds and he'd touch bare skin. "Tell me to stop, Kat."

She whispered, "Don't stop."

The first contact he made with her skin was damn near electric. He expected sparks to fly, but instead her skin acted like his opposite, cool and smooth. His hands were warm. She moaned as he massaged her hands, then spread his palms upward over her arms.

"Why do I want this?" Her question, most likely rhetorical, came out with a bit of anguish.

"Forbidden fruit... I can't be with another client, and you're my partner's cousin." At those sobering thoughts, he backed up. "We want what we can't have, a simple explanation."

"Sure, simple." She reached up, wrapping her hand around her throat, and he wanted to reclaim the territory from her, to mark it as his. "Best we call it a night, wouldn't you say?"

"I'd say some other things, but it'd put me in a position I can't afford." He walked over to the love seat and grabbed his jacket. Slipping back into his wool and silk armor, he warded himself from falling prey to his lust again. It was the honorable approach for him to take, but why did being the honorable one suck? She walked him to the front door, and as he started his way down the steps, she called out to him.

"You're wrong, labeling what this is between us... You made it forbidden. Just remember I'm willing to label it an opportunity." Then she shut the door.

CHAPTER THIRTEEN

The workday had been brutal enough for Kat to crack open a cold one after she'd changed out of her work clothes and into a T-shirt and yoga pants. No more one-piece romper for her. The doorbell chimed right as she took the second sip of her beer and picked up her flash cards on the Beautification Board.

She set the bottle down and ran her fingers through her hair. Maybe she should've kept her romper on to show off her dressing talents to Dev. Therein lay her problem. Since their close call the other night, her body had entered a state of hyperawareness when it came to him. They'd spent the previous evening together, and every movement or action by his body had caught her eye. Ridiculous really, she'd been a virgin until her junior year in high school, which in some weird way should have translated into the ability to abstain from lust, want, and the male body.

Opening the front door, it was like déjà vu. Her nipples tightened underneath her T-shirt at the sight of his suit-clad body, his long hair pulled back in the ponytail, and the trace of a five-o'clock shadow on his cheeks.

Dev held up two bags of takeout boxes. "I hope you like Thai food."

"Red chicken curry?"

"You're becoming a mind reader now. That's my favorite, but I also picked up some pad thai with shrimp and tofu."

"Please bring all the delicious food inside." Kat stepped back and let him pass, then she went to the kitchen to collect plates, forks, and napkins. As she turned around, she ran right into Dev.

"Whoa, there. Need any help?" He outstretched his arms to steady her. She noticed how close they were, how this looked orchestrated on his part.

"I'm good. Did you want anything to drink?"

He still hadn't broken the connection of his hands braced around her forearms. The gaze he leveled at where their bodies connected made her nervous, and she attempted to pull away. Thankfully, he let her go. "Beer would be good."

"In the fridge, on the door. I've got a couple of local craft brews in there." She had to yell since she'd hightailed it out of the kitchen to avoid the lingering tension.

Fuck.

The whole comment she'd made the other night about them being an opportunity, not forbidden— shit. She'd thrown the gauntlet down. Regardless, the statement had seemed to make things worse. In a way, that made things better. Lines were blurred, a bit confusing, and they acted a little awkward around each other. She warred between pushing him further or keeping a safe distance.

Dev walked back into the living room, open beer in hand. "How about you serve up your plate and I'll start quizzing you?"

Grabbing a plate and opening the first container in the bag, she nodded her agreement.

"Okay, Jim Hunt, what's he most famous for?"

A big scoop of red chicken curry plopped onto her plate. "He's notorious for his charity work with—"

The doorbell chime echoed throughout the room.

"Expecting company?" Dev set his beer down and moved toward the front entryway.

"No, and contractors aren't scheduled to do more work until this weekend. Maybe it's a salesman; could you tell them I don't watch cable television?"

She heard the door open, Dev's greeting, and then a female voice. She waited, placing the carton of food back on the table. The front door shut, and two pairs of feet could be heard.

"Kat." Dev rounded the corner looking apologetic. "She said she wouldn't leave without making sure you were breathing and conscious."

Betty followed him into the room wrapped up in a maroon jacket and black slacks, her blond tresses swept up into a fancy updo with a pair of chopsticks—her signature look. "Because Kat doesn't have a boyfriend and isn't inviting men over to her house except for contractors. Unless there's a new business in town, contractors don't wear expensive, tailored suits."

She'd been a little vague when her friends had asked how she was spending her weekends, and even though she'd mentioned her cousin to Betty, she'd never gone into detail on the favor she'd owe in return for the money.

"Hi, friend," Kat said while she grabbed a fork from the cutlery on the table.

"Hi, yourself. Is that red chicken curry?"

Kat nodded and lifted up the plate she'd loaded down but failed to take a bite from. "Want some?"

"Yes, please." Betty sat down on the couch next to her and grabbed a plate and a fork. She picked out all the chicken, dropping it back into the container.

"I'm Devid Esposito." Her smoking hot dinner companion stuck out his hand to Betty, which she took in a brief but sturdy shake.

"Hello, sorry for my lack of manners. It's been a long day, which I'm sure Kat mentioned, and we starved ourselves trying to get everything done. No lunch break at all."

"She didn't mention it." He grabbed his beer and headed off to the kitchen. "I'm going to get another plate."

The look on his face, a combo of surprise and hurt, reminded her how there were plenty of elements of their individual lives they hadn't shared with each other. They worked together on this one piece. The day job crap and other mundane aspects of their worlds were still kept separate from everything else.

"He's hot," Betty whispered between bites of her chicken-less curry. "So who is he?"

"I can't explain right now, but he's helping me save my house."

"Oh, really? So you won't need the money?"

Kat shook her head, scooping the discarded chicken and more of the curry onto her plate. "Not exactly, I'll still need the money, probably… I don't know. At this point the idea is to get the city off my back, to get them to ease the deadline dates."

"How?"

Good question. One she didn't have the answer for. Dev talked about her pleading her case to the rest of the decision-makers on Pru's project, but what would they do? Make a few phone calls and get the city's inspection board to back off, to cancel the inspection and her violations? The specifics had never been discussed; there were also no guarantees.

"We're still working on those details."

"What details?" Dev came back with another fork, another plate, and two extra beers. "I wasn't sure what you wanted to drink, but I grabbed a bottle of each beer Kat had."

He offered the two to Betty, and she grinned up at him—one of her perfect grins—and a twinge of jealousy rocked through Kat, the emotion fierce and sudden. "Either one works. Most of the brands Kat enjoys, I enjoy, too."

Dev didn't respond to her friend's version of the megawatt. Shockingly, he pulled his keys out of his pocket and popped the cap with a bottle opener from his key chain. Of course this suave, ready-for-anything man kept a bottle opener on his key chain. "Here you go."

Betty murmured her thanks, and then Dev crouched down in front of the coffee table to make his plate.

"So ladies, what details?"

"The ones about how you're going to save Kat's house."

Damn Betty and her big mouth. As Dev's focus strayed to the carton of pad thai and getting it scooped onto the plate without spilling it on her rug, Kat nudged Betty with her elbow.

"What?" Betty mouthed silently.

The pad thai carton plopped onto the coffee table, then Dev rocked back on his heels to a standing position, picked up his plate, and took a seat on the loveseat across the room, fork in hand. "Excellent question, and our goal is to get Kat face time with all the members of the triple B at their celebration dinner. If she can convince them her house would be better spared, left alone, then they will call off the city's hounds."

"But if they don't?" Her friend was voicing all of her fears, the concerns she'd been shoving into the back of her mind, ignoring.

"We can cross that bridge if we come to it."

Everyone ate in silence for a moment, and the possibilities, the fear, sunk deep into her bones. There were no promises, no expectations, just estimations of what might happen. She could go to this party and look like an idiot and be treated by these people like she'd been treated by her parents, dismissed and ignored.

"What are my chances?" The question came out sounding a little more serious than she intended.

Dev didn't answer right away. This time, she looked at him as he chewed a bite of his dinner, eyes on her and calm as lake water on a windless day. "Excellent, but they increase exponentially the more information you know about the board members and the more confidence you feel. The fear in your eyes right now, the doubt, it's got to get kicked to the curb, or we've lost before we've even begun."

"Are you scared, Kat?" Betty reached over and rested a hand on top of hers.

She set her plate down on the coffee table and took a deep breath in an attempt to dispel the demon eating her up. "Yes, I'm scared shitless. This is my house, my safe place, and some crazy woman is trying to take it away. I'm sorry, not trying—she is taking it away from me. I've got one shot to talk to a bunch of dudes I've never met and convince them to go against their partner's wishes to save this material thing that has no value to them, no significance. It's a lot of pressure."

Dev stood up and crossed the room. He placed his plate next to hers and leaned down opposite of Betty. "Kat, look at me."

She looked up, meeting those deep brown eyes of his. The safety she experienced when around him reflected back at her, and the determination in his face washed over her.

"You've got more than a chance, trust me. I wouldn't be helping you if I didn't believe we can get your house saved."

"Thank you." Those were the only words she could muster, and she wanted to believe him and to see the woman he saw because she must've been something special to earn such faith and dedication.

He could still see her doubt; she sensed it when he pulled away and stood up. Reaching behind his neck, he adjusted his ponytail. "Tell you what, take the rest of the evening to rest. Download a bit since you've had a long day at work. Review the flashcards if you want to. We can pick things up tomorrow night."

Betty patted her hand. "I think that's a good idea, and I can stick around if you change your mind and want to do a little studying. I'm staying to finish this delicious curry, but I'll help in whatever capacity."

Kat laughed a small chuckle, which was what Betty'd intended, if her smile was any indication. "Thank you, both of you."

"No problem. I mean to be helpful, not stressful. Text me later if you need me." Dev grabbed the carton of pad thai. "I'm taking this delicious stuff with me. You ladies can keep the red curry."

Then he left, out the door without another word. His lingering invitation to text replayed in her head, something he'd never offered to her before, a chance to talk over the phone outside of their working partnership.

As soon as the front door clicked into place, Betty got up and peeked around the living room corner, appearing to check and make sure he was really gone. "All right, Kat, no more keeping secrets to yourself. What the hell is going on?"

***

Dev pressed send on the last email for the day and started the process of closing down every open window and file on his computer. Picking up his phone, he checked for messages. No luck. Kat hadn't bothered to reach out to him at all. He'd hoped she'd give him a shot, a chance to be the person she'd voice her concerns too.

Until Betty had shown up and raised those questions, he never would've suspected Kat's fears about the party. She'd put up a good, positive face on the surface. Deep down her fears swirled around like a slow, invading infection. Something he couldn't fight. Only she could, and he believed she'd defeat it with the right motivation. Sex is not an option for motivation.

Even if he wanted it to be, those thoughts were based purely on how much he wanted her, a separate concept from the party and the goal to save her house. How could he win both battles? Defeat the dragon, win the princess, and save his kingdom?

A knock came on his office door, and Victoria didn't wait for his acknowledgment before she opened up.

"You have a visitor." Her face, all wide eyes without the usual displeased smirk, told him she was surprised.

He pushed himself out of his seat ready to greet Kat, to be a comfort and a support center, but when Victoria stepped to the side, his sister Juanita came forward. The smile he'd held faded, and he tried his best to tamp his reaction.

"Don't look so disappointed, mi hermano. I'm here to find out what's become of you."

Victoria crept out of the room, no doubt wanting to avoid being dragged into the conversation. She shut the door behind her, giving him privacy with his sister. In the years since they'd worked together, she'd become familiar with his family. They were a close bunch, and the fact that his younger sister had shown up, instead of his mother, served as the warning salvo.

"I take it you're supposed to report back if you found me alive?"

"Yes, and I was told to deliver a message. If you're not at dinner Sunday night, our mother makes no promises about not showing up here with lunch, whether your schedule is clear or not."

Dev walked around the desk and approached the smaller woman. She'd never gotten the tall genes from their father's side of the family. Nope, she stood a little over five feet, similar height to their mother, a tiny, fierce creature he'd do anything for. He'd been one of those over-protective brothers. She'd expressed disdain for his antics to scare off boyfriends and the usual anger at his teasing.

"I'll be there. Now, what else made you volunteer for this mission? Because last time I checked, you hated being Mom and Dad's message service." He pulled her into a big bear hug, wrapping his arms around her small body and letting her sink into him.

She gave him approximately five seconds before she stepped back and leveled a serious, furrowed-brow look at him. "Just wanted to see you, and maybe a certain secretary messaged me and said she was worried about you. Thought I might be able to pry some secrets out, starting with who in the hell did you expect to walk through that door? Because it wasn't me."

He stared at the wall past her, gathered his thoughts, and debated on whether he should lie or not. The problem with being close to a sibling, a person who knew all the dirty secrets and challenges, including his crap with Pru, was it made it damn near impossible to lie to her. To lie to his hermanita would be equivalent to betraying the foundation of who he was. So, he told the truth.

"I thought you might be Kat."

"Kat? Who is she?"

"Have a seat and give me a minute. Maybe I can explain this without you thinking the worst of me."

"When you put it like that, you don't inspire confidence." She sat down in an office chair, and he perched on the edge of his desk.

Before he could stop himself or think better of it, the whole story came out. It sounded a bit like an episode of a crazy reality show, maybe one of those pranking, comedic acts. He shared how his ex was attacking his partner's cousin, trying to steal her house and that she was coincidently the same person he'd taken on as a pro bono client.

He left out the part about being attracted to her, and that the sexual tension was difficult to avoid. Not to mention, Kat's blatant announcement that she was completely cool with them pursuing whatever this thing was between them.

On some strange level, coming clean to someone lifted a burden from his shoulders and a heavy dose of tension he'd failed to recognize building over the past several weeks.

"Pru and her project are going to take this woman's house, and you're helping her save it?"

He nodded, pursing his lips and waiting for her judgment. His high-school-teaching sister heard crazy stories all the time; angst-filled teenagers bred them like a fish laid eggs. She could put everything in perspective for him.

"How do you get yourself mixed up in this shit?"

"I stumbled into it. This was supposed to be about getting my 'mojo' back, according to Mark."

"Mark's an idiot, but I won't even touch that subject with a ten-foot pole. Besides all those points you mentioned, you haven't told me why you're attracted to her yet."

He nearly choked on a swallow of water. "What are you talking about?"

"Brother, you're talking to me. The look on your face when I came through the door was not a look of my-client-is-here. No, you possessed a bit of the doe-eyed look I catch sight of between my students who suffer from cases of Bambi twitterpated."

"And? Does it matter? I'm not making the same mistakes as I did with Pru. Nope, I'm keeping this business-related if it kills me."

"Then you like her?"

"I do. If it weren't for her being a client, I'd want to date her, or at least see where things go."

"Sounds like you're almost to the point." Juanita cocked her head to the side and gave him a grin. The one she often gave when she'd solved the world's problems without lifting a finger.

"Come again?"

"She's technically your client until she's completed the makeover, and this party is her big reveal on all the conversation tips, the hairstyling, and the new wardrobe she's been breaking in. If she survives the night, she's done. The client portion will be wrapped, and you can see where things lead. She does like you, right?"

Dev laughed. "Yes, I think so. She kissed me, which gives me the impression we have something."

"You didn't mention that before."

"It wasn't any of your business, and I thought we both agreed not to talk about those kinds of things, which saves me from wanting to hurt someone."

His sister had said all the right things, reassured him, and shown him the path to simple freedom. All he needed to do was last another forty-eight hours, and the cherry on top of their sundae would be possible.

Then doubt crept in, thanks to the same voice with the winning plan. "What's in it for her, though, besides the house? I mean, it's kind of silly that she needed a makeover if she's been trying to get her house up to code."

"Good question, and I've got no clue."

CHAPTER FOURTEEN

Kat pulled up to Beauty Magicians on Thursday afternoon still debating on whether she wanted Chad to work on her hair or take a flying leap. Since Tuesday night she'd heard nothing from Dev, except for a dismissal text on Wednesday.

Family thing came up, will have to skip tonight's review session.

Maybe she'd scared him away with her startling confession about fearing the party. Combined with her statement and actions in the days prior, she probably looked a bit psychotic. Sure, she kept challenging her fears, ideas, and negative thoughts with Dev's positive affirmations.

Outside of that, Betty had commented on the spontaneous combustion she was sure they'd experience in the bedroom if the looks they kept trading were any indication. *For fuck's sake.* Her friend picked up on the attraction; she obviously sucked at hiding her lust glazed thoughts.

The memory of his gaze burned a path on her mind and the longing in his eyes made her want to call her cousin Mark and tell him to take his contract and shove it. If she and Dev wanted to rip their clothes off like born-again nudists and fornicate in every position ever invented, Mark couldn't stop them. They were adults, damn it.

At the same time, thoughts like that scared the shit out of her. She'd cooled toward the idea whenever her mind leaned toward the next steps. A true fear boiled in her brain of him wanting more from her than hot, wild sex between the sheets. More meant opening up, sharing parts of herself she'd rather keep safe. She'd admit to a growing respect for her hotter-than-hell image consultant, but to trust him with everything emotional? Insanity.

Not to mention, he'd backed down against the wave of desire she'd been ready to surrender to the other night. While it was pretty impressive to see him hold back and not react to the crazy tension between them, it was maddening too. Maybe he wasn't as affected by their attraction, or this truly was a case of being addicted to a damsel in distress like Mark had predicted.

No way to know without asking, and she'd decided somewhere in the last twenty-four hours she was too chicken to find out.

A knock on her window and she turned her head, coming face to face with Betty and her blond hair in those familiar chopsticks, with magical makeup and a grin on her face.

"We're five minutes late." Her voice came through the window muffled, but understandable.

Taking the keys out of the ignition, Kat committed to the appointment. If only she hadn't told Betty about it Tuesday. Betty had a weakness, and it involved the dreaded word "pamper." In fact, Kat earned another compliment again as she got out of the car.

"Your hair still floors me. A perfect trim. My stylist can't even do that. Thanks for letting me tag along. I want to meet this master genius of hair."

"No problem, as long as you promise to leave me out of any future visits."

Betty gave a light chuckle. "I think it's funny you're so against the process of beauty on the outside. It's okay to like those things, to enjoy looking good."

"I know it's okay, but I don't like them. It doesn't make me feel right."

"How would you know if you never really tried?" Betty took the lead then, walking into the salon without another word.

Her comment stung a bit since she judged Kat for not doing the makeup, the nails, the hair, and all the things. In her opinion, she'd tried multiple times, and each attempt had left her with a hole inside her. The few minutes where she thought she looked good dissolved into a mess when the eyeshadow got in the corner of her eyes or when her face broke out into a dozen zits. Nails and hair required upkeep, and she didn't want to deal with it or the associated cost.

Still, she walked through the door determined to give up control over her hair, at least for one day, especially since it meant saving her house.

Chad greeted them within minutes, Ace not manning her post at the front desk. "Hello, Kind Kat. See, I can come with nicknames too."

An elbow to her side and Betty whispered, "Introduce me."

"Chad, this is my friend Betty. She's real impressed with the trim you gave me last weekend."

Her stylist blushed, surprisingly, at the attention paid to him. "Thank you, but it's the hair, not the artist."

Betty grew shy standing beside her too. "Still, I'd like to see you work your magic."

"Then, by all means, let's get started on my miraculous idea. I've been thinking about it for days."

Escorted to the chair, Kat sat down and waited as the drop cloth was put over her. Chad excused himself to get a few supplies he seemed to be missing, and that's when Betty pounced. "All right, I've got the notecards you gave me, and I'm ready to start the review, but first, what about that guy?"

"Clarify?"

"The dirt, the down low, his life story… give me something." The girl had the hots for her hunky hair stylist if the look in her eyes said anything.

"I know nothing. This is the second time I've been around him. His orientation, no clue. Aspirations, no clue. In the market for a date or a fling, no clue."

"You're not very helpful."

Kat laughed at the look of exasperation on Betty's face. Her friend let out a small huff, which blew a loose strand of hair away from her eyes.

"I'm not helpful, but I agreed to let you come because you said you'd quiz me."

Chad came back then, hands full with a bottle of hair product, a packet of combs, hair ties, and clips. "Somebody raided my station while I was away, so I had to steal a few things back."

"No worries, I'm working up the courage."

Immediately Chad put a hand to his chest and pulled off a stricken, wounded look Kat could see, thanks to the mirror. "You don't trust me."

"I trust you too much. My friend is going to quiz me on things I need to know for tonight. Will that be all right?"

"Yes, as long as you turn your head when I say to and no comments on the hair until I'm done."

"Will it be that bad?"

"I want it to be a surprise."

"Ooh, I love surprises," Betty said, clapping her hands together.

"You, fact cards."

Betty nodded. "Right."

She reached into her purse and pulled the index cards out. Chad had started combing her hair out by the time Betty called out, "Richard."

Thirty minutes later, her scalp felt like she should have no hair left, and she'd successfully rattled off details to three of the four board members. Now to get the last one, Colton Kinyon. She'd blundered the first two passes, horribly so. "He made his money in gas and then sold off the majority of his company to a co-op. Did some investing in, wait, um—"

"Don't tax yourself it's—"

"Hush, I'll get it. Investing in commodities trading."

Chad stepped in front of her, blocking the mirror, and sprayed something in her hair. "Give the girl a gold star. Even I know that's right."

"Friends with the millionaire, Charming?"

Leaning down, he grinned at her. "As a matter of fact, I'm his barber."

"Can you be both friend and barber?" Betty inquired.

"I certainly can, if needed," he replied as he pulled away from Kat, looking over his creation. "My masterpiece is complete. What do you think?" He stepped out of the path of the mirror and she took her first good look at her hairdo.

"It's amazing." Betty's words were spoken softly with reverence. Kat took in the braids lining the sides of her head, the top ponytail with its small braids, and "poofed up" top. It wasn't a style she'd pick out for a swanky get-together.

"Are you both sure this is the right look for me?"

"Yes." They both spoke in unison.

Then Chad whirled her chair around to face him. "Think Viking queen, the warrior woman. You're entering a lion's den; this hairstyle gives you strength. Shows you're willing to step out of your element. It's still an updo, but with a little heathen, a little wild."

"Betty?"

"I agree, and with the dress, plus those heels you have, it will be perfect—edgy and a completely different fashion. They won't know what to think of you, but everyone will want to talk to you."

Too bad she didn't want to talk to anyone. *For the house, this is for the house.*

The mantra is what kept her going, helped drown out the fear.

"Then let's do it."

Betty and Chad shared a high five and a moment of something else, but Kat vowed to stay out of it. If her friend wanted to know more about the guy doing her hair, by all means, more power to her. She rocked her body so the chair faced the mirror again. The person staring back at her appeared stronger, fiercer than anything she could've cooked up. In a way the hairstyle gave her power, confidence like Chad promised.

Is Dev going to like this? Only one way to find out.

"Betty, quit chatting my stylist up and take a photo of my hair, with my phone."

Her friend did as requested and then handed the phone back over before she started gathering their things. Kat quickly sent it off with a short message about Charming's selected style for the evening.

His response proved equally short and left room for plenty of doubt. *See you at seven.*

***

Dev parked the car outside Kat's house and took a deep breath. He wasn't ready for tonight, not since he'd seen the photo Kat texted him of her hairdo. She'd looked regal and fierce; Chad had promised a transformation and delivered. The man truly worked miracles.

He didn't want to remember the other thoughts he'd had, but they came back regardless. How her hair would feel wrapped around his hand while he kissed her. Things he didn't need to do. Somewhere between the last time he'd been with her and now she'd become temptation personified. He knew the price but still couldn't erase the thoughts from his mind. His sister's advice, stirred with fears, trickled into the mixture as well.

Refusing to wallow or debate about them all night, he got out of the car, straightened his suit jacket, buttoned it up, and marched to the front door, determined to keep his mind from the gutter. Doorbell successfully pressed, he waited, hearing the familiar clack of heels on the other side. But, when the door opened, it revealed Betty.

She frowned at him. "You look fabulous, but we have a problem."

"What's wrong?"

"She won't come out, something about embarrassing herself."

"Is this about her shoes?"

Her friend shrugged her shoulders. "No idea."

"Take me to her."

Leading the way, Betty guided Dev back to Kat's bedroom. He couldn't help but notice the whole house ablaze, lights on in every room. Her bedroom looked different from the last time he'd been in here; clothes tossed all over her bed, boxes filled with papers on the floor. Kat wasn't to be found anywhere. "Where is she?"

"In the bathroom," Betty replied, pointing to a closed door he hadn't paid close attention to last time. She knocked on it. "Kat, Dev's here. It's time to go."

"I can't go. I feel like I'm going to be sick." Her voice filtered through the door, sounding awful.

Dev motioned to Betty to give him a shot, and they switched places. "Kat, can I come in? I think I can make that nausea go away."

The lock disengaged, and he tried the knob. It gave easily. His first look at her as the door swung open was more erotic than he'd imagined possible. Kat had her arms braced against her vanity, lower half thrust out. The little black dress Sam had picked out shimmered and accentuated her gorgeous curves, including her fine-looking rear end. Plenty for a man to grab a hold of in the heat of the moment. Coupled with the black heels they'd both agreed on at Nude, she was breathtaking. Add in the hair, and she'd become a seductress, a no-panty-hose, bare-legged siren. Thank goodness the October night ran warmer than most.

The look she gave him was pained and vulnerable as she held up a stick of eyeliner in her hand. "I look awful, a mismatched mess."

"You look fabulous and are going to turn everyone's head. They won't know what to do or think. Your ensemble is perfect."

She let go of the vanity. "You meant that." Her words were not a question but an acknowledgment of his statement.

"I don't say things I don't mean."

"I know... but it doesn't stop me from asking." She turned, and the dress let out a little swish, the skirt flowing with her. "Now, how do I get rid of this queasy stomach?"

Dev smiled, unable to help himself. Even when she didn't feel good, Kat still kept herself matter-of-fact, all business. If she truly were using him, this wouldn't be the way to go about it by standing here in a state of weakness and trying to be strong, but accepting her need for help. He lost himself a bit and took a deep breath before responding to the first direction. "Close your eyes."

Kat hesitated, but only for a minute. When her eyes were shut, he stepped closer.

Keeping his voice low, designed to invoke a sense of peace, he spoke the next set of instructions. "Breathe in through your nose and out through your mouth. With each breath out, envision your nervousness leaving, your fears. Replace it with strength, confidence. No one will laugh at you. At the least, they will ignore you, and the most, they will engage you in conversation and want to know more."

Her breathing continued, and after thirty seconds—"Now open your eyes."

She did, and her shoulders relaxed, the tension melting away, and her frame straightened up.

"Feel better?" Betty asked from behind him.

"Yes." She nodded her head once. "I think I can do this. I'm ready."

They all migrated to the living room, Kat collecting her purse, which she bemoaned about. "This is why pants are perfect. They have pockets for keys and cards. This dress-and-purse stuff is for the crazy ladies of the world."

"Hey!" Betty sounded only a little offended. "I'm not crazy."

"You took time off work to help me get ready for a party you have nothing to do with," Kat replied.

"That's not crazy; it's called friendship. And now I'm going home to my dog and a bottle of wine. You both have a marvelous time." Betty stepped up to Kat and gave her a brief, barely there hug before she turned on Dev. "She better make it home safe, or you'll have to answer to me and two other women."

The woman's no-nonsense, dead-eyed expression gave him a bit of a chill, and he replied, "Yes."

Betty clicked her way out of the house, and once the door shut behind her, Kat asked, "One last time, are you sure I look okay?"

"The scary feelings coming back?"

"Maybe a little."

He wanted to touch her to soothe the nervousness, but being in the living room brought back to mind the near kiss the last time he'd been there. Better to get out the door. "It will be fine, and you look wonderful. Let's get going."

"If you want to review anything in the car, I need to get my index cards."

"No cards. No reviewing. We're going, and we will have a good time, at the least."

She nodded in agreement and readjusted the strap of her purse on her shoulder. "Let's get it on."

Twenty minutes later they'd found a place to park and walked into the fancy 2Squared Hotel. The dinner was being held in one of the conference rooms. Fancy and elaborate, no doubt one of Pru's ideas. The hotel stood in the heart of downtown and attracted celebrities all the time. Pru and Dev's idea for downtown had sprouted after the hotel was built, over dinner at the Digs restaurant. Since their breakup, this was the one place he'd refused to come back to. This had been the location of their first anniversary, where they'd decided to move into together. It was also where he'd decided enough was enough. Fitting he'd walk in here with a different woman on his arm, one he found himself more interested in. Kat had curiosity, a flair for the dramatic, and a sweet enthusiasm he wanted to explore to its fullest extent.

They came up to the hostess.

"Two for Bentonville's Beautification Celebration." Dev handed over the invitation.

A quick glance by the hostess and she replied, "Follow me, sir."

They walked across the bar area and past the crowd of folks talking, through a set of double doors. Once inside, the hostess bid them a good evening. Back along the left wall was a replica of downtown Bentonville and the surrounding blocks. Small green and purple flags with the board's logo were planted in front of the houses that had agreed to the remodel. They approached it slowly, moving around a couple of people standing there. No one Dev knew had seen them yet, nor had anyone greeted them.

Kat's face turned ashen. "There's a flag in front of my house."

"Don't let it get to you. It's a show-off piece." Dev whispered.

"But she may as well already have it. I don't have the rest of the money."

"Stop. Those kinds of thoughts will end up driving you crazy. Let's mingle; dinner will be served in about twenty minutes. We've got time to get a drink." He didn't mean to, but he put a hand on the small of her back. The contact sent a tingle up his arm as he guided her away from the model and right into Pru and her godfather, Jim.

"Dev, you made it." The look Pru gave him, the open admiration, immediately turned sour as she glanced at Kat. "And you brought a guest."

Jim didn't seem the least bit affected by Pru's disapproval and stuck out a hand toward Kat. "I'm Jim Hunt, Treasurer and board member. You are?"

"Kathleen Baum." She shook his hand, and Dev didn't appreciate the gaze Jim leveled at her bosom. A spiral of unwanted emotion circled in his belly.

"What do you do, Kathleen?"

Pru didn't wait for Kat to answer. "She works for a marketing company pushing papers."

The venom in her words was visible to everyone and pissed him off. He'd seen the same type of attitude ruin a woman's self-esteem. So he did the next best thing. Dev wrapped his arm all the way around Kat, loving the feel of her waist beneath his palm. A small tug and she fit right against him. Heat, chiffon, and soft women nestled in beside him. His slacks tightened in the groin area, and he willed his semi-arousal to disappear.

But the movement evoked even more anger from Pru. "Her house is also on the verge of being condemned. It's the little one off Central. The two-bedroom, tiny thing with the tile roofing. You remember, Uncle Jim." She wrapped an arm around her godfather's elbow.

Jim frowned. "I don't believe I do remember; regardless, I'm sorry to hear that."

"Me too," Kat replied. "The house has been in my family for nearly seventy five years. My great-grandparents bought the property and built the house from their savings."

The words appeared to touch a soft spot for Jim, just like he knew they would. History was very important to him, as it was for all the members of the board. It's how Pru had convinced them to agree to the project. "Why is it condemned?"

"Outdated wiring, plumbing, and a few other issues. Of course, I never knew about them until a surprise inspection by the code department."

"Uncle Jim, I see a few people I'd like you to meet. We'll leave Dev and Kathleen to get settled." Pru's voice sounded a bit panicked because the truth of her deliberate deception hovered right at the surface. No doubt the board members weren't familiar with her tricks.

"Mr. Hunt, I haven't seen the other board members here this evening. Are Hugh and Richard in attendance?" If they couldn't work Jim, they'd move on to the others, but it wouldn't hurt to find out where they were within the monstrosity of the room.

"I'm afraid both of them had pressing obligations this evening, but Kinyon's wandering around here somewhere if you don't mind putting up with him." Jim started to walk away with Pru, but as they passed, Dev whispered, "The truth will come out."

Pru shot dagger eyes at him and then click-clacked off. If her reaction was any indication, the night could only get better.

CHAPTER FIFTEEN

Kat survived the fire. Once Purple People Eater left them alone, things had gone swimmingly. There were dozens of people to meet, and meet them she did. Dev introduced her around the room. A lot of the folks he knew from dating Pru, but it seemed the Purple People Eater's circle of influence didn't include a mean girls group.

As they sat down to dinner, Kat caught a glimpse of Mark a few tables over. Maybe him seeing her tonight would secure the rest of the money by proving she'd finished the makeover, which gave her the light at the end of this fucked up tunnel. The strange thing was, Dev hadn't talked about beyond tonight, and her stomach gave a twinge at the idea of this being the last time they spent together. Over the last month, he'd become a part of her life, particularly her weekends, and they'd come to find a lot of things in common. Sure they spent most of their time talking tips and development topics, but then she'd make a movie reference or mention a silly nickname and he'd pick up on it.

Tonight, the urge to kiss him had come on strong. Especially when he'd walked into her house earlier and taken away her fears, calmed her down by declaring her a beauty. The admiration in his eyes made her believe him. There'd been a moment after Betty left that she'd sworn they might have shared a kiss. Now he walked over to Mark, who stood up from his chair. They clasped hands, and Dev pointed to Kat. Mark's eyes went wide, and the two began talking.

"Is this seat taken?" asked a male voice from beside her, the tone rich and cultured.

She swiveled in her chair and made eye contact with smoky grays, a tan face with grayish-brown hair, and a matching goatee-mustache combo. He smiled at her with perfect teeth, white and pearly.

"No," she replied. "Not at the moment."

"Then I'll join you." He slid into the chair, a knee brushing against hers. It didn't creep her out, but made her more aware of her new acquaintance as a man. A niggle at the back of her brain screamed familiarity.

"Colton Kinyon, nice to meet you."

Ding ding ding, we have a winner. This was the one man Dev had insisted she talk to tonight, but he'd grown facial hair and a tanned since the photo for the board had been taken.

"Kathleen Baum, and likewise." She stuck out her hand. "I was told you were the man I needed to speak with."

"Oh, really?" His eyebrows went up, and he gave a secret smile. "I'm happy to help however I can."

He'd probably regret saying such a thing when she got done with him. While she didn't have strong religious beliefs or bind herself up in a church like most of her family, she did believe in signs. This man—the one with no ties to Pru or Dev outside of the Beautification Board, of which he served as Vice President—sitting at her table, one of many with empty chairs, appeared to be a sign.

"How can a house on the Beautification Board's list of prospects get removed?"

Colton appeared surprised by the question, but regained his composure as fast as it took to drink from his wine glass. "Before I can answer that, I'd have to understand why they would want to be removed. The houses selected are all in need of updating, remodeling, and we're doing the owners a service otherwise unavailable to them. It's not often a bunch of millionaires would offer to spend their money to fix up houses they will never live in or gain an asset from."

The elegant words struck a chord with her—a somewhat negative one. "You have a point, but typically when someone remodels their home, they get a say in how the house looks. Based on the paperwork, these owners have no say in the final product. It's the discretion of the board what the inside and outside of these houses will look like, which takes away from the history of the house. Ruins it. How can you say you're preserving anything when the homes are bent to your every idea and whim? While no monetary gain is earned, playing God with someone's home is a reward in itself."

Leaning toward her, Colton gave the most apologetic look—softened eyes and a downturn of his lips—a sad face. "My dear Kathleen, you're so passionate about our project. I take it you have a house on our list?"

She nodded, afraid to open her mouth and utter an expletive. "No shit, Sherlock" would have been fitting.

"Have you accepted the contract?"

"No, for the reasons I just stated," she replied.

"Ah." He said, sounding like a doctor who'd just been told some secret. "Then you're the lovely, fiery young woman I've heard so much about, the one who cannot afford to bring her house up to code. Why would you want to keep living in a death trap?"

"It was my grandmother's. Two generations of her family were born and raised in the home. I'm the second female to own and live in the house. There's history you can't begin to understand—"

"One errant spark and the history crumbles to dust." He interrupted her, the arrogant ass.

She wanted to stamp her foot and resort to the easiest tactic in the book, name-calling. Instead, she took a sip of her beverage, a fruity Moscato, and glanced around the room. Waitstaff had begun to put plates on the tables with dinner near the front of the room. It wouldn't be long now before everyone would sit and eat, discussing all the good work being done, as if this project was the greatest in the world, a charitable endeavor people should be appreciative of, instead of the reality where they were selling out houses' histories like cows at auction.

Colton touched her hand, and she started. "Kathleen?"

"What?" She didn't tug away like she should, the warm, callused palm a welcome heat source in the chilly room.

He removed his hand from hers, politely. "Do you have any plans for taking care of your ancestral home?"

"I'm working on getting things updated now. It's taking a bit of time and some money, but coming along."

"But therein lies the problem, the funds for the upkeep. How much is it putting you back?"

Anger rushed through her veins at the question, and she couldn't admit she'd entered into a deal with her despicable cousin to get the money. "A pretty penny, but what matters is I retain control of my home. I won't be a visitor, and the history of my family won't be cast aside for a fake one."

"We're the devil, aren't we?" This time, Colton smiled, big and wide without guilt or the appearance of shame.

She shook her head in disbelief. "A devil with money pouring out of your checking account. How do you see this as right? You don't even care about how this perverts history instead of preserving it."

"Good evening, cousin." Mark's voice came from behind her, and she looked over her shoulder to see him with his typical lowball of whiskey in hand. His red-and-black suit made him look more flashy than usual. *Well hello, Satan.*

Colton piped up then. "Cousins? Mark, you're related to this enchanting young woman?"

"Yes," Kat spoke before her cousin could. "We have parents who share the mother who, until her death, owned the house I live in."

Instead of responding to her, Mark focused his attention on her companion. "Do you mind if I borrow her for a minute?"

"Not a problem. I need a refill from the bar anyway." Colton got up and left, giving Mark a chance to slide into his seat.

"Didn't expect to see you here." The sassy tone in her voice came without volition. Maybe it was because Mark had no smile, no life. He looked absolutely bored and cold.

"The same would go for me, but Dev mentioned something about your house being on the chopping block and that this party was a perfect chance to test out what you've learned about the board members. You haven't been running your mouth about our little agreement, have you?"

"No, my lips are sealed. How am I doing with the board members?"

He took a sip of whiskey and gave some weird half smile, "Horrible. If the angry way in which you talked to Mr. Kinyon is any example of what you've learned, I'm afraid to see the rest. I heard you ticked off Dev's ex too."

"From what my image consultant says, we have common enemies. She's after your business and my house." For once she'd like to align with her cousin on something. to be working together because so far her deal with him felt terribly one-sided.

"She's not our enemy, but as important as any client. We have to ensure she makes money as much as we do. That's the purpose of investors. They give the funds, and the business makes the moolah to pay them back. The investors also ensure business decisions are sound, and speaking of, Dev tells me you're done. If he gives you the gold stamp tonight, then it's all over."

Her heart jostled with joy and sadness at the announcement. The goal of passing the inspection and saving the house was within her grasp; she just had to last through dinner. "Consider my part of the deal complete."

Mark pushed out of the chair. "We'll see."

***

Dev got back to his and Kat's table with fresh drinks in time to watch Mark stalk off, Colton Kinyon take a chair next to her, and dinner to be placed in front of him. The way Kinyon grabbed hold of the back of Kat's chair as he sat resonated within Dev. Primal, territorial emotions invaded his being, which seemed unlike him. He didn't get jealous.

Sure, this woman held his interest more than any in the past, and he'd shared sexually charged moments with her that had never led anywhere, thank the Lord. When Mark had quizzed him on why he'd brought her, he'd done his best to make it all about work, about the consulting. He'd proudly confessed she'd impressed him over the past several weeks. She wasn't changed, but equipped for social events, and this happened to be the final test.

The word "final" set off a reality bomb inside him. They'd been building up to this moment for the last two weeks. *A one-time performance and after this, then what?* Did they see each other on weekends or go for runs or out to eat? Would she want him to come on shopping trips? Use her newfound style and tips to get a new job or maybe set up a competitive company? If his sister were here to offer a suggestion, she'd predict the worst. Somehow he couldn't imagine Kat being as two-faced as Pru, but he did have a ton of unanswered questions and no clue on when to begin asking them. The only questions that mattered were where he fit in after tonight and why the hell was he worried about it?

"Your dinner's going to get cold," Pru whispered into his ear.

He fought every instinct to stay still and not jerk away from her as quickly as possible. Without looking at her, he parried, "What is on the menu tonight, besides humiliation tactics and glowering stares?"

"You're still holding my comments on your arrival against me? I was caught by surprise, and I didn't say anything untrue." Her reaction was typical, fluttering a hand in the air to dismiss his truth and replace it with one of her own.

"You didn't say anything helpful, either. But that's okay because everything you do has some reason, some justifiable purpose in your mind, right?"

The words came out angrier than he intended, the reality of their relationship brimming to the surface again. The cruelty he saw so often destroyed women's self-esteem and confidence, and she wielded it like a reverse mirror, one side closeup and personal, the other pulled back away from the imperfections.

She didn't faze, though, didn't yield. "Maybe you should consider eating; a hungry stomach can turn the most pleasant person sour."

"Great idea." Grabbing onto the out she'd given him, he didn't say goodbye, just walked over to the table and slid into his chair. Kat and Kinyon were already eating. "I got you another Moscato."

Kat looked up from a plate of salad and chicken breast. "You were gone a long time."

He leaned in. "Long enough for you to get cozy with Kinyon. Make any headway?"

The man in question conversed with a couple on the other side of him. Dev hoped she'd been able to share her story. This was the only investor he didn't think Pru had her hooks into.

"No, Sweet Talker here is pretty convinced he's doing the right thing. He firmly believes those who can't afford to take care of their houses should accept the deal the board is offering, even if it takes away the homeowner's rights." She didn't keep her voice down or try to hide what she'd discussed with him. In fact, her comments turned Kinyon's and the couple's attention on them.

"I can't help but think you're talking about me." The smile Kinyon wore soured.

"Let me be clear." Kat stabbed through a bite of chicken and held it up in the air. "I am."

For a moment Dev envisioned a bull seeing red, the matador taunting, and she'd be run down. Then the man she'd so blatantly bad-mouthed threw his head back and laughed.

"You've got brass ones, young woman. Calling me out like that, I don't know a single person who would ever do such a thing."

"My grandma always said lies get no one anywhere. I'm a firm believer in speaking the truth."

"Even if it hurts?"

"Even then." Kat ate her bite of chicken, and Dev let himself smile. She'd wowed someone with more influence in his pinky finger than she possessed in her whole body. A self-made millionaire who constantly expressed an attitude for not taking crap appeared to be willing to put up with hers.

"A piece of advice," Kinyon lowered his voice a bit, but Dev could still pick it up. "Don't ever change, and if you ever want to get a different look at the city, call my office."

The man then put a hand over Kat's, an intimate gesture. She appeared a little surprised, but Kinyon grabbed his plate, got up, and left them with a parting greeting. "I better mingle with a few other folks. Wouldn't want to monopolize your time, or I'd try to steal you away from your date."

"Oh, he's not my—" Kat cut off as he walked away.

The words were a blow to his ego a little bit, creating the sudden desire to be more—a date, a companion, or at least somewhere higher on the scale. "But technically I am."

She eyed him with skepticism. "Really? Last week that wasn't the case. I'm the client, the cousin. Off-limits, remember?"

"Is that what you want to be?" He whispered the question into her ear, felt her shiver. Her fork clattered against her plate.

A little wrinkle appeared on her forehead as she replied, "I want a lot of things, but I'm familiar with being limited to less."

He gripped her fork, lifting the metal utensil with its single bite of chicken up to her mouth. "Eat."

Her lips wrapped around the prongs, and he could feel every movement, including her tongue touching the meat, her lips using a gentle pressure to pull the succulent bite off the fork. The room, the problems, the guests fell away and left them. He'd started this, driven by her ability to dismiss the contact they shared, the intimate nature in their familiarity. The lines had blurred weeks prior, and after tonight, she wasn't a client but his business associate's cousin.

"Aren't you hungry?" She asked this before taking a drink of her wine. He watched her swallow, traced the path down the slender line of her neck, then her ample chest and curves.

"Not for food." A dangerous sentence, but he couldn't help it. The words lingered between them, the air thick as he set down the fork and slid his palm over hers. Feedback from a microphone echoed through the room's speakers, but it didn't encourage him to break the contact. In the last five minutes, he'd decided to throw caution to the wind.

Pru started speaking, her voice droning on about the board, the beautification of downtown Bentonville, and all the wonderful families willing to allow the board to help restore their homes. Dev didn't care about it; he wanted the woman next to him alone. He wanted to run his fingers into her braids and strip the chiffon dress off and reveal all her skin and the body he'd been tempted by since he'd met her.

"Let's get out of here?"

She nodded her assent, and they stood from the table, moving toward the door quickly. Hopefully, no one would notice or care they were gone.

In the car, once they were both settled, Dev looked at Kat, her breathing slow and steady. His heart pounded in his chest. If he wanted to have second thoughts, now would be the time. "My place?"

"Sure." She looked at her lap, linked her hands, and he could sense the hesitancy.

"Are you sure?"

"Yes, but what about you?" The natural concern in her question touched him.

"You passed tonight—got dressed up, mingled with people you didn't know, and impressed a millionaire—all of that without changing who you were, only refining bits and pieces. I have a feeling you'll be getting your house back. Our business contract is complete. At this moment we are two consenting adults who know each other."

She smiled. "Then let's go."

CHAPTER SIXTEEN

Kat couldn't believe the turn of events. One second she'd been trying to keep her patience with Colton and process her cousin's attitude toward her. Then Dev had swept her away with his sudden change of heart. He wanted her, and let it show. She hoped Mark missed their exit for the simple sake that it might complicate her getting the rest of the money. She agreed, though, with Dev's assessment; their business arrangement was complete. The next steps were up to them.

Dev's apartment rested in Rogers, a good fifteen-minute drive from the Bentonville Square. The car was waved in by the gatekeeper, and they parked at the second building. She waited for a minute, taking in the all-brick facade and large patios on the outside of each apartment, which gave Dev the opportunity to open her door for her. When she put her hand in his, he pulled her out of the car and into his arms.

"I love this dress, your hair." He mumbled the words, eyes on her lips.

"Thank you." Why the hell she experienced a sudden wave of shyness, she had no clue. But his words made her feel beautiful in a way no other man had. Like earlier, she could tell he spoke the truth by the lack of a smile on his face. He spoke the words stone-cold seriously, and this time they dripped with desire.

"*Ay Dios mio*, the things I want to do to you." He ran an index finger down her cheek, allowing his hand to mold against it. Then he pulled away, the giant fucking tease. "Let me show you my place first."

She almost stomped her foot and demanded he kiss her, but instead, she let him lead the way, the whole moment still so close to a dream. She'd imagined where he lived before but never pictured this place. They went up one flight of stairs, and he was the first door on the right. He had to let go of her to open the door, but once done, he held her again. She liked how he wanted contact with her body. Once inside, he shut the door and locked it.

She trailed away from him and walked toward the big living room window, which overlooked a small lake and, across from there, a golf course. The moon illuminated a path on the lake, bringing to mind childhood memories of night fishing with her grandmother in summer, and she stood transfixed.

"Are you okay?"

"Yes, just enjoying the view."

His question had her turning to look at the rest of the room, the white sectional and glass coffee table, the matching end tables and glass lamps. Everything was clean and pristine, and light-reflecting colors dominated the room and appeared brighter thanks to the moon and the window. A kitchen was off to the right with a breakfast bar and stools. He didn't keep a messy place.

"I'm a little embarrassed I even let you in my house," she said as she sauntered toward him.

He chuckled. "I have a housekeeper. If it weren't for her, this place would be a disaster."

The tension between them thickened. They both stood, mere feet away from each other, locked in a staring contest like gunslingers awaiting the clock chime to draw their weapons.

"Damn, looking at you like this... face the window." The command, so different from how Dev normally acted, caught her off guard. She paused, and that had him grabbing her hand, caressing it with his fingers. A soothing, calming sensation washed over her. "You don't have to, but I need to slow things down. You're lighting me on fire."

She smiled and turned, his fingers trailing away, loosening as she went.

"Walk toward the window."

She responded with a slow roll of her hips as she took multiple steps forward. His eyes were on her; she could feel them boring into her body. The power she had over his desire emboldened her. She slid her palms down the sides of her dress, past her hips, flattening the poufy skirt.

"Stop."

She froze like an escapee in a spotlight, palms near her upper thighs, looking out those big windows on a crystal clear fall night with the stars twinkling. Her heart pounded in anticipation, like in those scenes in a movie before something big happened.

He moved then; she didn't have to turn to know it. The unmistakable sound of his slacks, the light swish they gave as he walked. She had exposed herself, given him a chance to catch her off guard. Why had she kept her back to him? *Because you're going to explode if he doesn't touch you, and you're still afraid.*

Afraid it was a joke, a farce made to destroy her completely. She'd already come close to losing everything. Now there existed one more person to rip away her faith in the idea that someone somewhere would want her as she was, falling apart house and all.

One arm slipped around her waist. Dev's suit jacket was still in place as his hand flattened against her stomach. "I got jealous of your hands for a minute," he whispered, hot breath against her ear. "I wanted to be the one sneaking under your skirt."

The words heightened her awareness as his hot, smooth palm slid underneath the dress and touched her bare thigh. Then glided upward to the silk of her thong. She couldn't move or think. It had been a while since a man touched her there, and all her snarky, witty comments failed her as two fingers breached past the thin barrier and touched the folds of her vagina.

"This is a surprise. A thong?"

She shuddered at the touch, and his other hand moved to the back of her neck, offering support. The way he touched her, reached out to her, stole her words away.

"Breathe, *Hermosa*. May I continue?"

"Yes." The word came out on a moan.

Each breath she produced paired with him furthering his exploration of her body. Her nipples tightened against the fabric of her strapless bra, and she wanted him there, wanted no clothes between them. Through a faded, transparent reflection of him in his patio glass door, she glimpsed his hand up her dress and her eyes wide, mouth in an "oh." Her desire increased, the scene ten times more erotic with a combination of touch and sight. One finger slipped inside her, then another. She tightened around him, and he groaned, "So tight and gorgeous. Your expressions... show me more."

He whispered more wicked nothings in her ear, dirty encouragement, and she bucked her hips to connect, searching for some momentum. He pulled his fingers out and found her clit, stimulating it with flicks and teasing.

"Right there."

He pinched the little nub, and she bit back the scream threatening to escape. The sensations were nearly too much, and then he spoke more naughty things. "Imagine me above you, entering you. Can you picture us together? Your legs wrapped around my waist, sweet heat joining us together. I see it."

Moaning, she leaned back against him, feeling his erection press between her ass cheeks. The heels were bringing her right in line with the part of him she wanted to be impaled on. She was so close, right near the edge, and her legs locked. Sensing her rigid movement, Dev quickened his pace, focusing all attention on her clit. Her breaths turned into pants, the shortened to gasps. He coaxed the sounds spilling from her. He mastered her without effort with each stroke, every caress. When he let go of her neck and reached down inside the bodice of her dress to pinch one of her nipples, she exploded.

"I'm—" the only word she got out as a short light burst behind her eyes and her legs turned to jelly. Dev held her as the last twinges and shudders from her orgasm worked their way through her body.

"I can't tell you how amazing you looked, *hermosa*."

"What does it mean?" She squirmed in his arms until she faced him. Those eyes of his appeared darker in the light, pupils big, as if they were taking in everything—thoughts, feelings, her very soul.

"*Hermosa?*"

She nodded, leaning up to kiss his lips with a soft touch. Her attempt at gentle, leisure kisses fell apart in rapid succession, and they battled with tongues once more. Except this time, her hands roamed, cupping his erection and giving it a gentle squeeze. He pulled away then.

"It means beautiful, but I call you that."

The words were not as formal or well put together, but she loved how he was a mess like her. His hair loose, shirt untucked, and eyes darting across her figure as if he couldn't decide what to do next. She knew what to do. She wanted to bring him to a quivering, unable-to-think state, similar to the one she'd fought through. He always gave to the shelter, his work, to her. For once she wanted to give.

"Then let me show you something beautiful," she said as she dropped to her knees.

***

Dev never wanted a woman naked so bad before. Sure, seeing her sink to her knees fully clothed proved hot, damn hot. But he wanted a chance to explore her body completely naked and at his discretion. For now, he'd let her take control to give him a chance to simply exist. She kept her eyes locked on his, and he watched her lips part, her tongue darting out. Then she loosened his belt and freed the button on his slacks from its mooring. He couldn't look away from watching how she licked her lips. The tentative, teasing way she took the zipper between two fingers and eased it down the teeth made him shudder. She changed her focus from his fuck-me eyes to his dick as she pushed the flaps of his pants aside. He sighed as cool air hit his thighs, replaced with warm heat from her fingertips as they crept across his skin. When she finally got her hands on him, he sighed in relief. That's when she looked at him, all blue-eyed wonder staring him down, and she held the whole package and squeezed gently. He moaned.

"I've been wondering about this for a while." Her words caught him off guard, and she focused on his erection now.

"Really? Then I can say without shame I wondered what this would be like."

The downright wicked and sexy grin on her face touched him somewhere he'd never expected to be touched again—in his heart. Her wanting him without a need to get something made him melt. Her devious, playful side turned him on.

She started with a gentle grip that quickly turned firm. "Then let's turn your wonder to reality."

He'd always been a huge fan of blowjobs, loved and appreciated receiving them, selfishly took them whenever offered, and kept his eagerness locked up so his previous bedroom partners never thought him too greedy. This tactic had earned him many blow jobs, and he'd become accustomed to the tentative ways women approached the act.

When Kat put her hot mouth around him and swallowed him to the hilt, cupping his balls in one hand and his shaft in the other, he almost spilled his load right there. His jaw dropped open, and he tried to get the words to come out to convince her to slow down. But no, she was engaged on a mission to make him lose his damn mind, confirmed by the way she fondled him, kissing the tip of his head, before starting all over again.

She set the pace, and he closed his eyes and gave in to the sensation, attempted to imprint the feel of her tongue and mouth around him. Even the occasional graze of her teeth felt more arousing than he'd ever thought possible. When her hand on his sack reached back to the little area between his scrotum and anus, he lost it.

The world went dark for a moment, and all he knew was that his release had found a home. She didn't pull away as his cum burst forth into her mouth. No, she drank it all, sucking and swallowing. He finally came down from his momentary high to watch her sit back on her heels and then stand up.

"Not my favorite thing to do, but I couldn't let you ruin the dress," she said with a wink.

"I'd have bought you a new one." He didn't bother closing his pants, nor did he care about anyone on the other side of the window. The only thing of importance stood right beside him.

She put a hand on his shoulder. "What else would you do for me?"

The question echoed in his ears like a single gunshot, an open invitation to extend this beyond oral in his living room to something far more. He should say no, stop the madness. Leave them both with some sort of boundary intact, but at the same time, if this was the only night they had together…

If nothing came of them beyond this chance to clear out all the lust and insanity, he wanted it to be a night worth remembering. It'd be unfair to them both if they didn't explore the possibilities.

"Let me show you." The words flew out of his mouth, and he turned, hoping she'd follow. He walked past the furniture back toward the front door. "Take your shoes off and leave them here."

Dev followed the same instruction he'd given her. Kat didn't hesitate either, grin still on her face with eyes in full-on seductress mode. Then they took the walk down his hallway. Normally, he'd give her the same tour all visitors received, with introductions to photos of his family and a special trip down memory lane from his childhood. Instead, he bypassed everything with his brisk walk.

Pru had been the last woman in here, over six months prior. He didn't want to analyze that. No, he wanted to create new memories to wipe away the bad. This would be a chance to forge a future without the past weighing over him like a thundercloud.

"It's beautiful." Kat stopped beside him, both of them facing the king size bed covered in a black, goose-feather comforter. Underneath were flannel sheets, perfect for the fall and a way to keep warm as the night cooled down further.

"It'd be even better with you on it. Naked."

She smiled big. "That's something I can do." Then she turned, exposing her back. "Would you mind undoing the zipper and my bra clasp?"

"I can certainly assist you, my fair lady."

"He doesn't sleep with her in the musical."

The zipper came down with ease, and she gave a shake to make the whole thing slide down to her feet. He worked on the bra next. "No, but I wanted to believe he wanted to. I would have succumbed to temptation." The metal teeth released from their holes. "There, all done."

Kat cupped her bra to her bosom, rotated, stepping out the dress, and faced him once more. "Is that what you're doing? Succumbing?"

She dropped the bra then, practically throwing it away from her body. Those flesh color breasts, with dark pink nipples made his mouth dry up.

"I'm surrendering." He reached out, pinching one nipple between his index finger and thumb.

"With far too many clothes on. I need you naked for mutual exploration."

He leaned in and pressed a kiss to the top of her breast. "Your wish is my command."

Stepping back, he shed the suit coat first. The belt, trousers, button-down shirt, undershirt, boxers, and his socks followed in rapid succession. When he finally stood naked, a pea-sized lump took up residence in the center of his chest. That small ball, the size of a vegetable, was the insecurity he recognized in himself. He willed his courage to look at Kat, to accept her judgment.

"You look amazing." Those three words snapped him to attention, eyes open, on her.

"Thank you."

"You say that like you doubted how good you look."

"It's always a possibility." Funny how they both stood there naked, exposed, and he'd become self-conscience. He'd gone years without experiencing similar emotions. "Dreams and imaginations can be misleading."

"Or, thankfully, tamer than reality. If I'd known you looked like this, all toned, ripped... hell, I would've given into this sooner."

The words dislodged the kernel of doubt and fear stuck at the forefront of his mind. He stepped toward her. "Thank goodness I came to my senses and decided we should stop now."

She reached for him, both palms gripping his upper arms, pulling him closer, their nipples touched. She gasped. "I know you're being sarcastic... at least I hope so because I'm afraid it's too late for that. I need you."

"Where?" He loved this, the drawn-out tease. This type of foreplay hadn't existed with his ex. He silently vowed to no longer compare the two. "Show me."

She traced the muscle of his left arm until she grabbed his hand. After she guided it to her warm, wet center, he flicked the nub of her clit and basked in the dilation of her pupils and the way her other hand, on his bicep, tightened like a vice.

"So sensitive."

"Fuck me," she begged. The syllables were drawn out, and he wanted to know every sexual sound she made. If it took all night, he'd discover each one and let her discover his. The exploration would be exhausting and marvelous.

"Lie down on the bed."

She followed the direction, like she did all others, flawlessly. She swayed her hips as she backed up. He knew how his flannel sheets felt against bare skin and had a momentary flare of jealousy as she pushed herself onto the bed, elbows and arms working in tandem with her feet in a spider crawl toward the headboard. He grabbed his slacks and dug through his pocket for the condom he kept in his wallet. He ripped into the packet, rushed and eager. She started stroking her nipples, teasing him.

"I like it when you rush." She said the last word nearly on a moan. Her hips bucked at her own efforts, and he wanted to make her twice as wild.

Climbing on top of her, condom in place, he pushed on her knees, and her legs fell open, exposing a wonder of the world—pink, glistening flesh. He wanted to taste her.

"Don't you fucking dare." Her expletive put him on alert.

His *mujer hermosa* was rough and direct in bed, and he liked it. "I don't get to taste you first?"

"We have all night, and I need that marvelous dick of yours driving me past the point of coherent thought."

He laughed a low, villainous thing. "Then by all means, don't ever say I didn't take direction as good as I gave."

"Less talk, more action. We're off the clock."

Without comment or providing warning he plowed inside her, loving how those tight channel walls gripped him, attempting to stop him from pulling back.

"More."

So he gave more, holding onto her hips and setting a brutal pace. Within minutes he'd worked up a sweat and so had she. They both grunted, panted, reveled in each other's sounds...at least he did. She whispered then, two words, but he wanted to be sure he'd heard correctly. "Louder, Kat. Tell me what's happening."

"I'm going to—Dev!" The warning of her orgasm was replaced with his name.

He loved how she surrendered to him, loved being the one who could make her come apart. The relentless efforts on his end continued, seeking the same precipice she'd crashed over. He leaned down and took her lips in a rough mash of tongues and teeth. The fruit of his efforts started in his member and radiated downward to his toes. He flexed his legs, locked them, and then he roared, letting the animal he'd become free. He didn't want to pull out but didn't want to crush her as she lay beneath him still and quiet. Moving, rolling over, he disposed of the condom. When he rolled back, she faced him.

"Ready to go again?" Her face lit with a grin, eyes and cheeks still basking in the afterglow.

"I'll need a bit to recover if it's okay?"

"Perfect." Then she snuggled in close to him, head on his chest.

He wrapped an arm around her shoulder trying not to feel humbled by her content and comfortable way of just being with him. Love. He'd never expected it, hadn't planned on it... but with her cuddled against him, he couldn't get the four-letter word out of his mind.

"Just a few minutes and then more fun." She said the words with a yawn, and as her breathing deepened, his eyes began to close.

CHAPTER SEVENTEEN

When Kat opened her eyes, she saw sunlight streaming into the room through a pair of black-patterned curtains, which caused momentary confusion because she had no east-facing windows in her room. Then realization dawned about the warm body behind her and the manly arm smattered with dark hair draped over her torso. A smile found its way to her lips at the memories of falling asleep after so much pleasure and letting her desires reign free. No other way to describe the experience. She'd wanted him in every way—a different stance than with previous partners. If he would've asked for just about anything, she may have agreed. *Scary.* The thought brought back the blowjob, his fingers and hands—his cock. She shivered.

"Good morning," Dev whispered. He gave her a gentle squeeze, then got up from the bed as she found her voice.

She rolled to face his fully naked body standing up, an erect dick saluting the chilly air. "Good morning," she managed.

He smiled and glanced down at himself before looking back at her. "Like what you see?"

"Immensely."

He brought that sex kitten part of her roaring to life, similar to how he'd inspired emotions last night that she didn't want to analyze. She found herself wanting more of the domestic scene this moment represented. The desire flared for a kind, warm, compassionate man to hold her tightly each night. There was a safety in such an action that she'd failed to find or experience elsewhere.

"How about a bathroom break, breakfast, and then whatever we want?"

"Sounds fantastic."

The perfect chance to get her head on straight and wipe away the fantastical ideas of more, which had been playing around in her head since the moment she'd reached her orgasm a second time. Scales were tipped during their nighttime adventures; she'd somehow left herself open and susceptible to the most idiotic of emotions and ideas of how they could be like this all the time, maybe something more than the casual fling. It should've been just a fling, one night to expel all this desired and attraction. She hadn't expected it to be as intense as it had turned out to be.

He walked off into the bathroom, and she glanced around the bedroom, taking in a better idea of Devid, the man. The master suite he'd furnished with all black furniture against white walls. The design stuck out in contrast, but was the opposite of the living room. He'd put in a lot of effort to make things look a certain way, something she never would have thought of.

When he came back, he tossed a T-shirt and a pair of shorts on the bed. He'd already donned his set. "Thought you'd like some clothes in case golfers are out this morning."

"That's ideal unless you want to put on a show?"

"I'd never expect you to be into that, but..."

"I'm joking." Kat laughed and slid out from under the covers. She pulled the T-shirt over her head and into place. "But you should've seen your face."

"You definitely got me a little scared. *Ay Dios mio*, you're beautiful."

"*Hermosa*, right?"

Dev grinned. "*Si*. I'm tempted to postpone breakfast."

She slipped into the shorts, shaking her head as she pulled them up. "No, you've got my stomach thinking about food now. You deliver that, and I'm all yours."

"Then," Dev approached and wrapped his arms around her waist and pressed a soft kiss to her lips. "Let me meet your requirements."

The next kiss they shared deepened, involving tongue and the promise of so much more—at least another memorable experience. Then the doorbell rang. Dev's forehead rested against hers. "Probably the FedEx guy. I'll start coffee and food if you grab that for me?"

A request which lent to the continued domestic vibes she'd been experiencing since the moment she woke. "No problem, is it something fun?"

"A little gift for the shelter."

"Ooh, now I'm dying to know what it is." She'd been impressed with his work and his dedication to the women. To be reminded of his kind heart and everything he did for others put her in a danger zone; she wanted to keep this going. One night, one more day really, wouldn't be enough. "I'll meet you in the kitchen."

She kissed his nose and vaulted out of the room, skipping to the door. The day was off to a fantastic start. For a moment she could forget the house, her cousin, the deal for money. She opened the front door, eyes searching for a box on the ground beyond the door. Instead, she found three-inch purple pumps. The same bright, eggplant color as—Kat let her gaze travel up the legs, past the matching skirt and jacket set in khaki tan with a purple blouse, to hair drawn up in some fancy ponytail with stiff curls spiraling outward near the crown of Pru's head.

"Good morning. I thought I'd find you here but never believed he'd have the balls to send you to answer the door. Dev!" The way she shouted his name sounded like a screeching cat. For some reason, Kat stepped to the side, horrified and in shock at how the good feelings from moments past had shriveled into a giant black well of nothing. The analogy didn't make sense; this didn't make—

"Kat?" Dev rounded the corner, and she saw him stop short and glance at Pru, who amazingly remained silent. "Please shut the door."

He gave the direction, and she saw the immediate change, every part of the happy and romantic him fled in favor of cold and detached. She'd missed it before, getting the pleasure of slowly opening him up and watching his interactions with people he actually liked.

As soon as the lock clicked into place, he asked, "What are you doing here?"

Kat rotated back around to face the showdown, the music. *Fuck all.* She'd really believed they would get away with it, enjoy a little bit of happiness.

"Catching you—with her. Can't say I'm surprised, but slumming is not you. It's also a bit embarrassing, and I'm tired of looking like a fool."

Silence and anger started to course through Kat's veins. If Dev—

"I don't see how any of this is your business."

"She's your client, at least that's what Mark told me. An official one on Bona Fide's books, and you're sleeping with her."

"She's no longer a client; her makeover is finished, all done, as of last night. No harm, no foul."

Pru shook her head. "I don't think so."

Fear rattled the angry animal inside Kat. He couldn't lose his job; too many people needed him. "It's my fault. I threw myself at him."

A look of pity got tossed her way. "Honey, I used to date this man. I know he doesn't do anything, physical or otherwise, without wanting to. You're not the first, I was. You won't be the last, and this latest snafu is the final straw." She focused back on Dev. "I've given you plenty of time to sow your oats and get this crazy predilection for damsels in distress out of your system. Instead, you dragged Bona Fide back into it. The board will hear from me."

Dev's cold facade faltered then. His business, his livelihood was being threatened.

Kat'd had enough. He didn't deserve to be harassed in his home, nor did he have to put up with it, but telling someone to fuck off wasn't always easy. "Do whatever the hell you want, but we won't take your bullying and threats anymore. Please leave."

She opened the front door back up and extended an arm towards the chilly October morning.

"This isn't your home; I don't think you can or have authority—"

"Leave, Pru." Dev didn't look completely himself, but Kat had helped him. At least she believed she had. He didn't need this woman or her accusations here.

Pru stomped her way to the door, footsteps echoing on the tile near the entrance. "Fine, you're a pair of liars who can fail together without a job or a house."

Kat froze. Her momentary joy and righteous indignation were over.

Her enemy sensed it, saw Kat's horrible attempt at a poker face. "I know all about the money; you may as well admit it out loud."

"What money? You've truly lost it," Dev said from behind them, his confusion clear.

"Have I? Your lover doesn't deny it."

Kat didn't want to say anything. Crawling into a hole and dying was a preferable punishment. So she'd settle for silence and pray Dev backed her up.

***

Dev was still reeling over Pru showing up with her mouthful of venom for him and Kat. Her threats held truth. It'd be difficult to get out of this. Then he'd seen Kat stand up to Pru and force her hand, easily do what he'd always been so afraid to do when they were here at his place. Kat played the role of a hero until the mention of money. One phrase and she retreated; it scared him. Pru's accusations scared him. He wouldn't get to the bottom of this mystery without cleaning up the first problem.

Incidentally, the problem started talking. "You should ask her to tell the truth. You've been used, just like I got used by you."

"That's enough. Don't you remember the effect of verbal abuse? We were together because we wanted to be. Now please leave."

"This isn't over."

"With you in my life, it never is."

His ex stormed out the entrance, heels echoing in the vestibule behind her. He shut the door and then gingerly took Kat's hands. Her face angled downward. He didn't know what she thought, but there was no excuse for what she'd gone through in the last ten minutes. "I'm sorry. This is not how I planned our morning."

When her head snapped up, guilt and tears brimming in her wide eyes, he knew something Pru had said held truth.

"Maybe we should sit, and you can tell me what the hell is going on."

"Okay," she replied with a nod.

So he held onto her and walked into the living room, took a seat on the couch, and brought her with him. She tugged at their connection, and he let her go, then watched as she readjusted her ponytail. The braids from yesterday were still in place with minimal damage. Chad was truly a miracle worker.

"So, tell me what the hell this money thing is about?"

"I'm afraid to say. Let's talk about it later; I'm starving." She glanced around wildly searching for anything else, grasping at a new topic with her eyes as much as the words.

"Kat? Come back here, to me. I may not like it, but I'd rather learn about whatever this is from you than from someone else."

She sighed, pulled her feet up onto the couch and tucked them under her. "This happened before I knew you, really knew you. Even when we first met, I didn't like you. I'd heard rumors, made some rash judgments."

Dev raised an eyebrow at that, but it wasn't surprising she'd disliked him. He hadn't been too keen on her either. "Comes with my profession, but you're not telling me anything new."

"I needed money for the house; you know how much it means to me. Anywho, no banks would give me a loan, no payday thing would cut it. A friend with money didn't exist, and my parents could care less. So that left…"

She had since started looking at the ceiling, talking to the air instead of him. Shitty how his gut told him this tied back to his partner too.

"Mark," they both spoke at the same time.

Her head went level, eyes landing on him. "Right. A deal with my asshole cousin. He refused to give me anything out of kindness or to save his grandmother's home. He hates his dad."

"I'm familiar with his attitude toward that side of the family." He'd been along for both rides with a front seat tour as Mark's dad was arrested and convicted.

"Then you may understand that it's tough to be around someone who thinks you'll turn into a criminal any second. Moving on, I agreed to the deal, and he gave me some of the money up front and promised me the rest after."

Dread and a little anger at his partner came with Kat's unspoken words. A deal and money were one thing, but, "What was the deal, Kat?"

He didn't want to know, but deep down the truth needed to be spoken.

"I get you to agree to give me a makeover and complete it."

His heart dropped to his gut; he'd been ready to hear this. But like any bad news, it still burned him everywhere. Jumping off the couch, he paced the living room, flexing his hands over and over. The efforts didn't get rid of his urge to hit something. To pile drive through the wall and expel some of his frustrations. His best friend and business partner didn't trust him to find his way back on his own. Naturally, the next question was, "So the whole thing was fake? Did you dress down, pretend to have no wardrobe and social challenges in the workplace to gain my help?"

"No! That's the crazy part. I gave you a tough time, but everything I told you about me was true. The clothes, lessons, conversation, and body language tips you gave helped me last night and at work. I've never gotten so many compliments in my life."

"This hurts, Kat. I've had someone hide their personality from me before, lie to me to get what they want. The fact you hid something, lied to me..." He shouldn't have blown up, but it hurt. To know she didn't trust him with the truth, had made a deal, and while they'd grown closer she'd continued to hide part of herself from him.

Kat stood there and squeaked out, "I'm sorry" before the tears started to fall.

Dev resumed his pacing, grabbed a box of tissue on one pass near the kitchen, and dropped it on the couch by Kat as he made his way back.

She sniffled, and blew her nose. "Thank you."

Over a couple more laps, he watched her mouth open and close, like a fish on land. He hated this whole situation, yet it appeared he wasn't the only victim. He had to give her the benefit of the doubt, right? "Why, once you finally got to know me, didn't you say anything till now—since you got caught?"

"I couldn't. Another part of the deal. If I mentioned the money or contract to anyone, especially you, the deal was off."

Inside he said Hail Mary's, thankful his instincts had been spot on from the start. She'd been holding back, but not for the reasons she'd given him. Maybe she wouldn't have hidden anything intentionally. Before he could formulate his next question, she kept going.

"Dev, I wanted to tell you. But losing my house over the respect of some guy I've only known for a couple of months? Even after last night—which was the best, I'd like to add—I couldn't give up my home, one of the few things I own, for great sex, a charming, caring personality, and a business owner who probably isn't looking for anything long term. Once Mark finds out, I'll lose the house, too." Tears sprang anew, and she grabbed a fresh tissue. "I'm fucked."

He hated seeing her like this, sad and hurt. The situation looked so different now that he had the whole story and knew that she didn't deserve the anger he felt. No, he'd save his temper for the right people. Plopping down on the couch beside her, he grabbed the tissue from her hand and dabbed at the droplets of moisture on her face. "*Hermosa*, no more tears.

This face deserves smiles and joy. I can't stand it, seeing you like this. Damn Mark for putting you in this position. Pretty shitty of him not to help out with this, which, in my family, is important. I'd never leave a cousin in this position. I won't leave you in this without help. We're in this together." He had to fix it, looking at her now. They'd gone through enough bullshit, and if he could control one thing, it had to be this. "I'll make everything right and see this through."

"How? You have enough problems to deal with."

"I work with your bastard cousin; I can talk to him, convince him to do the right thing. Besides, you didn't tell me; Pru did. I have a suspicion she learned about it from him as well. You shouldn't have to face this alone, not when you have a friend who can help you." His best friend seemed to be more like a thorn in his paw. Dev wanted to clear the path. He stroked both of her cheeks, all red and tear-stained. She still looked every inch the warrior. Fierce and vulnerable. "What other ridiculous rules did Mark give you in the contract?"

"Only one, I couldn't sleep with you."

He smiled. "Well, I plan on breaking that one again."

Pressing a gentle kiss to her lips, she responded, immediately opening for him. He pulled back before they went too far and he got lost in her scent and taste. "Are you sure you want to break the rules again?"

"Might as well."

CHAPTER EIGHTEEN

They wound up back in the bedroom, the shirt and shorts they both wore quickly discarded, in favor of being naked. The kisses they shared dissolved into a mutual exploration of necks, collarbones, chests. She couldn't get enough of his lips on her skin and vice versa. She threw her head back and let him ravish her neck, nibble a trail to her ear lobe.

"Tell me what you want."

"To feel this way... all over."

She loved when he set to his task, kissing, nipping, biting her everywhere. Her sides, breasts, stomach, thighs—and then he stopped. "I didn't get to do this last night."

There were bad experiences, memories of her last boyfriend that lay just beneath the surface. Of his unhappiness with her hair or the fact his oral efforts never yielded an orgasm. Everything had been so wonderful with Dev, but she couldn't let him do something he didn't enjoy... When she opened her mouth to speak, he put a finger to her lips.

"No. I beg you. Don't deny me this."

The chocolate puppy eyes, the downturned lips, and the sound of those words. Another chunk of ice fell away, and the final barrier she'd kept firmly in place dissolved. Scary to think she might give him whatever, whenever. For the moment, she'd live in the here and now.

She nodded her agreement and fell back against the pillows. The first touch of his tongue to her clit made her shiver. He repeated the action before trying out other efforts, from her labia to her center, mimicking the movements of his cock. How she wanted that part of him. Then he pulled back.

"One moment." He said this before opening the bedside drawer. She expected a condom. Sure she was incredibly turned on, but there was no rising pressure, no urge to thrash or throw herself around. Instead of a condom, he came back with a vibrator. A black, sleek-looking thing the size of a pickle. "Now I'll get to taste you."

"You're serious?"

"I want to taste your orgasm on my tongue. I can tell it won't be easy to get you there, but I love a challenge." The look he leveled at her—serious, sexy, and fucking hot—made her want him to succeed.

"Anything I can do to help?"

"Forget the bad experiences and let me give you a new one."

She pushed the doubts away once more as he resumed his position, tracing her entrance with his tongue. The vibrator took his place, a cold object nestled against her vagina. He re-focused on her clit. Then he turned the damn thing on a slow setting. It shot tingles up her spine, and her muscles immediately contracted as her body generated fresh, natural lube. His attention to detail and pleasure was something foreign to her; no man had ever dedicated this much focus to getting her off.

He chuckled against her sex before nipping her clit with his teeth. She jumped this time, and as she came back, toward the mattress he pushed the vibrator in. A rhythm soon formed, maddening and delicious. He'd bite, tease, and then pump her with the vibrator. Then he'd move slowly. The constant ebb and flow between fast and turtle's pace got her going. She was lost in the sensations, the need to have his mouth and the speed. Soon her body became so sensitive, honed like a well-strung instrument. He played her like a master. The end came sooner than she expected, starting at her center and radiating out to every part of her body.

"Dev."

The vibrator disappeared, replaced with his hot tongue lapping at her like a cat at a bowl of cream. He cleaned her of her orgasm, devoured any trace of her release. When complete, he kissed her. She tasted herself, her pleasure on him, and if anything, she wanted more. He'd enjoyed himself, and she reveled in the power such a thing gave her.

The intensity of her climax became overshadowed by the way he kissed her. Dev stripped away her worries of intimacy, of attempting to please her partner. No, he believed in pleasing her, and that jarred something loose in her mind. Only her Gran had ever cared more about taking care of Kat versus taking care of herself. Dev did the same, and she wasn't going to survive this. No, he'd be imprinted on her heart.

Getting lost in his kiss and the way one hand tweaked her nipple, she failed to notice him sheath his cock. Then he buried it in her, setting a brutal pace. She loved the rough way he drove into her, replacing his earlier ministrations with something wild and rabid. Then he slowed once again.

"Why?" The question came without thought, sounding more like a plea because she wanted it rough and tumble to the finish line.

"I don't want to rush this." He groaned, lifting one of her legs, to go at an even deeper angle.

Each slow thrust drove her to a new level of torture, and her eyes drifted shut in an attempt to drown the intensity.

"Look at me." His words were insistent, and when she didn't respond right away, he stopped moving. "Kat, open your eyes."

The soft sound of his voice did her in. She looked up at him and was unprepared for the adoration and emotion she saw there. He openly admired her, whispering words in Spanish as he made love to her body like some sort of love song. The slow procession leading them to release caused her body to arch off the bed.

"Please Dev, hurry… I need to come."

He increased the pace and refused to let her stop looking at him, to break their connection. If eyes were the windows to the soul, then she sold hers during the final stretch toward the finish line.

They arrived in the victory circle together. This time, it was both of them losing control, letting a part of them explode free.

He shouted. "Kat! ¡Ay Dios!" As his breathing came back to normal he let go of her leg and rolled onto his back.

She missed the weight of him on her. Scary, as she'd not been a fan of closeness in the past. He interlinked their hands, a sweet reminder of how he wasn't like the others before him. Her Gran had always said a man who worships a woman is a keeper. Why had that thought popped into her head now?

"You're a miracle, you know that? I can't get enough of the sounds you make."

His words caught her off guard, and as she turned her head to respond, her stomach grumbled. She groaned, trying to mask the worst of it.

Dev laughed. "Even the ones from your hungry stomach."

"Really?"

Dev rolled to face her, caressing one cheek with his free hand. "All of you deserves admiring. Now, give me ten minutes, and then we'll have brunch."

Once he left the bed, the feel-good endorphins started to fade, and she dreaded the coming week, the confrontation Dev would have with Mark and Pru's next move. Those fears proved she'd saddled herself with an even bigger problem—a possible broken heart.

***

Dev walked into Bona Fide on Monday determined to keep his dread under wraps. He tried to hold on to his anger on Kat's behalf toward her bastard cousin who'd convinced her to enter a fucked up business deal for the money. Sure, some of his anger he'd save for Pru. That evil woman needed to leave him and his personal life alone… leave Kat alone.

The weekend they spent together proved the connection between them wasn't a fluke. They'd spackled and repaired the holes in her hallway walls, gone for a jog. Every hour a new adventure. He'd almost asked her to come to his family's Sunday dinner next weekend, but refrained in order to keep things light. Besides, if he brought her to dinner, they'd think it was serious. A part of him wanted things to be serious, the same part of him that had gotten lost in her body and sucked in by her open gaze as they'd made love in his apartment. There had been a few times after that, including a passionate, rushed encounter against her front door. Pru had been to dinner; his family hadn't liked her. Mark had been to a million dinners, and his family loved the bastard.

Think of the devil and he will appear. Mark walked out of the breakroom, coffee cup in hand, and headed toward his office.

"Hey partner, wait up."

His friend stopped mid-stride. The look he cast back at Dev was not happy or angry— unreadable, like the emotionless man he'd become over the years since his father's incarceration. When Dev caught up to him, his words were equally noncommittal. "What's up?"

"How was your weekend?"

"Great, except for the phone call that woke me up Saturday and sent the very attractive blonde I'd brought home the night before scrambling from my bed."

"Pru's yelling will do that."

"Funny how you know who it was. Bet you can tell me exactly what she said too." Mark was never one to beat around the bush; he also hadn't gotten the moniker "asshole" without reason, either.

"Your office," Dev point to the door ahead of them.

Mark encouraged him to pass. Once in a place of privacy, a monument to the connections his partner had made thanks to Dev's genius idea and Mark's anal retentive financing talents, Dev spoke. "Pru's claims are crap. She's just jealous."

"Afraid that's the problem. The claims aren't in her mind. She asked me at the Beautification Board dinner who Kat was to you, and I told her a client and my cousin, so you can see the problem we're in. You slept with a client."

"You and I both know that's bullshit because we said this would be a pro bono deal."

"Not according to Bona Fide's records; we've got the paperwork." His friend's pompous attitude—as if Dev was the bad boy, the undependable one when Mark had convinced his cousin to sign some bogus contract— grated on Dev's nerves.

"If you're talking about that shitty deal with the money, that's between you and Kat, not Bona Fide."

"No, I am talking the profile paperwork, expenses filed, all that shit. She's got a file here and everything."

"Fine, but who told Pru about Kat's deal with you, and why the hell didn't you just give her the money? Kat has met all my requirements for the makeover; she completed your agreement."

Mark shook his head and set his coffee cup on the edge of his desk. "But sleeping with you was a deal breaker. While I'm pissed Pru found out about your little sheet romp, thanks for saving me a bunch of money. If you get some new clients quickly she may forget. At least the other investors will be more forgiving, and you've proven you're ready to help female clients again. It's all a win-win."

Dev curled his hands into fists and kept them at his sides to prevent them from flying at Mark's face. His partner moved behind his desk and sat down. Then Dev took a seat, but the action didn't quell his thirst to physically harm the man.

"Let's not change the subject. We slept together after she completed the makeover. A loophole. As for Pru, she can whine all she wants. You're the one who told her about Kat being a client and set her on a jealous tirade. You even told Pru about the money. With Bona Fide, it doesn't really matter until the board is aligned. Unless you're going to fuck me over like you did your own family."

"You keep implying I care, but she's related to my rat-bastard father. I could give two fucks what happens, though my mom might complain."

For the first time ever, Mark disgusted him. Sure, he possessed the ability to be cruel, crude, and even crass, but the caring person Dev had known had disappeared somewhere along the way.

"What happened to family first?"

"When your father steals for years and gets busted with your teenage brother robbing a classmate's house and tries to sell his son up the river for a reduced sentence, then talk to me. She's related to him; the fact she hasn't tried to steal before is a surprise."

"You can't relate people to other's actions."

"Really? Then Pru's nasty ways are not influenced at all by her dead husband's abusive tendencies and her tyrant of a mother? Kat's mother had a few shoplifting issues years ago. Says something."

"Says you're an asshole."

Mark took a sip of his coffee and smiled. "I've never refuted that fact, and the contract we have trumps everything. It states Kat must abstain from any physical relationship with employees of Bona Fide for six months following the completion of the makeover and the stipulations of the contract."

"*Culo.*"

"Changing languages doesn't affect the result."

Dev stood and slammed a fist on Mark's desk. Words weren't cutting it. "You can't possibly keep on this course of action; she needs a break. She's been fighting against a force nearly impossible to beat. We've been in the business of helping the downtrodden for years, no matter what. It'd be great if you offered this up out of the goodness of your cold, misshapen heart."

His partner smiled, a sarcastic thing. "Well put, and is this thanks to the magic pussy you got to sink into or because she's in distress? With you, I never can—"

Dev didn't let him finish. No, he clocked him with the same fist he'd used on the desk. He vaguely heard a door open behind them, followed by a clearing throat. Mark's chair leaned back on impact and now rocked forward with a small squeak.

"Sorry to interrupt your boxing session, but I just received the strangest phone call," Victoria said from the door.

"Who?" Dev didn't take his eyes off Mark. Nope, he let the full force of his anger burn through his facial expression.

"Some guy named Daniel from a local paper. He wanted to know if I cared to elaborate on the allegations that my place of employment was a high-end escort service. There were a few other horrible things mentioned, but I hung up without a comment. Should I be worried?" The fact the tone of her voice hadn't changed from calm and collected to freaked-out demonstrated not only her faith in him but her unflappable composure.

"Let me follow up on it. No sense in worrying when it's probably another bogus reporter looking for some sensational story, all right?" Dev wouldn't mention the real possibility of Pru pulling a stunt to oust him. No, at this point it'd be better to keep everyone calm and hope for the best.

"I'll let you handle it then, and I'll leave you two to your exercise." The door shut behind her, the audible click of the door latch his cue.

"I'll see you next Friday for the board meeting. Otherwise, shut the fuck up, and I'd burn that contract. Consider this your final warning. I listen to you disrespect everyone, be negative, and generally act like an asshole on a daily basis. Disrespecting Kat and talking about her in a crude manner is the line for me. From here on out, it's work and only work between us. If you weren't my partner, I'd fire you."

Mark held onto his jaw, massaging it gently as he scowled. "That fucking hurt."

"Insult your cousin or me again, and there's more where that came from."

"All right, but even if I wanted to, I couldn't help her. I don't have the money. My savings are invested; you know this."

Dev wanted to slug him again but settled for slamming the door behind him as he left. The asshole never intended to pay her from the start. How to make this up to Kat? How to fix it? At the moment, he didn't know.

CHAPTER NINETEEN

It had been five days since Kat had seen Dev. They'd parted Sunday, and she'd done her best to stay normal, focusing on work and all the other shit she needed to do. The whole week passed with only a few text messages, basic conversation really, with no heartfelt declarations, dirty messages, or confirmations of when she'd see him again.

Today, she worked from home, waiting for the contractor to show up to finish the work in the kitchen with the insulation and sheet rock. She clicked and clacked away at her computer, putting the final touches on a logistics sheet for some upcoming laundry soap event. Then she sighed, removing her hands from the keyboard and placing them against her head. No use.

Dev wandered back into her mind regardless of what she did; every stray thought brought a memory to the surface. There were his kind and caring ways, like opening doors and getting her a drink refill from her kitchen before the glass was empty. How he didn't blame her for the contract with Mark. According to him, she'd been put in a hard place. The option she'd chosen was the lesser of two evils.

Then they'd bonded over action movies and Chinese takeout. The whole weekend had given her a taste of perfection, of life with someone worth spending it with. She'd become a damn sap.

In fact, outside of the scheduled contractor, she'd heard nothing. No words from the city or Purple People Eater meant she had an opportunity to go on the offensive. The likelihood of Mark giving up the money to her became less practical the more she thought about it and with each passing hour. She picked up the phone and dialed Colton's office. Time for her to stop waiting around for her knight in shining armor to show up at the door.

"Hello, Mr. Kinyon's office. How may I help you?"

"Can I speak with Colton please, my name is Kat. You can tell him we met at the Beautification Board dinner a few nights ago."

The secretary cleared her throat, "I apologize, but Mr. Kinyon is unavailable right now. Would you like to leave a message?"

The runaround, something she'd become familiar with. "No, let me just set up a meeting for next week. Monday, afternoon?"

"I'm afraid his schedule is full; the best I can do for you is take a message." The firm, disapproving sound in her voice gave Kat the impression this lady thought her call involved a sales pitch. Thanks, but no thanks. The last thing she'd be interested in is selling.

"A message will work. Tell him I'd like to discuss my house some more and getting it removed from the project. Let him know I am not giving up, and here's my number."

She recited off the ten digits and enjoyed the way the secretary's dismissive tone became a tiny bit more subdued. "I'll make sure he gets the message. Have a nice day."

The connection ended, and she tried to refocus on the work while fighting the urge to text Dev and ask how things had gone with Mark. Did Dev get her cousin to give him the money? A million questions had come and gone in the last few days, the worst being guilt-ridden ones wondering if Dev had experienced discomfort in confronting her cousin.

She should've done the hard work instead of sending him to do it. The funny thing was, Dev had wanted to do it. He'd practically promised he'd get the money from Mark—not officially a promise, but pretty damn close. He'd heavily implied she'd have what she needed, made silent commitments and verbal ones. Non-verbal commitments were also implied, but on another level.

They hadn't been able to keep their hands off each other. Like magnetic attraction, touching grew into sex multiple times over. She'd woken on Monday a properly satisfied woman. Her natural glow drew attention from her friends, Ana being the first to call it out, and Betty giving a sly grin with a wink. Betty had cornered her yesterday threatening bodily harm if she didn't get the details soon.

A knock sounded at the front door, and she went scrambling to get it. Could be the contractor or Dev. She tamped down the bit hoping for Dev as ridiculous bullshit. She needed to stop fantasizing for more than what she'd already gotten. Of course, her hired help stood on the stoop, smiling with his sandy-blond hair, white T-shirt, and jeans. He looked adorable in that cute, want-to-pat-your-head way. She'd taken to internally addressing him as Sandy because she could, and his name escaped her every time she'd tried to recall it.

He bracketed both hands on his tool belt, slung around his waist. "Good afternoon, ma'am."

"Afternoon." So polite, she liked that.

"I came over to finish the kitchen today, if you still want me to."

She nodded, damn tired of her kitchen looking like a Tasmanian devil had whirled through.

"Wonderful. Before I get started, my boss wanted me to make sure I get the next payment from you."

"We originally agreed on me having it by Friday." Dread bubbled up inside her; she didn't have the two thousand yet. Nope, she'd spent everything Mark had given her from before. The last of it had paid for all the materials for the kitchen and the paint and spackle to fix all the holes left by the electrician across the other rooms. *Shit.*

"I understand." Sandy ran a hand through those loose locks of his. "But if I don't receive the payment from you today, I can't finish the work. At least, that's what I was told."

"What happened to a job well done first? I mean seriously, you want me to pay for services I haven't received. You could drop dead in there, and then, who will do it?" She tried to sound outraged, offended, and summoned all her anger at the situation, even though she had no room to talk.

Sandy frowned. "I apologize, but my boss is already giving you this work at a discount, and how do we know you won't skip out on payment? It works both ways. Now, will you cut the check, or should we postpone?"

Sandy had claws, motherfucker. "I'll have to postpone. Can you come back on Monday?"

"I'm not sure. I'll let my boss know, and he'll get back with you." He had a mulish look and turned around, stomping off to his truck. Southern gentlemen were polite until pissed off.

Kat thought about offering farewell salutations, but instead she shut the door and slumped against it. The deadline on the house inspection was only a couple weeks away. She'd never get this work done without the money. Maybe Dev knew some contractors who'd work for beer and pizza. Paying for food and alcohol was the best she could do under the circumstances.

She should've offered the same to Sandy. She stayed there, sliding to the floor, her brain searching for a solution, anything not involving dancing naked on a stage or begging folks for help. For a brief second, she contemplated one of those sad, sob-story posts on a fundraiser website. The problem was saving a house didn't compare to those with medical bills or in need of paying for a funeral for a loved one. There were a million better causes than helping poor her find a way to finish code updates on an ancient home.

The phone in her hand rang and vibrated. She picked up without a second thought or checking the caller ID, ready for something, anything to distract her. "Hello, Kathleen speaking."

"Hello, this is Daniel from the Arkansas Morning News, is this Kathleen

Baum?"

"Maybe, depends on what you want." She didn't read the news, nor did she want to be a part of it, but silently she hoped for bad press on the Beautification Project.

"I'm doing a piece on Bona Fide Image Consulting, an investigative piece into the allegations about the head consultant sleeping with his clients. Your name has been brought to my attention. Would you be interested in answering some questions about your relationship with Devid Esposito?"

Kat ended the call with a press of a button and no verbal response. Not the distraction she'd been looking for. At all. She wondered if Dev knew; if he had any clue about the article coming his way or any idea of who had gotten such a thing started. The urge to warn him, to save him, came without effort. She thought about calling the reporter back, giving a positive interview, but the risk of the fool spinning her words was too much of a possibility. The phone rang again, and this time, she decided to tell the asshole off, to give him what for.

"Now, listen here, Daniel from the Arkansas Morning News, I don't know where you get your story ideas from, but you might want to double-check your sources. I hear the going verdict on libel cases usually awards the victim and not the publisher."

"Really?" An unexpected voice filtered through the phone. "I'll have to remember that next time Daniel decides to publish something unflattering. This is Kat, right?"

Fuck. She'd told off the wrong man. "This is."

"Colton Kinyon. My secretary gave me your message, and I had a spare minute. When you launched into your rant, a piece of beauty, by the way, I figured I was talking to the right person. You're fantastic when you get fired up about something, you know that?"

"Thank you, I guess." She shook off the compliment. Seemed he flirted on the phone as much as he did in person. "What can I help you with?"

"Actually, I believe you wanted my help to discuss your home and its place with the Beautification Board, correct?"

Holy shit, the bad luck was finally spinning in the opposite direction. Maybe good-thought karma existed. "Yes, that's right."

"Good. Would you like to meet for dinner and discuss?" His voice, a few months ago, would have been temptation all on its own. Now she only granted access to her personal time and body to one man.

"If that's the only choice I have, fine, but I'd prefer to keep this professional, Mr. Kinyon. My house is at risk, but I won't sell myself to save it."

"You don't ever mince words, do you?"

"I think you became familiar with my brand of speech when we met the other night."

He laughed, the deep bass echoing through the receiver. "It's not the only option, but a man has got to try to get a beautiful woman to go to dinner with him now and then. I want to put you in front of the entire board, with the exception of Pru. She appears to be a little prejudiced toward you, and I'd like everyone to hear your side of things before we get her involved with a decision. Does that sound fair?"

The heavens were opening up, rainbows pouring down, and birds singing merry tunes. "It sounds more than fair."

"Great, I'll need you to come to my office in a week. We'll have the meeting at one o'clock in the afternoon. You'll get exactly thirty minutes to speak to them and plead your case. If they like what you have to say, we'll work on getting the code enforcement department to back off."

"I can't thank you enough, Mr. Kinyon."

"You could call me Colton and let me take you to dinner."

Her turn to chuckle. "I'm flattered, but still have to decline."

She wanted to tap dance, to jump up from her position on the floor, put on her heels, and tap out a celebration. "Is there anything I need to bring?"

"Yourself and whatever information you want to present that you think will persuade them. Show us why your house should be excluded, why it's not as important as all the other homes we're renovating. Because I'll be honest, I still want to fix your house."

"But not under my terms?" The past forty-eight hours she'd been leaning toward attempting to renegotiate the original agreement because Colton was right. The house needed to be updated or at least get some work completed to ensure it survived another hundred years. The Beautification Board seemed the easiest way to ensure success in that corner, especially if Mark didn't pony up the money.

"I don't know. What are your terms?" Colton asked.

The statement gave her hope, and she silently prayed no hope-sucking monster would try to steal this one piece of glimmering light, one chance at securing her gran's wish. "You will hear all of them at the meeting next week."

"I look forward to it. And, Kat?"

"Yes."

"Feel free to call me anytime, if you change your mind about dinner. My secretary will email you an invite for the meeting." The man switched hats with ease, blending business and pleasure, and it bothered her that he'd gained access to all her information. She'd only left a message with her home number.

"How do you have my email?"

"My secretary works magic," he said with a laugh. "Goodbye, until next week."

"Goodbye." She hung up the phone, not certain if she should be weirded out by his confession of a magic secretary or grateful for not having to be responsible for getting any information to him. Standing up, she pumped both fists in the air, celebrating the momentary triumph. She'd done it, somehow, without having to put forth any real effort, and Mr. Kinyon had come through for her. A foreign concept, people doing the right thing. If this kept up, she'd start looking for flying pigs.

She had a week to get a presentation together and convince a room full of old men to let her keep her home. If ever she needed Dev it would've been now, but this battle she needed to win for herself.

***

The article came out on Saturday morning. A shock-and-awe piece that was less-than-flattering. Dev found himself thankful for the small favors, including the fact that Kat's name had remained out of the article. Regardless, he couldn't put off seeing her anymore, not that he'd refrained from coming over on purpose. In fact, he'd spent the week trying to solve both of their problems. He knocked on her front door, waited for the telltale signs of acknowledgment, the sound of footsteps on her wood floor or the snick of the dead bolt being unlocked.

Kat's facial expression, the sad eyes and half-smile, half-grimace turn of her lips, told him she'd read the article. "Dev, I'm sorry."

Her arms spread wide, and he entered them, seeking the comfort he'd become addicted to. Her scent enveloped him, and he savored the long seconds that he got to hold her in his arms. The urge to be a provider of good news was defeated by the defaming publishing piece and the fact he'd have to disappoint this woman who deserved so much more. He'd take this momentary peace, this chance to bask in what might be in their future, after he'd fixed all these ridiculous problems.

To prepare for this visit, he'd donned his dark suit of armor and polished shoes and left his hair down. When she finally pulled back, interlocking her arms with his, he couldn't stop his body from becoming aroused at her visual perusal. She smiled then, a wide grin full of happiness that he couldn't reflect back to her. There would be no saving the day, no sexual romps, and no more getting lost in what they could be. Instead, he let his face possess the seriousness of a pallbearer and separated himself completely from her embrace.

"What's going on?"

The worst thing ever. "Can I come in?"

She threw the door wide and stepped back. As he passed, she reached out and touched his arm. That's all it took, and he gave in to renewing their embrace. He shut the door, and then he pressed his lips to hers. The kiss was incendiary, like a spark to a pile of paper, burning hot and fast. While, it was great to find comfort in one another, to let his frustrations melt away beneath her touch, they needed to talk. Communication was preferable to locking up all the bad things they were going through and throwing the key away. She broke the connection first, and his stomach knotted up at the light in her eyes. A light he'd put there, one he'd have to extinguish.

"Before things get out of control, tell me what's wrong?"

He sighed. "Mark doesn't have any money, and I can't see you anymore."

The week had been hellacious, super busy, and he'd been fielding emails from board members at random intervals over the last couple days. They wanted to know more and expected Dev to explain himself at the investor meeting next Friday.

None of the crap, the run-in's with Pru, the awkward conversations with Mark, or the accusatory attitudes of the board compared to the article this morning and having to come here to deliver all the bad news. He wanted to keep them going, to stick together through this.

The internal debate between staying with her and sparing her from being drawn into his mess lasted until he'd pulled into her driveway. In the end, protecting her from being exposed by the local media won out. Selfishness wasn't in his capabilities deck—especially when she'd suffered lies from so many people, even been tricked into a shady deal, which Dev still couldn't wrap his head around. She was actively fighting to keep her home. The Beautification Board wouldn't appreciate the extra publicity, he was sure.

At the sight of the absence of hope, the light in her eyes dying out, he pulled her back in for a hug, holding her close and murmuring endearments. "*Hermosa*, I don't want to, but you've seen the article. This situation is bad."

She shook her head against his chest, words muffled when she spoke. "No. It's shitty, and we know who did it."

Taking her with him and refusing to let go, they went into the living room and sat on her couch. She'd started to cry, and he pulled out his handkerchief. This moment he'd planned differently, to involve something more uplifting, but he found himself wiped, only able to offer comfort instead of ready-made solutions.

Dabbing her tears, she released a half-hearted laugh. "Life's no fun without challenges, so we can weather this together. As for the money, no worries. I've got a meeting with Kinyon and the board next Friday. A thirty-minute shot to convince them. With your help, it will be no problem. I don't have any solutions for Bona Fide, but a little bedroom brainstorm sounds like a good plan right now."

His brain short-circuited at her reasoning, how she dismissed his concerns and worries with simple acceptance. She'd be ruined, destroyed—an unacceptable option—and as far as the meeting went, he had another idea. "You don't have to go to the meeting. I've got another plan."

"What's that?"

"I'll give you the money." It sounded simple enough. He had the savings, his personal nest egg, to pull from. "Call it me replacing Mark and giving you the cash for your contract."

"Absolutely not." Her face, red from the tears, settled in firm rebuke.

He'd never expected her reaction. No, she had to accept the money as his means of helping, the only way he could for the moment.

"Why? It's money. I don't need it at the moment, and you did complete the contract. The only reason Mark isn't paying is that he doesn't have it. He promised money he couldn't deliver. This will be like me giving him a loan."

She stood, moving across the room. The action held weight as if she'd broken the tether holding them together. He wanted to gather her back to him, to stop this day from becoming worse.

When she faced him, she looked downright pissed. "That's as bad as the whole excuse we made about me not being a client. I justified it, so did you, but the fact remained that technically I was a client, right? That's why we're dealing with this article now."

"We're not dealing with the article. I am. That's why I'm saying this thing between us has to stop for the time being. I've got a board meeting Friday, and technically you were not my client when we slept together. Maybe when we kissed, but things happen. We kept our relationship professional. I just have to provide the details to the board; they are worried about public perception. We're not a huge company, but we have a large client base. Rumors about that sort of thing could affect the bottom line. But I refuse to drag you into it. So far the news article doesn't know who you are, and we need to keep it that way."

He'd rambled to reassure himself as much as her. Sure, a part of him worried about the board's final judgment of his future with the company. As for the actual news about him sleeping with clients getting out to his existing client base—the cat was out of the bag.

"So, now I'm a paid lover and too embarrassing for anyone to know about." She paced back and forth, slow, measured steps, which set his gut to churning with disgust at how his words sounded to her ears.

"No, not in the least. I'm trying to protect you, keep you safe. This publicity won't look good if you want to go before the Beautification Board, but I'm also offering a way to avoid a fight where people might judge you for your association with me." He wanted to stand up and go to her, to melt away the issues with kisses. Like a natural predator, her posture and the tension in her frame told him to stay away.

"What happened to solving our issues together, not sweeping everything under the rug like we have something to hide? To sticking through all the bullshit, even the crap cooked up by your ex?"

"Sounds awful when you put it like that, and I already explained this."

She pointed a finger at him. "No, you justified it with fucked-up excuses; at heart, it's still dirty. Look at this from my perspective. You're amazing, marvelous, and talented. You engaged in sexual relations with your partner's cousin, a woman in desperate need of money, which you'd be giving me for nothing. That doesn't look suspicious. Then you add to that the idea you'll call things off for the sake of public image, and once everything dies down we'll be together again. Not a story I've heard before.

Anything you say doesn't really matter because I'd still feel the same way... used with the idea of owing you money or taking it for having sex with you hanging over my head. Waiting for you and hoping you'll stay interested, when leaving means you're not."

"What are you saying, exactly?" Dev stood up, worried. The words were one thing, but her demeanor, the crossed arms, closing herself off again... *Dulce Madre.*

"This has got to stop. I don't want your so-called help or money. I need to focus on a viable solution, and this meeting is the best option. I want there to be an us, but I won't be cut loose again, left in the dark waiting for you to figure out when I'm worth it. I am sorry, but I can't. In the past, I gave everything to help my ex and he repaid me with leaving and insults. My parents left me with my grandmother as soon as they decided I was too much for them to handle. You've decided to do the same thing, like them."

Those words were like a knife, worse than the confession about the contract. Somewhere along the way, he'd fallen for this woman—her brisk language, her carefree behaviors, and all her quirks. He found her endearing, incredibly sexy and soft in the all the places he was hard. But to say those things now would serve no purpose.

He'd be another man trying to bend her to his will, to convince her to take his assistance and carve out the strong ideals she employed to protect herself. Dev grasped her meaning, how she'd come to view him as the bad guy, as the man abandoning her instead of sticking to his commitments. Her fears were manifested by his need to protect. She'd never understand his ultimate goal, how he cared enough for her to keep her away from the worst of things to come.

"I can't change your mind?"

"Oh, Dev." She dropped her arms and sighed. "You're asking me to be okay with stuff I can't be."

"This isn't going to last forever."

"Yes, you're right, but the fact remains you're willing to sacrifice us, the 'us' right now, for saving your image. I can't be with someone now, or ever, who puts me second to themselves. We're either together, a team, or we're not."

More heartbreaking words, strong and empowering. He'd never seen a stronger woman before in his life. She stuck to her ideals, her guns. Here he'd thought to defeat the dragon, and she'd stopped being afraid of it. But he couldn't abandon his own fear.

"All right, I'll respect your decision."

Kat's frame relaxed, the tension lines on her forehead smoothed away. "I wish you luck and hate that I can't change your mind. Thank you for letting me leave this with some dignity."

"You're welcome." The words were hollow, and the guilt real he held was because he didn't respect the decision. In truth, he wanted to yell at it. To declare that love meant sometimes giving up what you cared about the most if it was for their own good. He'd let her have this moment, let her win because splitting up kept her safe. But as soon as the dust settled, he'd be back, and he'd lay claim to his princess.

CHAPTER TWENTY

Kat lasted about twenty seconds after she shut the door behind Dev before she broke down in tears. What started as some simple water streaks turned her into a sobbing, shaking mess. Dread climbed the emotional trellis of her body to gain a front row seat at her meltdown. She needed to gain some control over her reactions, but once more, she faced her problems on her own. The one man, the one she'd somehow given her heart to along the way, had offered her a choice that would leave her in debt to him. Not to mention she'd been waiting and hoping he would still be interested in her when all this grief with his company's public image was settled. Sure, he said breaking up was to keep her from being subjected to ridicule and being judging for something she shouldn't be judged for, but in her mind it was bullshit.

Love conquered all, right? In this case, it appeared not. She'd never shared her feelings; he hadn't either. They'd kept their relationship to the physical, which could be summed up as being her fault as much as his.

This mess called for an early bedtime. Sure, she could've called Betty, sobbed some more, and complained about how she was an idiot for falling for Dev after everything. Ultimately, she didn't want to hear the feedback, listen to the pity, or be encouraged to go out. Being around people would be a bad idea.

She'd solve her problems tomorrow. Right now, sleeping off another horrible day seemed like a good idea.

***

The article prompted an emergency powwow Sunday afternoon at Bona Fide. Dev, Mark, and Victoria sequestered themselves in Dev's office. He'd gathered them after his morning jog, which had gone from two miles to five. The extra distance hadn't cleared away the anger and frustration at Pru, the article, and the way Kat's words ate away at him.

The texts he'd received from Victoria over the last twelve hours were all about the message forwarding service receiving more than twelve calls, quadruple what they received on a normal weekend. Things were taking a turn for the worse, and then came the agenda topic addition from Pru to discuss, quote, "Bona Fide's bad press and how they would solve it," unquote.

They'd already spent a week answering Pru's request for more info. She wanted Mark to supply a complete P&L report for the year as well as a month–by–month breakout with analytic tracking, a detailed list of clients, active and non-active, and any clients owing the company money. He didn't feel sorry for Mark, who'd gotten stuck with a bunch of shit work, but he did regret Victoria getting roped into helping. She'd happily told Pru she was the worst, with a smile on her face, and once more Dev put up with Pru asking why he never fired such a rude employee. He'd never dignified her with a response and focused on keeping up with work.

Now they were all present with a bottle of scotch and three glasses. The newspaper sat on his desk. The headline for the investigative title read, "Image Consultant Caught in Shady Dealings—Bona Fide is not genuine."

"Have you both seen this?"

Mark stood and looked at it while pouring some scotch into a glass. "Yes, got an eyeful yesterday morning, or I decided to after my mother called to say she didn't believe it."

"I didn't read it," Victoria replied before getting her own glass of amber liquid. "But based on the messages, I've heard enough. Who published this garbage?"

"Some investigative reporter named Daniel. He doesn't name his source, but I think we can guess who it is." Dev wanted to call Pru and give her a mouthful, something as hateful and vindictive as she was. It wouldn't change the scathing article in front of him.

Victoria smarted off. "Not surprising in the least. What's the worst of it?"

"Basically"—Mark took a quick a drink of scotch—"our intrepid reporter accuses Dev of sleeping with at least two clients while they did business with Bona Fide, and the presumption has been made there may be more women who haven't come forward. There's also a mention or two of him using his charm, talent, and position to take advantage of women who are already suffering from low self-esteem. He preys on them and gets them to agree to things they never would have normally. The article muses that this may be why we're getting more patronage. Coupled with female consultants on staff and an increasing amount of male clientele, we may be running a very expensive *full-service* business."

Dev put the empty highball glass on the coffee table in front of him, and the scotch scorched a path down his throat. "They accused our company of being an escort service or brothel. Take your pick; either one damns us."

"That would explain all the clients canceling the need for services. Each call is either a corporation or some referral reneging on their appointment. Whoever said people don't read the newspaper is dead wrong."

"Salacious stories make good news. The shitty part is the assumptions are libel. They are based on an anonymous source we can't disprove, at least the parts about running an escort service anyway. The statement of me sleeping with two clients is technically true."

Victoria sat up in her seat, "What?"

"I may have engaged in some sexual activities with a woman who had ties to Bona Fide."

"Kathleen?" His wide-eyed secretary was damn smart.

"The one and the same."

Mark didn't say a thing. He sat there smug-faced, and polished off his first glass of scotch before refilling.

"How? Wait, I don't want to know. This royally fucked us, didn't it? You're telling me we don't have a court case. What can we do?"

She'd laid the fine points out perfectly. They were being bent over and told to enjoy the ride. From a public relations standpoint, the only way out involved proving they weren't an escort service. He refused to give Pru a win. Also, he wouldn't deny his time or activities with Kat. The only consolation was that she'd broken up with him and insulated herself from this nonsense, the fact that this little article destroyed his efforts to eliminate the obstacles to them being together notwithstanding.

"We can put ourselves at the mercy of the investors." Mark decided to chime in now. "Without those corporate accounts, we are sitting ducks. They comprised most of our net income for the fourth quarter. Them pulling out guarantees we'll need to let a few folks go. We could review the list today. I'm going to have to re-crunch all the numbers again, especially the forecasts and estimated P&L for the end of the year. It's a big fucking mess."

Victoria shook her head. "I can't believe you're talking about letting people go with roughly eight weeks to Christmas. You're an asshole, Mark."

"When it's true, it's true." Mark shrugged his shoulders.

"What would the investors want, any ideas?" He loved how even Victoria, at her worst, didn't replace her kind heart, unlike some of the folks in the room. She wanted the best for all of them like he did.

"They want Dev's resignation. At least that's what they promised to ask for in the past. With the PR nightmare, I imagine it will be much of the same. We'll have to restructure things and get a new face for the company."

Victoria turned on Mark, fire in her eyes. "The company is nothing without him." She pointed at Dev. "He built this damn thing from the ground up and now has to suffer because he fell in love with a woman and it pissed his ex off."

"Wait, wait, wait... I never said I fell in love. I said I slept with her."

The eye from this snappy, smart-mouthed woman would've intimidated most men. Dev flashed her a sassy look of his own.

"You punched your best friend earlier this week over a woman. Last time I checked, the Devid I knew wasn't a fan of physical violence. Calling it, and I quote, 'unmanly.'" She was right. He'd never wanted to hit things until the last two weeks. Violence and physical harm were things he'd left behind in high school. There were better ways to solve problems.

"Mark deserved it."

"I'd like to point out how you're both talking about me like I'm not here." Mark didn't sound upset by the fact but more bored than anything. "Also, none of this gets us anywhere closer to solving our problem."

The asshole in the room was right. Pru wanted his blood, wanted to punish him, and she'd try to convince the board it was his fault for the bad PR and that the only way to fix things would be to oust him. Hell, she could even harm the work he was doing with the shelter, tainted by association. He didn't want to call Theresa about the televisions he'd purchased for them. What if they refused the gifts? The number of things he could possibly lose because of one damning article from a jealous, hateful woman scratched at his heart, leaving it open and raw. The option to hide was not on the table. Mark and Vic were still going back and forth, the debate heated. When she stood up, Dev finally decided to speak.

"Stop it, whatever you two are arguing about this time. Mark's right; they will want me to resign. Bona Fide will have to change, but change can be good. Let's see what we can come up with to swing this in our favor. We should assemble a list of all the consultants, their feedback, etc. I think if we review them, figure out which one might be able to take on the mantle as the face of our company, it'd be good, right? Let's pull numbers and names for a PR specialist as well. I'd rather have a plan for whatever demands the board has and present them with viable alternatives to show we're capable. We can run numbers on employee salaries and expenses through the end of the year. No bonuses, no Christmas party, cut where we can. Mark, you can get all the info put together, right?"

His friend pushed himself to a standing position and nodded in agreement.

Victoria headed for the door. She looked determined and resolute. "Fine, I'll help wherever you need me to, but don't think for one minute you're going to escape confessing your love for Kat. In the meantime, I'll be gathering all the information on our consultants."

"Love is for saps; we wouldn't have to give up our Sunday if someone had kept his dick in his pants."

The comment, another offensive bullshit sentence, pushed Dev over the small edge he'd been skirting. He did love Kat; the need to shout it from the rooftops was not required, though. Protecting her and supporting her were the greatest expressions of love in his opinion. The dick in his pants even knew that, obviously, since he'd split from her yesterday.

Splitting from her, losing the chance to be with her because of this mess... He wanted to take this out on someone, and his friend gave him the perfect excuse. Dev stood, walked around the desk, and sized up his buddy, who'd been a star of the wrestling team in high school as well as a football player, like him, for all four years. Except Mark had given up working out on a regular basis; he'd started to look a little soft, especially in the middle.

So he gave him what the bastard seemed to be wanting, a sucker punch right to the gut. Dev enjoyed watching Mark drop to his knees, and Victoria chuckled as she walked out the door. She'd leave them alone to finish their business, and he doubted she cared what happened to his friend, a friend who could be partially blamed for this fiasco.

"What the hell was that for?" Mark groaned

"I think you know."

"I don't deserve a punch if it's true. You didn't keep it in your pants, and we are stuck with the repercussions of it, love not being a factor at all."

This time, he punched Mark in the face; the moan of pain the punch elicited made Dev feel a tiny bit guilty. But if it resorted in blood being produced to get this asshole to stop saying derogatory comments, even admit to being in the wrong, then fine by Dev.

Except Mark decided not to take this punishment without giving a bit of his own. He pulled himself onto the chair and then kicked Dev square on his thigh before delivering his own punch to Dev's jaw.

The reverberating pain was cathartic to his already bruised heart and ego. It reminded him he was still alive and able to combat the problems ahead. Yes, the physical contact improved his mood. So he punched Mark again, square in the center of his pretty-boy face.

Hands flew up to cover the nose he'd just hit. "Sonuvabitch. I think you broke my nose."

"Let's see."

Mark removed his hands, and the pointed beak had no blood, only red skin. Dev touched it, and Mark let out a yell. "Ow, don't do that."

"You wanted me to see if it's broken; it's not. Do you want me to fix it?"

"No thanks, get away from me." He pushed Dev away and sat back in the chair, grabbing the rest of the scotch as he went. "Again, what the fuck?"

"Your negative attitude and derogatory comments have no place here. I told you the other day."

"Fuck that, you're lucky you're a friend. Nobody else would be able to get away with what you did." Mark took a swig. "And it's not like I lied, so screw you."

Dev wanted to grab the bottle and smash it across Mark's face, but he'd never been a violent man. His thoughts about physical displays continued to change the more he heard Mark speak. The crazy part was that his own partner really thought he hadn't helped contribute to this situation. "This is partially your fault too. You know that, right? You told Pru who Kat was, and though you haven't admitted it, you told her about the money."

No response. None at all, just more scotch-swigging like a pro.

"Refusing to confess, even now? You're caught, red-handed, and guilty. You fucked over your cousin and your own business. Pretty impressive for a week of hard work. I want to know your side of the story before I tell you to get the hell out of here."

Head shaking, Mark looked defeated. He also looked a bit like Kat; they had similar cheekbones and eyes, for all the dumb fuck didn't want to be compared to her. Damn, Dev missed her so much. He wanted to call her to regale her with how he'd punched her cousin. He'd never told her the depth of his feelings, never told her he loved her, but it was too little and most likely too late.

"Pru lied to me, like she lied to you. The plan didn't involve articles or getting rid of you, none of this nonsense with the board either." He paused to touch his nose, wincing as he did.

Dev lost any chance at remorse with those sentences. "Don't stop there. For what it's worth, you may as well deliver the whole, sad tale."

"It's worth a lot. I messed up. But I wanted things to be right here at the office. Pru turned into a damn monster after the breakup, and I thought maybe you both needed to work things out. I told her about the deal with Kat. Especially because of the Beautification project, I felt obligated to keep our big investor informed, whatever. Anyway, she promised this would be the perfect thing to get you back on track and liked the idea of the makeover. I told her the night of the dinner this was Kat's last night; that's why she came to your place the next day. She said she wanted to rekindle things and get back to where you both started, except she found Kat there, which had the opposite effect. Now everything sucks."

"No, what sucked was your attempt at matchmaking. You know what she did, how she tried to take me places and make me a circus performing monkey. Then she'd contradict everything I said, demeaning my advice. I was like a one trick pony to her and her friends. She got jealous about my other clients, made snide remarks about them. It had to stop. She took over my life, was needy and abusive. I was just too dumb to see it; I believed she'd been misguided, and somehow if I loved her enough, I'd heal her.

Once I finally saw the light and ripped myself free of the abuse and issues, you came along trying to helping us fix something not meant to be fixed."

Mark frowned, scooting around in his seat, no doubt trying to get comfortable with an uncomfortable conversation. "We never talked about the breakup in a lot of detail. I knew some of that, but not everything. Jeez, she came to me Dev. You have to believe me, she told me you'd been hesitating to commit. I got her jealous tendencies and being a bit of a bully, which was clear every time she came to the office during work hours. But she'd told me she was getting help for it, seeing a counselor or something. I wanted to help you. Are you really in love with my cousin?"

"You made a small thing, huge. Moon huge. No, Jupiter huge. I'm going to lose my job. I could lose my position with the shelter. This is one of the worst days of my life. And I told you in detail what happened with Pru, but per your usual M.O. you didn't listen to a word I said."

Dev went back and sat down; laying his forehead against the desk so he could stare down at his sneakers. They looked foreign on his feet, in the office. He always wore polished, business black shoes to the office. These were the opposite, his running shoes, designed to allow him to carry himself anywhere, away. Except this time he couldn't run. There was nowhere to go, and the future involved things he didn't want.

Mark cleared his throat. "You never answered my question."

"I don't want to answer your question."

"Then I guess I'll get started on those numbers. I want us back in here in an hour or so."

"Fine." His single word response was rude but effective because Mark left without rebuttal.

A true friend, indeed. Bereft and lost, calling his family to talk to them would open up topics he'd rather not get into, even if they meant well. He had no one to turn to. Kat wasn't an option for him. No, he'd need to figure this out. Solve the situation before asking for help. Too bad the person he'd once relied on for those types of things had become the type of person he hated. Mark was self-absorbed and only worried about himself. The business piece had his attention because it affected his paycheck. Deep down Dev got the impression his friend cared for little else anymore.

Before he could play knight in shining armor to the woman he loved, he'd need to battle his war and survive.

CHAPTER TWENTY-ONE

In the few days since she'd broken up with Dev, she'd gotten drunk at Louie's, fine-line detailed the contract from Pru, started preparing her presentation for the board and suffered the remnants of a nasty hangover. The ideas she'd produced were not ideal, including renegotiating the renovation contract or asking for additional time on the code inspection due to the fall weather. If she got the extension, her friends promised to pitch in any Christmas bonus they received, even Betty, who normally spent her extras on an additional payment toward her mortgage. She truly surrounded herself with some amazing people. Things were looking up, except she missed Dev.

She missed talking to him, even his stupid assignments, and the ability to text him randomly. So far he'd stuck with the respect thing. No calls, texts, or surprise appearances at her house. It wasn't like he'd done any of those things before, but still, there had existed the possibility. She'd refrained from doing the same. There would be no crazy girl syndrome or attempts to fix the ache in her heart. Somehow he'd propped up a little home inside there. Maybe when he'd staunchly defended her, or made love to her—or all the things they'd done together. Ridiculous how one guy had become so ingrained in her life, her mess. She wanted him back.

The risks were too great, and being hidden away until PR issues with his job blew over was something she refused to go along with. All her friends agreed. She needed to focus on securing her situation; he had to focus on his. After she won the house, then she could start searching for a good man, someone who didn't have a crazy ex or a fancy company to worry about. No point in dwelling on something she couldn't affect right now.

As it stood, she had two days left before the meeting. Her focus needed to be how she'd save her house by making counteroffers and all the horrible things she didn't really want to do. Saving her house involved a lot of sacrifices, and she hated it. Everything was coming together thanks to help from Betty and a couple of other friends, too. They'd read and re-read bits and pieces for her, giving near immediate feedback via email. If she focused hard enough, she didn't have time to miss Dev. Nor his smile or the way he'd call her *hermosa*.

Natalie, the HR coordinator at Ying Yang, and another friend had phoned her about the article. Natalie's husband, Marshall, had mentioned he knew Dev and read the whole thing shocked. Then it got worse when the article got double the coverage, moving from digital to print. All the implications and references to the possibility of Dev being a player and scam artist, plus the inferences to Bona Fide offering escort services, made for salacious news so exciting even local television stations were mentioning it. Kat's name so far had been kept out of things. To Dev's point she was safe, but hiding in the shadows frustrated her. The idea she'd been a dirty little secret hurt.

The rude informant who started the mess, likely fearing for her own reputation, chose to remain anonymous, of course. Kat could count on two fingers the people capable of doing such a thing, Pru being the most likely choice because Kat didn't believe her cousin had the balls.

She heard a car outside and looked out the window out of habit. The devil himself parked in her driveway and got out of his car in dressed-down attire. It looked odd to see her cousin in jeans and a T-shirt. He always dressed the consummate professional at family dinners. Surprise propelled her from the couch to the front door. She opened it to greet him, but stopped short when she saw the bruising near the bridge of his nose and around his eyes.

"You're looking a little worse for wear. Did someone decide you were enough of an asshole that you needed a lesson?"

"Hardy-har. A bundle of jokes and smart ass comments. Your lover did the damage you see here." He pointed to his face, and she tried not to smile or get curious. She wanted to ask how, to know the details—anything to hear something about Dev and how he was holding up with the additional coverage of the article.

She settled for a safer topic. "What brings you here?"

"Can we do this inside?"

Funny he'd ask that, since letting him in was the last thing she wanted. She'd decided months ago to un-invite him from anything to do with her house or anything of Gran's, for that matter. He'd set her up for the downfall and cared next to nothing about it. But maybe if he saw the damage inside, the work still needing to be done...

"Fine, for a minute. I've got shit to take care of and no time for a waste of space."

He followed her into the house, looking around like a kid walking into a fancy restaurant. "It still smells the same."

"Yep, I use the same soap Gran did. Something about cloves and lavender makes me think of home. I'm headed to the kitchen; you want a drink?"

Shaking his head in the negative, he trailed after her. "What's with all the pictures missing. There were holes here?"

"Renovating. It's like you forgot I said the house had a gazillion code violations. It needs updating, hence holes and Gran's knickknacks and photos packed up. If the Beautification Board had their way, the whole inside would be redone to their specifications and decorated in their style. No personal touches at all. I'd have to stick Gran's stuff in a storage unit, if I can afford it."

She grabbed the teapot and stuck it under the faucet. Once full, she set it to boil on the stove and grabbed her favorite mug. The kitchen was still in shambles, most of the innards of the outside walls exposed. No insulation installed and no sheet rock. All of that was stored out in the shed for later use.

"This looks like a wreck. What code violation is this?"

"I may have opened my big mouth about doing a kitchen renovation about six years ago, and they called me out for not having insulation in the outer walls. Something to do with fire hazards and fire code, the new stuff has special treatments to prevent burning and catching fire."

"Crazy, just crazy."

When she finally turned around, Mark was leaning against the back of a chair at the kitchen table, staring out the window into the backyard.

"What do you want?"

He nodded toward the backyard. "I remember the Fourth of July celebrations we'd always have here. The fire pit out back. Lighting up the sparklers and dancing around like heathens. We caught a jar full of lightning bugs that one year, remember?"

"Yes, and then you dumped them down Andrew's pants."

Mark laughed, "Oh, yes. Yes, I did, got in so much trouble. Good memories."

The teakettle whistled, and she pulled it off the burner, pouring the hot water over her loose leaves in the small strainer. "Nice trip down memory lane, but get to the point."

This time he took a seat. She joined him, tapping her fingers against the tabletop as she waited. His eyes were still focused on the outside, and then he glanced around the kitchen once more before looking at her. "Dev loves you."

"If that were the case, he'd be here saying it instead of you and he wouldn't have asked me to keep our relationship a secret because of a stupid article."

"Maybe, but did you ever think he wanted to protect you? He spent so much time helping you, he's afraid to taint your chances of saving your house with his name. Then he locked those feelings up but did a shitty job of it. Anytime I mention you, he gets all tight-lipped, if he's not punching me." Mark touched his jaw as if the words recalled a specific memory.

"Dev doesn't hit people."

"Tell that to my nose. It hurts, and he did the hurting. He's a mess without you. Trust me, I'm getting firsthand experience. Not the first time he's hit me either. Did the original damage about a week ago trying to pry money out of me I didn't have. He was willing to give you some, enough to save the house, or so I heard."

She drew her hand in the air. "See all this? Those memories you keep reliving, they're our history, a past I don't want to lose. I could've taken the money from him, accepted it, but then he'd have been paying me off for being with him. If you think Pru wouldn't have questioned where I got the money... she's on your board of investors, on the board for the Beautification Board and she had to have acted as a source for the newspaper article. She's out for Dev, gunning for him with the goal of a head-on collision. I was willing to get caught in the crossfire, but instead, he wanted to push me away, keep me quiet like some dirty little secret. Love is not hidden away; it's brought out in the daylight for everyone to see, to acknowledge that they can't break it with some bad words or insults.

Sorry, I got on a tangent, but bottom line is this house is all I have. If I lose it, I don't make enough to get a place to be on my own, not with the debt I'm still trying to clear away. I refuse to let the board destroy the memories of our family because they think it would improve the rich background of the community, but I won't accept hush money or sell myself in the process. I'm not doing it."

He got quiet, thoughtful, which in her mind might prove scary. Mark's silence meant plotting, and with her latest endeavors, it seemed he always plotted against her. "Fine. I get it, but you care about him right?"

"I do."

"Would you say you love him?"

"Even if I did, what the hell is the point? Love isn't going to do much for him or stop Pru from getting her way." Kat took a sip of tea, letting the bitter taste linger in her mouth before swallowing. Yep, life was like a cup of tea—warm, inviting, then bitter and cold too soon.

"She doesn't have to win. If you love him, you'll help him out. And he's going to need it this coming Friday. The board basically wants to put him on trial to decide whether he should remain with Bona Fide. They are talking about asking for his resignation. Dev's plan to help is to get a new face for the company, but everyone knows the company is him. He makes Bona Fide a success. Someone else won't cut it."

"I may feel charitable toward him, but definitely not toward you."

Mark nodded in agreement. "Yes, I'm an asshole, and I'm sorry, all right. I jacked things up bad. I don't want us on bad terms, though. My mother will never let me hear the end of it. I'm sorry for lying to you about having money, for not telling you I didn't have the money to begin with. Dev was right."

"Right about what?"

"Can I have some tea now?" Contemplative, apologetic Mark scared the crap out of her.

"Sure." She got up and fixed him a mug of the same chamomile blend she sipped on, this time pouring it into Gran's favorite mug, one he'd recognize.

"Where the hell did you get this?" he asked as she set the mug down in front of him.

"Gran used to drink out of it every morning. It was her favorite, next to the one I made in my high school pottery class."

"Unbelievable. It's even got some chips in the rim and the handle." Mark gingerly held the mug up, turning it in a slow circle in his hands, and taking in the photos printed on it. They were all of him and his younger brother.

"She missed ya'll after your dad got sent away. I remember she'd look at this mug and then give you both a kiss, talking about how those kisses were love prayers."

Mark chuckled and wiped at his eyes. "She used to tell us that when she kissed us goodbye. We were supposed to hold those prayers and remember them anytime we felt down. Damn."

He swiped at his face in earnest now, and Kat realized this was probably the most emotion her cousin had openly displayed in years. She wanted to know what the hell prompted this sudden change of attitude.

"You never answered my question earlier."

"Hmm?" His response was muffled by the mouthful of tea he just drank. "What question?"

"How was Dev right?"

"He told me I couldn't hold grudges against you for my father's mistakes. He's right. You're not him; your mom's not him. Hell, Gran and this house didn't make him into who he was. I need to stop seeing him in everyone, and I can start with you. Can we try to put this past us?"

She wanted to say screw off to him and the cold, unfeeling monster who'd taken up residence in his chest, to tell him to get lost and take his sudden awakening crap with him, but he was family. Turning her back on him meant she'd stooped to his level. Not a place she ever wanted to be in. So she did the right thing. "You're forgiven for fucking me over."

"Thank you, and does that mean you'll help us?"

"No, I can't. I have a meeting on Friday with the Beautification Board. It's my one shot to get them to let go of Gran's house. I need to prep in the morning, and my meeting is early afternoon. Besides, Dev doesn't want me involved. He told me that repeatedly. Call me selfish, but where I rest my head is pretty damn important, and I need to respect his wishes as much as I'd expect him to respect mine."

Mark sighed before downing the rest of the tea. Setting the mug down he looked her right in the eye. "Fine. You know if you asked Dev, he'd help you get ready for this meeting. It could be a mutual thing."

"I need to do this on my own, without help or assistance from anyone associated with Pru. Better to run the show myself. Besides, I've got friends to help me too. I'm not all alone, and if this meeting doesn't pan out, I'll beg the inspection board to give me more time."

Standing, Mark offered a small smile. "Sounds like you got it figured. If they take the house, I know Mom would let you crash in my old room if you asked her. I also have a half-empty storage unit you could use to store Gran's stuff."

She stood herself and slugged him in the arm with a half-hearted punch. "Don't start being nice; it's creepy."

"Fucking bye, then. Forget I mentioned anything."

"Thank you." Kat walked him to the door, ready to be done with hosting company and get back to her presentation.

"Oh, hey, Kat."

"What?"

"I just remembered another thing Gran used to say: Put your value in people, not things. Things will let you down time and again, but people, if given a little piece of you, usually stick around."

"You're right. Maybe you should take that advice."

"Maybe you should, too." Mark walked to his car, and she shut the door.

Gathering her now too-cool mug of tea, she sat on the couch and pondered over his words. This house was not just a thing but a part of a promise to the one person she loved the most. She'd be letting the house down—Gran down—if she gave up now.

As for Dev, she hated seeing him suffer, but anything she said wouldn't make a difference. They'd been together in a relationship of sorts, blurred the lines of professionalism and personal interest. The risks had always been present in their interactions. The decision to throw caution to the wind was on both of their heads, and they were facing the repercussions. In this arena love didn't conquer all.

CHAPTER TWENTY-TWO

The bartender brought round *numero dos*, a double shot of vodka. Dev appreciated the fact that, after three nights, he and the bartender only had to make eye contact to get the next pour completed. He'd come to Louie's each time hoping to run into Kat on her own or even with her friends—for the chance to see her without looking like he'd been expecting to. She'd mentioned the place was a regular hangout after work at least one night a week, but no luck so far.

He refused to give in, and if anything, it provided a great place to people watch. Love, loss, friendly gatherings, there was always someone or a group he could make up a little story about in his head. Anything sounded better than how things were going in his corner. In a way, the bar had become a place for escape.

In the last four days, they'd identified a "new face" candidate and drafted a culling list and a restructured organization chart. Victoria despised it from the start, declaring a zombie apocalypse would occur before she'd report to Mark. Mark laughed at her outburst and politely suggested she could get a new job, which earned him a middle finger salute. The last couple days at the office weren't tons of fun—more clients lost and reports of a few people wanting to know whether they'd get refunds if Bona Fide went under. Horrible, awful things to hear as a business owner. Through all of it, the one thing getting him through the day was the random possibility he'd see Kat.

Instead, a familiar face slipped into his booth.

"I took the liberty of getting you another drink," Mark said sliding *numero tres* across the table toward him. "Vodka? You haven't drunk that in a long time."

"It's still my favorite. All the reports are done?"

"Yep, they are. Things don't look good at all. In fact, if I were a suspicious person, I'd say someone sabotaged us to make every report take a sudden downward spiral. Because that's exactly what they look like, the opposite of what I presented to the board this past Friday."

Dev shrugged, not surprised in the least. It was a good possibility that's what Pru wanted and why she'd engaged an investigative reporter, but they couldn't prove it. "Oh well, it is what it is. Thanks for getting them done."

"That's my job, isn't it? Are you drunk?"

"No, just tired of fighting, worrying, and battling against someone we weren't meant to beat."

Mark raised an eyebrow. "Really? Are you sure it's not also the fact that you are missing someone?"

Maybe he'd let his feelings show too much, but he refused to hide them now. No more hiding anything, and he'd be honest if it killed him. "Yep, I miss her… your cousin, to be specific. I don't know how, but she gave me something different in my life. I didn't have to worry about being someone special with her or meeting any expectations. She made me feel like I already did."

"I went to see her."

"What?" Dev tossed back *numero dos* and then looked at his friend, waiting for the delayed response, desperate for news.

"Yes, you're not going crazy. I really drove over to her house and had a conversation early this evening."

He shook his head. "No, tell me what the hell happened."

"I asked her to help you at the meeting Friday. She told me no; there's some meeting with the Beautification Board about her house. She didn't go into too much detail about it, but it appears there's a chance she could keep the house from being taken from her. Regardless, I told her you loved her."

"No, you didn't fucking say those words." The booze helped the curse word escape more readily. Normally he'd feel ashamed. At the moment he couldn't care less.

Mark nodded. "I did because you were too much of a pussy to tell her yourself."

He may have been, but, "Not your place to speak my feelings for me. I've got a good idea to punch you again."

"Before you do, I'd like to provide a friendly reminder that we are in a public establishment and laying hands on me may involve a call to the police. The last thing we need now is more bad publicity."

"Whatever happened to the 'any publicity is good publicity' school of thought?"

A shrug of the shoulders was followed by Mark tossing back his first drink, and then he said, "The way of the dodo. Like Bona Fide, if we're not careful. I also asked Kat for forgiveness."

"For what?"

"Screwing her over with the contract and being an ass. You're right; family should be a little more important. Honestly, the thought came to me after going over to that house that I hadn't been to the house in years. My grandma's place, I mean. It's still the same. Sure, Kat's things are there, but so is everything Grandma. It still smells the same too, spices and a little nostalgic."

"It's cool. I understand. Did she forgive you?" Dev knew too well the power of memories and how they could be cathartic as much as punishing.

"Yes, she did. Also, I forgot her main reason for not helping you—respecting your wishes."

"My wishes? The only thing I want is—"

"To keep her safe. According to her, you offered her money for the house and then told her she needed to stay away from you. Are you going to drink that?" Mark pointed at *numero tres*.

"Go ahead; I can always get another." Drinks didn't solve the big problem, though. "I said those things, but only because of Pru. We need to get rid of her."

"Is that an implication that we should get *rid* rid of her?"

Dev laughed; a loud, bellyache thing on an escape route to nowhere. "*Ay Dios mio,* no. I'm saying we need to buy her out of the board to get rid of her from our business. She needs to go the way of the dodo, and then it wouldn't matter. Kat could help me. I could help her. My past with this woman would truly be ancient history."

Then a light bulb flashed on. A bright idea stared him right in the face on how he could help Kat—the best way to help her and keep her home safe. "Mark, I gotta get out of here."

"I know what you mean. We need a vacation after this shit blows over. I say we head south for a few weeks this winter, maybe the Keys or Miami. Anywhere there's music, good food, and no stress."

"That's not what I'm talking about. I need to go home. There's a way I can help Kat, but I'll need a computer and a good eight hours of solid work. Grab the bill for me?"

"Sure thing, good buddy. It's the least I can do. Consider it part of me making up for the asshole attitude." Mark stood up then looked back at him before he headed off. "Are you good to drive?"

"I'll take a cab and get my car in the morning." Dev headed for the door and hailed one of the cabs off to the side; there were always two in this part of town waiting for the guy stumbling out of the restaurant or a bar down the street. He climbed into the back seat, anxious, ready, and hoping he could pull this off before her meeting on Friday. Even if his idea wasn't the option chosen, at least he'd help provide one additional choice.

***

"Welcome to Cafe Luna." The hostess greeted from her perch behind the desk. She gave a big smile, and Kat held up two fingers. With Betty in tow, she followed the red-haired woman to a booth and sat down.

"Thank you," Betty said before the hostess disappeared. Once she did, Kat got a mouthful. "Why didn't you talk to her? Use a few words."

Kat shrugged, tired and already a bundle nerves about the meeting, now one day away. "Sorry, I'm not feeling talkative, and I've barely gotten any sleep all week. The presentation I've put together is a doozy, but I think it will do."

"I've looked at it. You'll be perfect. Now, you need to focus on food. You can't present unless properly fed." Betty grabbed her menu and started scanning.

Kat followed suit, but her heart wasn't in it. She'd been thinking more and more about Dev and about Mark's words about her Gran ever since her cousin's visit, wondering if she'd made the right decision. Had she turned down the possibility of helping him too quickly? She hoped to wash away those thoughts by reminding herself that Dev wanted this, wanted them apart to keep her safe.

"Maybe I should've agreed to help Dev at his meeting."

Betty set the menu down and gave her a you-can't-be-serious look. "This is a conversation we've already had, and you know the answer. Helping him doesn't keep a roof over your head. In this world the only person you have to rely on is yourself. Family is good for some things, but not everything. I hate to say it, but so far your family has been a bust in being supportive."

Somehow the message sounded wrong. Sure Kat's family had failed to help with a lot, but her gran had been there through her whole life. She'd always been prepared for battle with some sort of baked bread, a warm hug, and a kind word at the ready to help solve her problems. Kat had relied on the older woman, especially in those first few years after her parents took off. They'd helped each other. Her grandmother always showed kindness to everyone, even when the situation may not have called for it. "I don't feel right about leaving him hanging. He's always helped me. I wasn't raised to abandon those who need help."

"Yes, but can he save your house if you're busy helping him?"

She thought about the answer to that one as the waitress came over and took their drink order. Would her grandmother have fought this hard for the family home? She'd liked to have believed so, but the honest answer was she had no clue. Gran had derived love from life, cooking or cleaning, even a good card game. The people surrounding her gave it substance. In fact, Kat had increasingly guilty thoughts when she recalled how her last conversation with Dev had gone. She'd minimized his feelings for her and dismissed everything for her fears of being abandoned. Mark had been right; loving people over things was better in the long run.

"I don't know."

Betty looked back at her menu. "Then, there's your answer, you don't—wait, I'm pretty sure the answer the other day involved a firm no. What's changed?"

"I realized I might have judged him too hard, thrown a few things out there without thinking about them. Mark had no reason to come over and tell me Dev loves me, none at all. He didn't even need to apologize, but he did. I have to believe that means something."

"Maybe, but if your cousin is so horrible, how impossible would it be that he's setting you up?"

The meeting with her cousin naturally had her on the defensive because it was Mark, asshole extraordinaire. She'd been fighting her natural anger toward him the entire time, even after she'd forgiven him. His words about Dev's feelings for her, though, those stuck and scared her. If he loved her, and she'd turned him away... "I don't think so, and setting me up for what? To make Dev look worse? Bona Fide is his business too. If it doesn't succeed, Mark won't either. Not only did he want to be forgiven for that, but for the whole situation with Gran's house. He even offered me room and board plus a storage unit if the worst happens. The cherry on the sundae? He said Dev loves me."

"You didn't mention that yesterday."

Kat shrugged. "Can you blame me? Everyone has firmly been in the leave-Dev-alone camp. Logic says to follow the advice of the many compared to the words of an untrustworthy person. But I'm sharing with you now because it's on my mind. If he loves me, then I need to show him I love him."

The waitress came back with their drinks and a bowl of rolls. "Are you ladies ready to order lunch?"

"Give us a minute, please?" Betty gave her sweetest smile, which disappeared as soon as the waitress moved away. "You love him? Is this serious?"

"Yes, I think it is."

Betty took a deep breath. "I'm not an expert in that area, but it's dangerous territory."

"Why?"

"Strings, there are always strings with love. I learned that the hard way."

"Then Betty, sweetie, you love the wrong type of people. He's never asked me for anything. Mark asked me to help. The only thing Dev ever wanted to do for me was give me money, attention, and time." She could've gone on and on with the things he'd offered her without reserve. "He's probably one of the most giving people I know. He gives time to the battered women's shelter, helping them with resumes and interviews. If he loved me, I'm pretty sure he'd never ask for anything."

Her friend shrugged and flagged the waitress down. "Time is strings. I'd be wary, and I still don't understand how he could've helped save the house."

The waitress, violet-haired and sweet, took their order. Once she'd left, Kat told the rest of the story that Betty failed to grasp. "He came up with those cards on the Beautification Board members. He taught me how to change my body language. I bet he has a ton of good tips for presentation and negotiation tactics. I'm entering unknown territory tomorrow."

"Then call him, if you think it'd help."

Kat rolled her eyes. "You're kidding, right?"

"Nope, I'm serious. Don't be wishy-washy. You either want his help and you want to help him, or you don't, and we'll eat lunch. The damn meeting is in less than twenty-four hours. Your last chance to get final opinions and thoughts is now. It's like the part of the wedding when you can still call everything off."

"Worried about weddings?" Kat asked.

"Not in the least, but a good analogy, right?"

"Yes, it is. The thing is, he might be worth it." In a split second, she saw it, her day with him by her side. A possibility of a future she'd barely dreamed of in the past.

"Worth what?"

"More than anything material I have. More than my house, my car, my bank account."

Betty scoffed. "You're crazy. I'd never throw away my security for a guy. That's nuts."

"People are worth more than things."

"Who said that?"

Her grandma, that's who'd said it. Mark's reminder of their gran's words filled her ears, though he'd botched the phrase a bit. She'd heard Gran utter those sentences hundreds of times, whether watching the news or talking with a friend who'd made bad choices—even when her son went to prison.

You put your value in people; things will let you down time and again, they don't last. People who get a little piece of you typically hang around.

A perfect reminder to show her she'd once again let go of the important things. "Someone I loved very much, and now I need to apply it."

"I hope this doesn't blow up in your face."

She hoped so too.

CHAPTER TWENTY-THREE

Dev had barely slept the night before, tossing and turning without any hope of getting well-rested. He'd tried counting sheep and drinking a glass of warm milk with cinnamon, as his *Madre* always encouraged, but to no avail. Instead, he'd given up on rest at around four in the morning and rose early to run, shower, and ensure the final touches on his presentation were complete. Then he sent everything off via email and headed into the office. Everyone showed up on time, as if they wanted to put their best foot forward. Preliminary discussions had already been held with their "new face," Stacy, in preparation for the worst. Even if he didn't lose his position, having someone groomed to take on the limelight seemed the intelligent thing to do.

Then the hours ticked by, fast and furious, leading up to the moment when he walked into the board room and took his place at one end of the table. Pru stood at the other end in deep conversation with two of the eight board members. She didn't have intimate connections to them all, but they knew each other from the country club. In a past life, they'd been associates of Pru's dead husband and now, by association, with her. Cultivating those relationships had taken time and determination on her part, which he'd never deny. They stood feet away, possibly talking about his future and what they wanted him to do.

He'd come up with the idea of Bona Fide, dreamed about it in his youthful high school days and into college as he watched women fall prey to assholes because of self-esteem or fail to put a dent in the glass ceiling due to being shy or soft-spoken. He'd been searching for a way to help, and help he had. Small stuff at first— volunteering for a suicide hotline and leading a positive image class at a local rec center. Then with Victoria and Pru's success came the full-fledged business, the promise of an investment group to give them the cash amount up front for space, a building allowing them to hold corporate sessions, to take on my consultants. His dreams were finally a reality and she wanted to strip them away. The same woman who'd worked alongside him to build him up. At the first sign of him moving on from them as a couple, she couldn't handle it.

He stared her down, watching Pru deftly ignore him, but he let those eyes of his bore into her. When she finally acknowledged him, he caught the first glimmer of a crack in her armor. She blinked and he didn't. Her skin took on a pinkish hue. He'd made her lose the staring contest and blush. Mark came in shortly after, a stack of portfolio's in his arms. The other investors filed in with the exception of three of them, Pru's biggest fans were not there. Dev looked at his watch, almost one. Kat's meeting with the Beautification Board may have had something to do with the board members's absence and he sent up a silent thanks to the Lord for this one little mercy.

"Are we ready to get started?" he asked trying to sound as innocent as possible.

Several of the gentlemen agreed, and everyone took a seat, Pru being the last. As the President of the Board, she got to speak for the group and hold the floor. "I'm glad almost everyone could come today. Thankfully, even without everyone, there are enough folks present to count as a quorum. We're here today to discuss the latest publicity challenge for Bona Fide, courtesy of Dev's personal activities. The article in the local paper was very damaging. As to the extent of the damage, that's what we're going to discuss. We will also discuss our expectations moving forward and hear any comments from the Bona Fide CEO and VP before we make any final recommendations. If we are in agreement, say aye."

A chorus of ayes filled the room.

"Then, Mark, if you please?" Pru pointed to the portfolios, which Mark passed down the table.

Mark cleared his throat. "If you'll please turn to page two."

And so it began, twenty minutes of debating over their previous meeting's proposed successes and the new proposed losses they'd suffer. Mark laid it on thick, with comparison charts and the whole nine yards by way of analytics with financials. When he finished, they asked Dev to speak, and so he did.

He detailed his professional relationship with Kat, mentioning it only turned personal after the client/consultant piece had come to a close. Pru chimed in with an ill-put comment about it being the same night, but Dev stuck to the truth. He even brought forth his understanding that she'd been a pro bono case, not an official client on the books, but a side project to help him gain his confidence again.

"In summation, I think whoever the article's source was is unreliable and damaging the company's good name out of spite toward me. I see it fit to ask for a retraction and potentially an interview from a competitive publication to get our side of the story out."

"But the source was correct; you've had relations with two Bona Fide clients in the past." This comment came from the oldest member of their board, Henry.

"Yes, true, but everything else was false, and I believe that deserves to be said. My reputation within Bona Fide and outside of it is threatened, but I wouldn't take any step unless this board decides to back me."

Another board member, Wilbur, spoke next. "We'll need time to consider all this information. May we ask for a few moments alone?"

Before Dev could say yes, the conference room doors opened, and Victoria stood there, a big smile on her face. "I apologize for the interruption, but a young lady is here to add some additional insight to the discussion, if it so pleases the board?"

Wilbur, Henry, and the others all nodded in agreement, except Pru. She'd gone sour-faced, and he felt the anger in her gaze as Victoria stepped aside and Kat walked in. He'd never been so happy to see her before, not because of what she might tell the board, but for getting the pleasure of seeing her again. She looked radiant, hair up in a high ponytail with her jumpsuit on and ankle boots.

"Good morning, everyone." Her voice sounded like music to his ears... Shit, he'd become a sappy mess.

"Good morning," went the chorus.

"I wanted to see if I could clear up a couple things because"—she looked at him—"it's the right thing to do."

Wilbur chimed in. "Then go ahead, young lady."

"You have Dev on trial for being in a personal relationship with me when I was a client, but Dev and I were always in a personal relationship. He did the consulting as a pro bono deal as a favor to Mark, my cousin. No money ever exchanged hands between us. All expenses were covered by my cousin. He didn't break your rules, and what's between him and me is exactly that... between us."

"Yes, but why didn't he say that, then?" Henry quizzed.

She shrugged her shoulders, and he basked in her beauty, her courage... for him. "Not sure, but it probably had to do with my paperwork being accidentally filed into Bona Fide's system. Once there, it couldn't be taken back without looking suspicious. Then there is the matter of him wanting to keep me out of this. He didn't want me involved or my character maligned as his has been. Would you want that for someone you love?"

Several of the board members shook their heads in disagreement.

Then Pru opened her big mouth, "Yes, but what about you and Mark? I have a copy of a contract stipulating that you had an agreement to exchange money if you received a makeover."

"Yes, there was an agreement and a contract."

No gasps, just silence. Dev wanted to pipe up and lay the blame at the appropriate party's feet. Kat, his *hermosa*, beat him to it.

"But the agreement between us was between the two of us. Nothing about it directly affected Bona Fide, and neither did Dev working with me. All business and meetings took place after hours or on weekends. He helped me prepare for a big event, and I made sure that any help he offered didn't impede his work here."

"What did he prepare you for?" Wilbur's question came with a serious expression and furrowed brows.

"He helped me attempt to save my house from being condemned for failing a code inspection via a meeting with those who could reverse the decision or give me funds."

Henry followed up with, "Did you succeed?"

"No."

Dev's heart thumped in his chest, all anxious energy coupled with hurt. She'd been fighting so hard and hadn't made it. Kinyon either never received his email or ignored it. *Damn.*

"But," Kat continued, "I'm not sure how things would've turned out since I skipped that meeting today to come to this one."

***

Kat hadn't planned any of this out, the entire process a complete fly-by-the-seat-of-her-pants job. She'd tossed and turned all night, and when she'd finally fallen asleep, her rest had been filled with nightmares about Dev, her home, and her Gran looking disappointed in her. She'd awoke in a cold sweat and immediately taken a hot shower. Sitting on her couch in sweats at five in the morning with a hot cup of tea, she'd pondered over everything all over again, weighing the possibilities and scenarios if she showed up at Bona Fide versus going to the meeting, and trying to determine which route held the most chance of success. In the end, she determined that not helping Dev would be something she'd regret for the rest of her life. To love someone and not do what you could for them… the end result was unthinkable.

Those had been the final thoughts pushing her out her front door and on a route to the Bona Fide office. She'd hesitated for only a brief second at a stoplight. Straight had meant Dev, and right would've possibly saved her house. She'd taken the rocky road by coming here and risking everything.

Her nerves became even worse when she'd walked in the front door and up to Victoria's desk. Victoria, for all her shock and surprise, had become super excited when Kat told her why she was there.

"Then you need to get in there right now. Come with me."

The secretary had marched right down the office hallway and toward their big conference room. Deep breaths and counting her steps had seemed to help. She'd heard Victoria introducing her, noted the acknowledgement to let her in the room.

Walking in, she'd expected a bigger crowd and to be looked at with disdain. Instead she noted interest, curiosity, and even, from her cousin, respect. From there it wasn't hard to start making her case, to face down the mob who wanted to hurt the one she loved.

"Well, thank you for that little summation, but this is a lost cause." Pru's snide remark could be heard throughout the room, and her dismissive physical reaction was in plain view of everyone. Kat found herself surprised Pru had let her true feelings show when the woman worked so hard to cultivate her image.

Kat refused to give her the satisfaction of being angry or to let the woman's attitude affect her own. Kat had lost everything today and pinned her hopes on the fact that Dev still wanted her. Love didn't pay the bills, but it certainly gave a person someone to bounce ideas off of. Maybe she'd get another meeting with the Beautification Board, or maybe she'd crash and burn. None of those things really mattered at this moment. "Is he a lost cause? Last I knew, his commissions are the highest at Bona Fide."

"They aren't anymore," Pru countered. "And it's a good chance they won't ever be again."

Other board members nodded in agreement. Whenever someone asked about this day, she'd cry "witch hunt" loudly and proudly. Pru wanted Dev's head roasted, based upon the daggers she'd been staring at them as soon as Kat had arrived.

Before she could rebut anything additional, her enemy added, "I believe it's time for a vote. The only solution to this problem is to have Dev's resignation. He's cast a horrible light on the company. I motion for resignation."

One of the board members who'd questioned her said, "Second."

Then a bunch of "nays" followed. Pru and the old man were the only ones wanting Dev to resign. Everyone else appeared to want him to stay. Both Dev and Mark looked surprised. The butterflies from her stomach and the fear gripping her seeped away at the board's decision. She sighed in relief.

"The board has spoken. Dev, you get to stay. For now." Pru sounded less than excited by the decision. No, the decision ruined her plans, and she was the first to gather her bag and stomp out of the room.

Kat wanted to challenge her on what "for now" meant, except she'd grown self-conscience in the past fifteen minutes. She's arrived to save him, to help without any thought to what it cost her. If she thought about the house, she'd cry, but a life not spent with Dev had already brought her to tears this morning. Her luck would be that she'd never find someone confident, stubborn, or perfect to spend every day of her life with. Now that one part of her mission had been accomplished, she needed the courage to ask for the other part.

The boardroom began to clear out, and she stood stock still. No one talked or looked at her, except Mark. He winked and then followed behind a few others. In moments the room was nearly empty, except for one person who still stood there.

Dev, looking at his phone and scrolling, had never looked sexier. Being without him for days had done something to her brain chemistry because she wanted to run to him, hop in his lap, and do all sorts of things were inappropriate for the workplace. The courage she'd lacked moments ago was renewed by being alone with him. When he finally tucked the phone away and looked at her, her heart pounded. Blood rushed to her ears and for a moment she lost the concept of sound. She saw his lips moving, but couldn't respond to his simple question.

He stood and rushed to her side. "Are you okay?"

"Yes," she managed. "Just excited to see you, to tell you."

"Tell me what?" He grinned before touching the tip of her nose with his index finger. "That you love me? Because you don't have to say it. I love you, and I already know."

"How? How did you guess?"

"You gave up your house, the potential to win it, for me. How do you feel about that?"

"Horrible, awful, devastated." She reached out to hug him, and he let her. The smell of citrus and spice against her nostrils, comforting and secure. "But houses are just that—houses, and they aren't worth more than people."

Dev chuckled against her hair. "Really? What genius taught you this?"

"My grandmother. I was too blind to see it. She never would've pushed for this so much, not if it caused other folks pain. I hurt you, said some cruel things, and thought the worst. Would you be willing to give me a second chance?"

"I am more than willing. Are you open to the idea that I don't think you lost your house?"

Hope bubbled up, fast and furious like a shaken soda. She'd have refused the emotion if she could've, but no dice. "I would love the possibility, but I don't think it's true."

Dev reached into his pocket and pulled out his phone. A few touches and swipes later, he flipped the screen around so she could see.

"You're fucking kidding me."

"Nope, *hermosa*. It's true; Kinyon loved the plan pitched to him about making the house a historic landmark, even agreed to do low-impact remodeling that won't take away the unique structure, inside and out."

She kissed him then, had to kiss him. There existed no other option in the world, and one kiss proved not enough. "How?"

"I put the proposal together and sent it to Kinyon this morning. Made it sound like it was all your idea, that I'd just reviewed it for you and approved. He obviously believed me, *gracias a Dios*."

"Yes, thank *Dios*, whoever he is."

"He's God, *hermosa*."

Laughing she pulled him in close again. "I had no clue."

"It's okay; I'm happy to teach you."

"I'll be happy to learn. Just... I'm overwhelmed."

"By what?" Dev pulled back, watching her intently.

"You, us, and the house. Oh my gosh, I get to keep everything. I get all the things, which is crazy." The day had turned into a miracle, a marvelous thing she'd never forget. "I love you."

"I love you, too. Are you ready to take the next steps?"

"With you by my side, I'm set."

CHAPTER TWENTY-FOUR

Six Months Later

"If you don't stop, we're going to be late." Kat's threat was rather empty since she giggled while Dev pressed kisses to her neck. His goatee tickled her skin.

"I love you, and I don't want to be late, but I can't help myself."

"All you have to do is wait two hours and then we can be back here and doing whatever we want."

Dev twirled her around in his arms, and she sighed at the way he held her close. "You promise?"

"Promise," she replied with a wink.

The last six months had been a complete whirlwind since they'd stopped Pru from ousting him and started the process of saving her gran's house, a house she no longer lived in. Dev had begged her to move in with him after two weeks. He hated going back and forth, and with the renovations to the house getting underway, it was easier to check in every day versus having her life interrupted.

Cohabitating turned out to be a wonderful, positive experience. They jogged in the mornings, went to work, spent three nights a week helping out at the shelter, and their weekends doing whatever they wanted. There were adventures, lots of love-making, and the beginnings of a wonderful partnership.

Kat had even been offered a job at Colton Kinyon's company, in his marketing department. The businessman thought she was a genius and didn't want her talent wasted at her previous job. The board still hired an outside PR consultant to help get Bona Fide back on track and overcome the bad press from the article and other things, much to Mark's regret. With Kat's insistence, Dev had also started a morning five-minute piece with a local radio station giving out personal image tips. Since then Bona Fide's business had boomed, and with Dev and, shockingly, Mark both in committed relationships, the image of the company improved drastically.

Now, they had to close the door on one more piece of the puzzle, the grand re-opening of her gran's house.

"You made it in time," Mark said, opening the passenger-side door on Dev's car for her.

"Of course we did. I wouldn't let him make us late."

She'd gone with a custom jumpsuit from Sam's shop today and would make sure any news articles mentioned the store. Part of her job within marketing was ensuring Kinyon's clients and partners received benefits from any work conducted in public.

"Yes, she made sure we were on time." Dev walked around the car, securing an arm around her waist. "Is everyone already here?"

"Yes, Colton is waiting for Kat on the front step to cut the ribbon."

Mark didn't follow behind them as they made their way through the crowd. No, her cousin hung back and gave her a thumbs-up when she finally got to the porch.

"I thought you might skip out on me, Kathleen." Colton accepted her handshake and then moved away. He still flirted with her from time to time, but respected her relationship with Dev and devotion to him. "I'm already handling everything since our head director skipped town. I didn't need to get stuck with this one."

Pru had pulled a big one over on everyone. One month following Bona Fide's investor board's decision to keep Dev on, both Dev and Mark had made a bid to Pru to purchase her shares in the company. Instead of selling to them, she'd sold out to Colton and even appeared to be done with it all. A month later, she took off for parts unknown and left the Beautification Board stuck without its head personality. Colton had kindly stepped forward, and thanks to him, the remaining parts of the project were completed on time. He'd also offered Kat a chance to make a little extra money working with the project. The extra dollars were the icing on the cake and had helped put the finishing touches on Gran's home.

"I wouldn't ditch you; this is a big day."

Colton gave her shoulder a squeeze. "You've done an amazing job and paved the way for other great houses like this one. With luck, we'll get all of the homes the board worked on to landmark status."

She smiled widely before reaching back to squeeze Dev's hand as he stood behind her. They'd done it. Colton offered her the giant scissors, and she took ahold of them. She aligned the ribbon between both sharp edges and pushed down. The tearing noise as the cloth of the ribbon gave way filled her with joy.

"We happily open Sawyer House today to the public. Sawyer House is a historical landmark home from the late 1890s and an intricate part of

Bentonville's history. We hope you'll take this special chance to tour the home and encourage you to make a reservation for a private tour or to reserve a room for tea in the future."

With that, the front door opened. She didn't follow the large group headed inside, having been given the opportunity to complete the tour yesterday. Her gran's legacy, knickknacks, and photos were still in place. Kat hadn't left everything. No, the favorite mugs and the afghan blankets they'd crocheted during her summer break between freshman and sophomore year, those memories and objects stayed with her. A few went to Mark and his younger brother as well, including the mug with their childhood pictures.

"Are you holding up okay?" Dev asked from beside her.

She nodded. "Yes. It's strange how I won't be living here anymore. I thought I'd raise my family here, thought I'd have kids playing in the backyard or roasting s'mores over a fire pit."

"Anytime you want to stay the night, you let me know, and I'll kick everyone out of here. I don't want you ever to think you can't come here whenever you want to. It may be a historical landmark, but you still own it."

"I love you." The only words she could say in light of his kind gesture. This is what the past six months had been, a magical time filled with sweet words and kinder deeds. "You're too good to me."

"You say that now, but you'll probably hit me in a few minutes."

"Why would I hit you?"

Mark laughed from behind them. "I think if anyone gets to hit him, it's me. So if you decide you want to punch him, Kat, please, let me do the honors. Better hurry. I think everyone is waiting."

"Waiting for?" She was so confused and a little concerned. "Is there something wrong with the house?"

Dev tucked her arm underneath his and guided her through the front door. "Come with me to the living room, and I'll show you."

As they rounded the corner, she found a big sign hanging above the fireplace mantle. The entire group that had been on her lawn was now gathered around the living room and spilling over into the kitchen area and a little into the hallway. The sign read, "Put a value in people, put your value in me."

She let go of Dev and took several steps forward. The muscles in her stomach clenched and her knees started to lock up. If this was what, she thought—*Oh crappity, crap.*

"Turn around, Kat."

As she swiveled around looking for the man she loved, tears filled her eyes. Dev crouched on his knees in front of her. Mark, Victoria, Betty, and her other friends Ana and Natalie, along with Dev's parents and his sister, Juanita, were all gathered there, along with reporters and countless others she couldn't remember at the moment. Surrounded by all her people, this was where he asked her, in the living room of her gran's house, and she'd become a blubbering fool.

"Kathleen Baum, here in this place, your grandmother's house, I ask you in front of your loved ones, will you marry me?"

She could make out the outline of the ring box, but failed to see the ring inside with all the tears gathering in her eyes and streaming down her face. Colton stepped forward and pressed a handkerchief into her hand. She dabbed at her eyes in a futile attempt to clear the moisture away.

"You may want to give him an answer, darling," Colton whispered to her.

"Yes." Kat laughed as she said it, probably sounding a bit crazy to everyone's ears, but she was so happy—ecstatic was a more accurate word.

Jumping to his feet, Dev removed the ring from the box and gently took her left hand. As he slid the ring onto the appropriate finger, the crowd around them cheered with joy. Dev pressed a kiss to her lips before whispering, "I love you."

Then he pulled her into an embrace while addressing their witnesses. "This one right here, ladies and gentleman, she's a bona fide beauty."

The End

ABOUT THE AUTHOR

Landra Graf consumes at least one book a day, and has always been a sucker for stories where true love conquers all. She believes in the power of the written word, and the joy such words can bring. In between spending time with her family and having book adventures, she writes romance with the goal of giving everyone, fictional or not, their own happily ever after.

Visit Landra on her website at landragraf.com

www.ingramcontent.com/pod-product-compliance
Lightning Source LLC
Chambersburg PA
CBHW070927250626
47159CB00009B/3151